SWEET AND VICIOUS

A NOVEL

DAVID SCHICKLER

THE DIAL PRESS

SWEET AND VICIOUS
A Dial Press Book / September 2004

Published by
The Dial Press
A Division of Random House, Inc.
New York, New York

This is a work of fiction. Names, characters, places, and incidents either are the product of the author's imagination or are used fictitiously. Any resemblance to actual persons, living or dead, events, or locales is entirely coincidental.

Book design by Glen Edelstein

Library of Congress Cataloging-in-Publication Data
Schickler, David.
Sweet and vicious / David Schickler
p. cm.
ISBN 0-385-33568-7
I. Title.

PS3569.C4848 S85 2004 2004047830
813/.54 22

Manufactured in the United States of America
Published simultaneously in Canada

BVG 10 9 8 7 6 5 4 3 2 1

for my beloved wife Martha
who heard a Voice . . .

. . . and for the Voice

Suddenly I realized
That if I stepped out of my body I would break
Into blossom

—James Wright

SWEET AND VICIOUS

CHAPTER ONE

Earth . . .

WE'RE DRIVING ON THE HIGHWAY IN THE BUICK when a hawk crashes through our windshield.

"Holy hell," says Floyd, and Roger and I say stuff too. The car swerves.

Brap, screeches the hawk. It's dying, then it dies. It's stuck through our windshield, its body on the hood and its head inside, like it's peeking through curtains, checking things out backstage. There are spikes of glass, I spill my Big Gulp, and the hawk has a squirrel in its talons.

"Dammit." Sprite fills the crotch of my jeans. I'm riding shotgun.

"There's a hawk in our windshield," shouts Floyd. He sounds awed or thrilled. He's in the backseat. Wind whistles in around the hawk's body, which is wedged tight. Roger, who's driving, fights with the wheel.

"There's a hawk in our windshield," shouts Floyd, "and there's glass everywhere."

Roger pulls over. We take deep breaths. It's six in the morning, no other cars around. There are ribbons of fog over the highway, points of dew in the roadside grass. Also, hanging dead before us is a red-tailed king of the skies.

"Wow," says Roger. He's got on black leather driving gloves.

"The hawk is holding a rat or something," says Floyd.

It's early May, the new millennium. I'm thirty-two and I bust people's heads for Honey Pobrinkis, a Chicago gangster. Floyd's my partner in the head-busting department. He wears his blond hair in a biker's ponytail, and he's as dumb as tundra, but he's got a photographic memory, which comes in handy. As for Roger, he's forty. He's Honey's nephew, but he's only a mob guy in the summer. From September to April, Roger attends the University of Chicago, where he's getting a master's in anthropology.

"Honey's gonna flip," says Floyd. "His car is fucked."

"Quiet," says Roger, brushing glass off his jacket. He wears a suit and tie wherever we go.

"Honey's ride has been fucked by a hawk and a rat."

"Quiet, Floyd," insists Roger.

I stare at the mangled former hawk. He's beautiful and lordly, but he's been dethroned. Just before the crash, I was actually thinking of animals—not hawks or squirrels, but sheep. The sheep I was pondering belong to Charles Chalk, whose head we're on our way to busting. Charles is Honey's diamond dealer. He lives west of Chicago, out Route 90, on a farm in Hampshire, Illinois. I visited his farm years back and admired his sheep. There were dozens of them. They were black and white and fenced in and they made noises that meant *Save Me*.

"Oh, man." Floyd gets out of the car, looks at the windshield. He whistles long and low, shaking his head. "Oh, man. We have witnessed the fucking of a Buick."

Roger finishes picking glass off his torso. He wears a porkpie hat, day and night, and under the hat is a black buzz cut with one weird white streak near the left temple. Roger's smart, built, and mean. I've never crossed him.

"Oh, man," says Floyd, "the hood's dented. If Honey were here, he'd kill that hawk, point-blank."

"The hawk died on impact," says Roger.

Floyd creases his eyes. "It got off easy."

I watch the hawk, whose fierce, shredded head hangs two feet before mine. I see no bullet wounds or other signs of why the beast kamikaze'd. What I see is the squirrel, out on the hood. Amazingly, he's wriggling free of the hawk's talons. He's alive, with pure white fur.

"Shitbox." Floyd, who's just twenty-six, makes a reverent sound. "The rat's still kicking."

"It's not a rat, it's a squirrel." Roger looks in the side-view, re-angles his porkpie. "You all right, Henry?"

I don't answer. The squirrel has liberated himself, and now he sits on his haunches, gazing at me through the windshield. There's some powdered glass in his fur, but he's still got a sporting chance in this world.

"Squirrels are brown." Floyd folds his arms. There's a cornfield behind him, and fog over the cornfield, and the sun's coming up.

"Well," says Roger, "this one's white."

The squirrel regards me. Other than the glinting powdered glass, his coat is free of blood or trauma, and his eyes are voids, black holes, like he could go on the news tonight, or home to the wife, or straight to hell, he doesn't care.

How far'd you fall? I wonder.

"Fine," says Floyd. "Three white guys, one white squirrel, one bashed-in Buick. That's the scenario."

The squirrel stares at me. I've seen dark, dead eyes like his exactly once, on a Cabrini-Green mark who owed Honey five grand last year. I cornered the mark around midnight outside a convenience store where he'd bought a six-pack of Schlitz. I got the guy in an alley and cracked his beer bottles over his head, but his eyes stayed gone, even when the blood trickled in.

"Yo. Henry Dante. You with us?" Roger punches the windshield in front of me, making me jump. The squirrel scampers off the hood, into the cornfield.

Floyd glares after the creature. "Fucking thing."

I blink at Roger.

"So, you're there after all." He notices my wet lap. "What'd you do, piss yourself?"

"It's soda," I say.

"Floyd," says Roger, "pull the hawk out and chuck him. Let's get to the farm."

Floyd stands in his jeans and his black tank top, which he wears year-round, heat wave or blizzard. His breath comes in vapors, and he watches them like they're crucial to the scene. Floyd loves a crisis. He once had a nonspeaking part in his high school play, where he tolled a bell to indicate a man's death. I hear about the bell frequently.

"Oh, man," says Floyd. "I was already having a lousy morning. Now Honey's Buick is fucked? This is the last straw."

Roger cracks his neck, watches the sky getting bluer, grins. Roger can do that, love colors one minute, club someone the next. He weighs only a hundred and ninety, but Roger's a Pobrinkis. He's killed men, led hitting crews. Floyd and I just do head-busting and bringbacks, so Roger's in charge.

"This is the straw that humped the camel." Floyd yanks out the hawk carcass, tosses it, pulls glass from the windshield like icicles.

"Broke his back, you mean," says Roger.

Floyd considers this. "No. Humped him."

"*Broke* the camel's *back*." Roger lights a cigarette. When he killed his first mark, he ran the guy over with a stolen cab, then left the cab on top of the guy, the meter running.

"This is the straw that broke the camel's back," says Roger. "That's what you were trying to say."

Floyd gets his defensive look. He purses his lips. "I said what I said."

"Straws don't hump camels," says Roger. "No wonder you didn't get speaking parts."

"Oh, man. Fuck you. I tolled the bell."

"Get in the car," says Roger.

Floyd reclaims the backseat, and Roger revs up, pulls out. I'm still thinking about the squirrel. Air gushes through the windshield.

"There's an absence in our windshield now." Floyd speaks over the wailing air. "There's an abyss."

Roger keeps checking his eyes at me. He likes my voice

more than I do. "What's the word, Henry? Hawk plummets from the heavens. Accident or omen?"

I've worked strong-arm for Honey Pobrinkis for seven years. Honey owns Chicago bistros, Vegas casinos, Canadian whores, the whole shebang, but his fetish is diamonds. He's the Adam Smith of the black market ice trade from Moscow to Mayberry. The rumor is, Honey has a five-carat, internally flawless back molar, but he never smiles or laughs, so I can't confirm this. Anyway, crewing for the Pobrinkis family, I've learned how to wait in cars, shatter jaws, keep my mouth shut. I've never killed anyone, though, or been on a hitting crew, or even wheelman for a hitting crew. I'm privately proud of these facts. My soul has a sporting chance.

"I don't know," I tell Roger.

Roger chews his Chesterfield. He half smokes cigarettes and half eats them.

"I believe in omens," announces Floyd.

"Floyd," says Roger, "would you do me the profound courtesy of shutting the fuck up?"

Floyd leans an elbow on each of our seats. He has a skinny orphan's frame, and marks never guess the crazy strength in his arms. "I just think there's omens."

Roger taps the steering wheel. "Forget the omens. Our concern is Charles Chalk."

Here's today's top story: Charles Chalk has stolen the Planets from Honey Pobrinkis. The Planets, I guess, are a glorious, amazing, sell-your-firstborn haul of ice, a seven-stone diamond collection owned by the same Spanish family since 1790. From what Honey tells us, back around the storming of the Bastille, a wealthy Barcelona prince named Don Canto was so in love with his sweetheart that he gathered from across the globe seven perfect diamonds, had each one cut to resemble a planet—Neptune and Pluto hadn't turned up in telescopes yet—and offered the gems to his love. Well, it worked, because prince and sweetheart married. They spawned generations of little dons who kept reliving the story, each giving his lady quite literally the world, marrying her, and stashing the Planets in the family safe till junior was born, et cetera. Anyway, the last living Canto heir died three years back, and circa last week, the Planets showed up on the Paris black market. Honey sent Charles Chalk to bid. Charles is a tall, bony septuagenarian on Prozac, but I guess he's a tiger on the job, and he got the Planets for forty million.

The trouble came last night around eleven. Roger, Floyd, and I were sitting at the bar at Ferryman's—Honey's South Side restaurant—and chowing calamari, when the bar's phone rang. Roger brought the phone to the corner table where Honey sat eating what he always eats—a bowl of merlot and sugar poured over blueberries. Honey listened, said "Very well" into the receiver, and hung up. He stared at his berries, then called us three over.

"That was Charles." Honey's lips, as always, were blue from wine and fruit. Also, his hair's like Roger's, black and buzzed, with that weird blade of white by the left temple.

"Charles is back from France," said Honey. "He's got the Planets."

"Congratulations, boss," said Floyd.

"He says he'll drive them into town in the morning."

"Cool," said Floyd.

Roger tossed Floyd a glance, because Honey was frowning.

Honey's a shambling six foot two, with a bulging torso. When he was sixteen, using his thumbnail, he sliced off the earlobe of his stepfather, Willis Enright.

"I just got a glimmer," said Honey.

I raised my eyebrows.

"About Charles?" said Roger, and his uncle nodded.

"Oh, man," said Floyd. "Flimsy old Charles? Are you sure?"

Honey stared at Floyd, and Floyd shut up. Honey's famous for getting what he calls glimmers. A glimmer is like ESP, or that warning tingle in Spider-Man's brain, except with Honey it comes when someone's about to betray him. On New Year's Eve, 1998, on the steps outside Jack Deck's tavern, where Honey and some other heavy hitters had just wrapped a sit-down, our boss got a glimmer not to share a limo home with Chester "Fish-Eye" Jones. When the limo exploded ten blocks later, blowing Fish-Eye and his driver all over Kedzie Avenue like party favors, Honey knew why Jack Deck had urged him to catch a lift with Chester. By noon the next day, Jack was kissing the floor of Lake Michigan, and Honey still had the broadest shoulders in town.

Other glimmers have warned Honey away from union meetings, Bulls games, and a prenup with his gold-digging second wife, Tasha. The glimmers come on suddenly, but they seal a person's fate. Of course, critics say Honey suffers not from visions but paranoid psychosis. Could be, but the guy's walking tall at sixty-five, and if you get a notion to rinse his blueberries with strychnine, he'll smell the idea while it's still in your doomed head.

"What'll Charles do?" asked Roger.

Honey sipped a spoonful of merlot. "He'll make for Belize.

He's got a house there, and contacts who could unload the stones easy."

Roger nodded. "You want us at the airport?"

"No, he'll drive," said Honey. "That wife of his hates flying. Go to the farm, at dawn."

That was that. We went back to our calamari, and I stared at a picture mounted behind the bar. The picture was twenty years old, a black-and-white of Honey and Charles at some church event, someone's baptism, with their arms gripping each other's shoulders. I wondered, as we finished our seafood, if I or Floyd or even Roger, Honey's flesh-and-blood nephew, might ever fall victim to a glimmer, might ever be fatally cast from Honey's favor like Charles Chalk. In fact, I'm still wondering this as Roger steers the Buick off the 90, into the countryside.

I pull my coat tighter around me. The morning air through the windshield is fresh and cold. It's May, and the world's waking up. As we pass farms and fields, giant ovals of fog drift over the land like alien ships, their tops lit by the rising sun. If this were a fairy tale, those ships would hold space folk, eager to reach out with glowing hands and pat local farmers on the back.

"Let's eat at Cleary's Pub tonight," says Floyd, over the wind. "Let's get shepherd's pie."

Roger pulls into Charles's driveway. The farm is a half mile into some woods.

"I'm serious," chats Floyd. "Let's have our tea at Cleary's."

"Our *tea*?" says Roger.

"Yeah. The Irish call dinner 'tea.' As in 'I was eatin' me tea.' They say that too."

"They say what?" Roger kills the engine, coasts along. If we were a hitting crew, Roger would rush in headlong, gun the

Buick down the driveway, pistols blazing, teeth tight. This is a bringback, though—Honey wants the Planets, but he wants to see Charles, too, alive, face-to-face.

"*Me,*" says Floyd. "*Me* instead of *my*."

Roger parks near the barn. "What the fuck are you saying, Floyd?"

"I'm saying what the Irish say. I'm saying *me* instead of *my*."

Roger removes his gloves. He wears silver stud rings on the middle three fingers of each hand. The second of the men he killed was a grifter from Milwaukee. Roger put a meat hook through the guy's sternum. I asked Roger once what he learned about in his anthropology classes, and he said, "People."

We get out of the Buick, which is midnight blue. Everything's quiet. I figure the sheep are in the barn, sleeping.

Roger checks the gun in his shoulder holster. "Floyd, look around, make sure we're alone. Then stay here and watch the driveway."

Floyd nods. He always quits yammering once a job starts.

Roger and I walk onto the porch, which features rocking chairs and a BB gun against the wall. The front door's unlocked. It opens into the kitchen, and when Roger and I breeze in, Charles and his wife look surprised. Charles sits at the table, wearing pj's, drinking coffee, maps spread out before him. Two suitcases are on the floor. Helena, who isn't even Floyd's age, stands in a thin flannel nightshirt, holding a pan of corn bread. She once posed nude for certain magazines under her maiden name, Helena Pressman. She married shaky old Charles a year ago.

"Good morning, Charley." Roger sits at the table. "Good morning, Charley's wife."

I stay by the door. Charles flicks his eyes at me, then out the window. His face ages about a century. To his credit, he doesn't start in with any pussy politics about how he was just coming to see us, et cetera. Charles knows about glimmers. He knows he's fucked.

"Hey, guys," he whispers.

I like Charles, and I wish he hadn't tried to cheat Honey. One time, Charles let me hold bottles of milk out to his lambs. When they got their mouths on the bottle nubs, they suckled like champs, loud and greedy.

"Charles," demands Helena, "who are these men?"

Roger looks her over. Neither of us has met Helena in person. She has fine, careless blond hair, green eyes, a lifetime of curves. I remember from a magazine bio that she has tremendous respect for Tibet.

"Have a seat, Charley's wife," says Roger. "Sit down here, right opposite Charley."

"I'll just go change." Helena sets the corn bread on the table, starts toward a doorway at her end of the kitchen.

"Helena." Charles's voice is high and thin. "Do what the man says."

Helena turns and scowls. When she sees her husband's face, her scowl dies. She's barefoot, and her nipples show through the nightshirt. She sits across from Charles.

"Let's all have some corn bread." Roger looks at Helena expectantly. She glances at Charles, who nods. Helena puts four pieces of corn bread on four napkins. When Roger reaches for his, Helena says, "I don't like your rings."

Charles draws in his breath.

"Women never like my rings. It's a grievance of mine."

"There's butter in the fridge," blurts Charles. "For the corn bread, I mean. If you want it, Roger. Butter can be good on corn bread."

I get my corn bread, return to my post. The bread's warm, homemade, and as I eat, I wonder if Charles has hidden the Planets somewhere groovy, like in the bellies of his sheep.

"The butter's probably hard, though." Charles looks nervously between Roger and me. "Um. It might crumble the corn bread. Ruin it."

Roger nibbles his food, sets it back on his napkin. "This is some fine corn bread. Yes, indeed. Fine, fine, fine."

My jeans are soaked from the Sprite, clammy. Through a window, I see Floyd on the Buick hood, rubbing his bone-handled butterfly switchblade. He keeps it stashed in his boot and takes it out to polish when nervous. Beyond the car is a pond. Above the water, fog swirls and burns in the light.

"Hey. Charley's wife." Roger stares at Helena.

Charles slumps his bony shoulders. Sad gray hairs loop out the neck of his pj's. I wish he'd made Belize.

"Can't we leave her out of this?" he asks Roger. "Please."

Roger gazes on at the woman. "Hey. Charley's wife."

"What?"

"You're Helena Pressman."

The woman tosses her head. "I know who I am."

"Please leave her alone," begs Charles. "I can get them right this second, Roger. They're here. They're in my study, the next room there, in a suitcase. They're all there."

Busting heads comes easily most days. Honey often sends me solo on collection gigs, because I have a face that opens wallets, and a discussion-ending southpaw jab. I'm also famous, I guess, for these two bulging, spiky knuckles on my left fist, the ones at the base of my index and middle fingers. Floyd calls them my devil's horns. I broke my hand once when I punched the brick wall in my apartment, and after the bones healed, two knuckles stayed sticking out, gnarled and toothy-looking. If I punch a mark's jaw right, my devil's horns leave a two-pronged scar after, like vampire fangs. I don't usually go for jaws, though—no need to waste a guy's face. I prefer soft tissue, rarely breaking ribs I don't mean to, or thumbs that don't deserve it. I rush marks fast, barely speak, no teasing them like Roger goes in for. I get the money or the goods, or I get to work. I never carry a gun, because pain scares people more than death, but also because I've been shot three times and survived, and to start packing might switch my luck. Plus, I'm afraid that with a gun I'll croak someone, and, like I said, I'm guarding my soul.

"Will you let me go to my study, Roger?"

"So . . . Helena Pressman." Roger picks at his corn bread. "Is that your BB gun on the porch?"

Helena licks her lips. Her gaze travels the room, from man to man. I see her register that I'm standing by the door, see her finally getting it. Also, the sheep in the barn are waking up. They're bleating for food, or release.

"Um." Helena buttons her nightshirt's top button. "It's for raccoons. For . . . scaring them off."

Roger peers at the maps, most of which show Mexico, the Caribbean, Central America. "Well, ma'am. We ain't raccoons."

"I'm going to my study, Roger. I'm going to get you what you want." Charles starts to get up.

Roger's hand goes to his holster. "Sit the fuck down, Charley."

Charles does. He sits, trembling slightly. He looks at the maps, then at his wife. Tears begin in his eyes.

"Charles?" says Helena.

"Helena, look at me." Roger still won't glance at Charles or away from the woman. "Charles isn't going to say anything more. He won't say one more word to you or anybody, because if he does, something unpleasant will happen to his wife. And you won't scream, or something unpleasant will happen to Charles. Understand?"

Charles whimpers. An artery beats in his papery neck. As for Helena, the blood leaks from her face. Her nightshirt is a fetching, homespun brown color.

"Understand, Helena?"

She nods. Roger stands, goes into the study. When he comes back, he holds a squat silver suitcase. He lays it on the table in front of Helena, clicks it open. He angles it toward me so I can see the Planets. They're set in a square solar system of black foam, with the Mercury diamond on the far left and the next six in a line to the right, in the order we learned in grammar school. They're stunning. Light hurries out of them into my eyes. The largest one, Jupiter, even has a small red spot on it, a beauty mark. And the Saturn stone has a ring etched around its middle. I imagine these Planets for a moment the way they were buried in nature, black, jagged, unpolished, hiding their hearts from men.

"Jesus," I whisper.

"Once I saw them," blurts Charles, "I—I wanted them for my wife. You can understand that, can't you, Roger?"

Roger bends close to the seated woman, his lips brushing her hair. "Well, Helena Pressman. Now what?"

This surprises me. On a bringback, once we have what we're sent for, we muscle the mark into the Buick and get gone. What's more, back in the city, Roger has Ferryman barmaids at his beck and call, plus some slinky U of C adjunct. He never messes with a mark's woman. But maybe Helena Pressman is too much to resist. Maybe Roger remembers too dearly the poses she's struck in magazines. For there in Charles Chalk's kitchen, Roger walks to the fridge, gets a stick of butter, then comes back and stands behind Helena. He holds the butter before her eyes, sets it on the black foam below the Planets. The butter is wrapped in wax paper. Roger takes off his tie, pulls Helena's arms behind her back.

"Hey." She struggles, but Roger lashes her wrists to the chair spindles. He takes out his gun, holds the stock against her cheek. "Please," says Helena.

Charles moans, makes to stand. Roger cocks the gun. Gutless Charley sits back down.

Roger leans to her ear again. "Now what, Helena Pressman?"

Helena's eyes are green danger, flicking between her husband and the gun. With his free hand, Roger reaches around Helena, hugs her chair forward. He takes the butter stick, unwraps it.

I clear my throat. "Hey, Roger. Shouldn't we get going?"

"Now what, Helena Pressman?"

I haven't felt for a woman in a long time. Three nights ago, I screwed Katharine Cleary, but she started it, pouring me pints at her brother's pub, tugging me to the cellar at three A.M., pinning me against a cold keg. That was just exercise, though. The last girl I cared about was Bella Cavasti, the daughter of the owner of Cavasti's Deli. Seven years back, we had an affair, and all two hundred and twenty pounds of me told Bella that I loved her. We kissed and kissed and whispered of our wedding, where we would serve egg drop soup. Then Bella broke me off for a Sicilian wine merchant, some crusty-eyed geezer fuckhead she met at a goddamn soup kitchen. They ran off to pursue charity and Chianti in the old country, and that's when I punched the brick wall, got my devil knuckles. I felt quicksand in my chest after that, and a gag reflex in my throat woke me in a sweat each night. I met Honey a few months later, started muscling for him. It chews up the clock, and I rarely have to think.

"Now what, Helena Pressman?" Roger sticks his gun in his belt. He still holds the butter stick. The Planets sparkle, and I remember Don Canto, their suave creator. I picture him in Spanish gentleman's dress, owning a sword, hugging a child. With his free hand, Roger reaches in Helena's lap, hitches her nightshirt up past her hips.

"Oh, God." Her breath comes in little emergencies. She wears no underwear, and she rams her thighs together. As she tries to lurch away from Roger, her breasts sway beneath the gown.

"Roger," begs Charles. "Don't." He grips the table, his knuckles white.

Roger's hand rushes to her throat, squeezes. His other hand still holds the butter stick. "If either of you speaks or moves again, I'll snap this neck like a fucking chicken bone."

Helena coughs and sputters. Charles sobs, but Helena's not crying. Her eyes are wide and dry. The sheep in the barn sound stubborn, angry.

"Good." Roger winks at me. His hand leaves Helena's throat, hitches her hem higher. "Now, Helena. Charley mentioned that the butter was too hard and cold for the corn bread. Now that I'm holding the butter stick, I take his point." He nuzzles her ear. "What's to be done, Helena Pressman? Is there any place we can put the butter stick to warm it up? You know, soften it?"

One time, Bella Cavasti and I stayed up all night long. It was summer and warm, and there was a carnival at Foster Ave. Beach. The rides and midway had shut down at one in the morning, so Bella and I tripped out to the waves. We made love in the sand, her mouth tasting pink from cotton candy, and we fell asleep naked. When we woke, there was a green sunrise over Lake Michigan, and we did that forever thing, sitting and sharing glances, not talking, but making plans. Then the Skee-Ball guy opened his booth early, just for us, and I won six hundred tickets for what I thought would be my bride.

Roger wedges the butter between Helena's quaking knees. Out the window, Floyd's chunking rocks into the pond. The barn's bleating like mad.

"Hey, Roger." I shift my weight from one foot to the other. "It's, um . . . it's just a bringback, right? Let's head out."

"Where can we soften the butter, Helena?" Roger steers the butter slowly up her lap, away from her knees. "Where can we soften it?"

Charles's shoulders twitch. He's really bawling now, spitting curses. Helena, meanwhile, maintains strict, excellent posture as the butter climbs her thighs.

"Come on, Roger," I say. "We should jet. Charles will come quietly."

"Let's warm up the butter, Helena Pressman." Roger watches her face with delight. He moves the butter higher. "Let's melt it right down."

Helena looks at me then. I don't know if she does it because I've started talking, or because her husband's a mess, but she looks at me deep, the way Bella did at the beach. A wide, searching light is in her gaze, green like that morning sky over the lake, and her soul seems to speak from her eyes, warning me that the sun might not rise this time, that it's not a guarantee, that night could suck dawn back into the pit and keep things black forever. *I don't want the black,* her soul says. *But if this bad breakfast action enters into me, I'll fall into the dark and never climb out.*

I stride over. "Hey. Leave her alone."

Roger glances at me. "Back off." He works the butter farther up her lap. Helena starts whimpering, deep in her throat.

"Leave her alone, I said." I grab Roger's right arm, the arm holding the butter. I squeeze till he cries out.

Dropping the butter in her lap, Roger stumbles back, rubbing his forearm. "Dante, you prick. What the fuck?"

"Charles is the mark, not his wife." I stand between Roger and Helena. The sheep are loud, and Floyd calls, "You guys hearing this? There's, like, animals out here."

"Charles is the mark, Roger. And we've got the Planets. Let's head."

Roger stares at me in disbelief. His gun hangs loose in his belt, but I think in his shock he's forgotten it. "What the fuck, Henry? You forget my last name or something?"

Helena bounces the butter off her thighs. It thunks on the floor.

"Thank God," blubbers Charles.

"I'm a fucking Pobrinkis." Roger swaggers forward, taps my chest. I'm six four, he isn't.

"I've killed five men," he snarls.

Still tied up, Helena hops her chair around the table toward her crybaby husband.

Roger shoves me backward. "I'm a Pobrinkis. If I want to grease up some centerfold, some farmhouse bitch, that's how it is. You stand and watch like the lummox you are, and then I don't tell my uncle to feed you your balls for supper. All right?"

I can't fully understand what's happening. There's Roger getting in my face. There's squeaky Charles and his caterwauling sheep. There's the Planets, winking at me from the suitcase, one for each year that's passed between Bella and now. Mostly, though, there's Helena Pressman and her easy blond hair. Even as she hops toward Charles, she's looking my way, singling me out, that high, green resolve in her eyes. I'm no sucker. I know she and I won't share a Belizean hammock, that I'm just a fence between her and hot buttered rape. As I watch her, though, something hard in me breaks open. She's a centerfold, yeah, but she deserves a sporting chance. So I fist up with a left and uppercut Roger's chin. My devil knuckles crackle, remembering brick, and something in Roger's face crackles too.

"Huh," groans Roger. He drops at my feet, coughing, blood raining from his nose. "Henry," he chokes. "Fucking dead, Henry." He reaches for his belt.

I kick his hand before it can close on his gun, then step on the hand, cracking finger bones. Roger howls, yanks his crunched hand to his chest, cups it like he's found a baby bird. I stoop, grab his gun, rake the butt across his face five or six times till his porkpie flies off and he blacks out.

"All right." I stand panting, Roger's gun in my hand, his body slumped on the floor. "All right."

I fish in his pockets, get the Buick's keys, and turn to Charles, who's untying Helena.

"Charles. You got a car?"

Charles nods, frees his woman. Helena tugs her hem to her knees, slaps Charles, runs around the table, kicks Roger in the head, keeps kicking. The fallen Pobrinkis groans unconsciously.

"Cut that out." I shove her away, close the silver case, grab it. I wave the gun toward the door. "We're leaving. Where's your car keys?"

Charles draws himself up. His face still wears Helena's slap mark, but he fixes his white hair like he's Chief Justice. "If you take me back to Honey, he'll kill me. You know that, don't you, Henry?"

I tap the gun. "Safety's off here, Charles. Where's your car keys?"

Charles points at a rack where coats and key chains hang. "The red one."

I grab a chain that holds keys and a red toy, a miniature pyramid. I grab two coats as well, toss them at Charles and Helena. "Let's go."

I herd the Chalks out onto the lawn. They put on their coats and stand barefoot in the grass, in the morning chill. The ruckus of the sheep is crazy.

Floyd lopes over, grinning, looking Helena over. "You the one from the magazines?"

Helena says nothing. The mist over the pond is dying in the sun.

Floyd peers at Charles. "Whatever you have in that barn is going apeshit, mister." He sees the gun in my palm. "Is that Roger's piece?"

Like the traditional me, Floyd never carries a gun, because Honey forbids it. In our early days, Floyd packed a .44 like Dirty Harry, but he kneecapped a bookie by mistake, and then, during a bender, he blew off the head of Honey's Siamese cat, Addison. Honey sliced off Floyd's left pinky finger in retribution.

"Where's Roger?" Floyd walks into the farmhouse.

I give Charles the Buick's keys. "You two have to get gone. Really gone."

Helena squeezes Charles's hand.

"Tasmania gone. Arctic Circle gone. And stay out of Belize. Honey's got that covered."

Floyd bursts out of the farmhouse, skitters down the steps. "Oh, man! What the fuck, Henry? Roger's down. Out cold."

We've crewed together for five years, and I like Floyd. I know his sister works at some resort in Daytona or wherever, and he knows about my Four Horsemen tattoo.

"Floyd," I say, "I'm really, really sorry."

"Sorry for what?"

I jack my fist into his nose, which crunches, caves in. I'm wearing my roomy denim jacket, which makes swinging easy, and I bring a roundhouse to his cheek. When Floyd reels back, I hike my boot into his stomach. The sheep take things up an octave, and Floyd sinks to his knees, hissing air through his teeth. When I kick him again, he doubles up.

"Stop it," Helena begs me, hopping up and down. With her nightshirt and bare feet, she looks young and out of place, like a Pat Boone fan.

I wave the suitcase at Floyd's befuddled, bleeding mug. "See this, Floyd? This is the Planets. The diamonds. Tell me you see them."

"Henry," coughs Floyd. "Planets."

"That's right." I drill him in the left eye socket. "I'm the one that's taking them. Not Charles, not Helena Pressman, me. Make sure Honey knows that."

Floyd paws his pockets, but weapons aren't there. I tug off his boot—where he keeps his switch—and toss it across the yard. His eye is swelling, fat and purple.

"Sorry about this, pal." I box-punch his kidneys. "But if I don't pound you, too, Roger'll be suspicious. I stopped him from raping Helena Pressman, by the way."

"Help," says Floyd.

"Stop it," screams Helena.

I turn to the happy couple, point Charles toward the Buick. "That's your car now. Where's mine, in the barn?"

Charles stands in his pj's, blinking severely. He nods.

"It's got gas?"

He nods again.

"What happened to the windshield?" asks Helena.

"Hawk. Long story. Now get out of here."

Floyd raises himself on one elbow, claws at my pant leg. Blood drips from his eye. He points a shaky finger at the three of us.

"Morally," he croaks, "we are not okay people." He collapses facedown in the grass.

I point the gun at Charles. "Get going, I said."

Charles tugs his wife to the Buick, and they roar away. I unlatch the fence surrounding the pasture and barn. When I fling open the barn's double doors, the bleating and baaing explode.

"Quiet, sheep," I say, but they only cry louder.

Charles's car isn't a car at all. It's a red Chevy pickup, maybe ten years old, but scrubbed clean. It stands alone in the center of the barn on a dirt floor. Sun pours from a high, open grain door. The rustling, freaked-out, damn-hungry sheep are cooped in stalls along the walls, maybe twenty critters per cell.

As I open the pickup, the sheep squeal. “Easy, fellas.” I toss the case on the shotgun seat, snoop around, and whistle. Charles was definitely planning a getaway. He’s removed half the jump-seat bench behind the cab and stocked that area with gas cans, a Spanish-English dictionary, and coolers of jerked beef, bottled water, and oranges. Not only that, but the back wall has a cut-away passage and the truck bed is capped with a roof. Charles and spouse have turned the truck bed into a nest. There’s a wide air mattress, a tandem sleeping bag, a Coleman stove, soup cans, a shotgun and shells, and a stack of tattered paperbacks with titles like *Little Julia Goes to Prep School* and *Little Julia Meets the Hombre*.

“Wow.” I key the ignition to life and start forward a few feet, but the sheep wail for mercy.

“All right, sheep.” I put the truck in park, then zip around the barn, throwing open stall doors. Skipping and rejoicing, the round woolly inmates surge past me. I get in the pickup and steer out of the barn, through the fence to the yard. I’m careful not to run over any sheep. For their part, the sheep make decisions. Some hightail it to the pasture, others stand around like idiots. A few follow the pickup.

As I crunch past the bleeding lump of Floyd, I roll down the window. “So long, Floyd,” I call. “Remember, I did you a favor.”

I move down the driveway. In the rearview, I see sheep criss-crossing everywhere. One gambols after me, while another, a baby, sniffs Floyd.

"Good-bye, sheep," I shout. I feel wide open, like I've got the horizon in my lungs. Grinning, I drive to the highway. My devil's horns throb from the morning's work, but the fog has burned away entirely. The sun's out for real, the Earth and her six closest friends are in the case beside me, and I drive northwest on the 90, thinking of the good deeds I've just done.

CHAPTER TWO

Grace

THE TWO POWERS THAT SHAPED GRACE MCGLONE in her youth were sex and Jesus Christ.

Grace had grown up a scarlet-haired only child in Janesville, a town in southern Wisconsin where corn and silence grew to sometimes oppressive lengths. She knew nothing of her father, Max McGlone, except that, while alive, he'd driven tractor-trailers across the country. According to Grace's mother, Regina, Max gave up his ghost in an unspecified but unchristian manner in the bunkhouse of Lou Feeper's Bozeman Truck Stop when Grace was just a baby. From four years old onward, Grace pressed Regina for details, but Regina, who'd turned Southern Baptist in her widowhood, remained tight-lipped, saying only that a woman was involved.

Regina spent her days managing Thou Shalt Read, the Christian bookstore she'd opened in the late 1970s, and her nights dusting the ramshackle house in which she and Max had planned to be fruitful to the tune of half a dozen children. While she dusted, Regina listened to her AM radio, which rested on the living room fireplace mantel. She set the radio nightly to the *God's Will Tennessee Power Hour,* a Christian gospel show that broadcast live from Memphis and featured the famous preacher the Reverend Bertram Block. Regina had fine, sturdy shoulders and cheekbones that had once won a beauty contest, but her face in widowhood fought off smiles. As her fingers dusted the metal screen that guarded the hearth she never lit, she drank in the strong wine of the reverend's voice.

"To whom will you give yourself?" asked Bertram Block one autumn night. "For whom will you lay down your life?" The radio crackled, as if transmitting from another world. Beside the radio stood two framed pictures of religious homage, photographs taken at one of Bertram Block's popular God's Will revivals, which he performed each summer in cities across the country. The first picture showed the reverend in close-up, wearing a dark suit as he presided over a revival tent from a raised stage. He looked eight feet tall and had angel-white hair swept back in a crashing wave. Tucked in his left breast jacket pocket was his signature accoutrement, a white handkerchief with the initials BB stitched in the fabric. The reverend stood with his hands on his hips, and the breadth of his shoulders beneath the suit made Regina believe he could swim across oceans or any other chasm the Devil might set between mankind and salvation. The second picture gave a panoramic glimpse of Bertram Block's faithful, and they must have numbered in the thousands, Regina thought. They were teeming bodies in cotton-colored suits, but their faces, turned toward the stage, looked stricken and creased, as if the reverend's words were cutting their skin.

"To whom will you give yourself?" demanded the wireless Bertram Block. "Before whom will you shudder? Whom will you serve?"

A car horn honked outside. Grace clattered down the stairs. It was October 1991, and Grace was fourteen, a high school freshman.

"Listen to this." Regina nodded toward the radio. "It'll change your life."

Grace tugged on a coat. "Tonight's the football game against Dutchess. Perry's driving, love you, see you."

"Home by ten!" called Regina.

Outside, Grace got into the Ford Taurus idling in her driveway. Behind the wheel was Grace's best friend, Periwinkle Danning, who was sixteen and a sophomore. Perry had cropped, licorice-black hair, Ds in biology and English, and hickeys on her thighs and belly. She also had twin upperclassmen brothers named Crimson and Forest, and a chillingly gorgeous older sister named Color. Perry's mother, Danielle Danning, was a reclusive expressionist painter with no husband and a mane of white hair that fell to her buttocks. As for Perry, she was dating Drew Barrister, the soccer team captain, whose bronze calves Grace admired as secretly and dearly as she did Perry's access to them.

"Tallyho, Ms. McGlone," said Perry.

"Tallyho, Ms. Danning."

A block from the McGlone house, both girls lit up Winstons.

Perry sorted through her Black Sabbath cassettes. "What's Mrs. Yahweh doing tonight?"

Grace winced at Perry's nickname for Regina. It did embarrass her when she and her mother stood in line at Todd's Supermarket and Regina denounced Hershey's Kisses as the ambrosia of Satan. But Grace didn't completely dismiss her mother's religion. Rather, she suspected that if God existed, he was a wild-haired symphony conductor, and humans his pit musicians. She felt that if God was real and wanted something from her, he would fix his burning eye on her, point his wand her way, and heaven would drop into her lap whatever trumpet she had to blow, whatever life she had to lead.

"The usual," said Grace. "Bertram Block."

Perry drove to the Oval Office, an egg-shaped clearing in the wooded bluff overlooking the James Madison High School football field. For decades, Madison students had made the Oval Office their sanctuary and proving ground. Cars parked there, joints got passed, songs got sung, bonfires and tempers flared. The clearing was encircled by monstrous oak trees whose branches climbed as high as teenage ambitions, and on many such branches were nailed wooden planks from which the contests on the school grounds below could be cheered or mocked.

"There's Drew," said Perry. She idled past rows of parked cars, nudged the Taurus into a remote Oval Office corner, where her beau leaned against a tree in his letterman jacket. During weeknight home football games that autumn, Perry, Grace, and Drew had a ritual. They all three met at the Oval Office just after kickoff. Then agile, boyfriendless Grace climbed to the upper branches of Uncle Treemus, the most mammoth oak tree on the bluff, where she could scout the cop cars that often raided the Oval Office for contraband. While Grace kept lookout, Perry and Drew clambered into the backseat of the Taurus, and, with Ozzy Osbourne wailing in their ears, they spent the remaining hours of game time making the Kama Sutra look like a Girl Scout handbook.

On this particular night, as she perched high in Uncle Treemus, Grace twisted twigs into her long red tresses and watched football boys smash each other fifty feet below. It was a lovely October night, with a copper moon and a warm, easy wind, and Grace wore her favorite blouse, a rust-colored care-worn thing from Pyle's Thrift Emporium. Sometimes, if the game was boring, Grace liked to read in Uncle Treemus. By flashlight, as she lay on a plank, she'd steal through the novels of Raymond Chandler. Tonight, lighting a smoke, Grace merely kept her eyes on Perry's brothers, Crimson and Forest, who played halfback and fullback for the Madison Colonials, and who tickled Grace to pieces back when she was a squirt. At fourteen, Grace now had smoothly swelling breasts and a tapering figure, but also constellations of freckles on her neck that embarrassed her.

"Touchdown!" shouted a referee below, and the trees around Grace applauded. Sharing beers and high fives, a riffraff of silhouettes moved in the oaks beside Uncle Treemus, but no other branch-squatters were as high as Grace, and they didn't intrigue her. What intrigued her were the twin Danning boys, butting their helmets together in the end zone, clomping each other in a touchdown hug. Grace dreamed them out of their uniforms, imagined their thick bodies embracing naked on the grass, her own body sandwiched between them. Grace was a virgin, but during her vigils high above the Oval Office she often fixated on Crimson and Forest and, on the playing fields of her libido, let them do to the insides of her thighs all the warm work that Drew did to Perry in the Taurus.

"Hey, Grace."

Grace jumped, dropped her smoke. She grabbed the edge of her plank and caught her breath as her cigarette, an orange firefly, fell to earth.

"I didn't mean to scare you."

Grace turned, already glaring. Just behind her on the plank squatted Stewart McFigg, a husky freshman loner who all but lived in the Oval Office trees.

"God*dammit,* Stewart. I almost fell."

"I'm sorry."

Her heart still churning, Grace gripped the plank with both hands. "And I dropped my cigarette. It could start a conflagration."

Stewart was hunched with his weight on his hands, like an ape. He hung his head, blinking at Grace through his bangs. "Oh. What's a conflagration?"

"A fire, dorkis. It was on our vocab list? From the Bradbury novel?"

"Oh." Stewart wore his perennial green vest jacket. His hair was black and long, almost as long as Grace's. It fell over his ears and temples in shaggy clumps, which he constantly pawed back. His friendly face reminded Grace of a pleasant, low-watt bulb, a bulb that she currently wanted to switch off.

Stewart flumped himself down. "You've got sticks in your hair, Grace."

She inched farther down the plank. "Really? Do I, really? Well, well, well, Philip Marlowe to the rescue."

"Don't worry, the sticks look pretty. Who's Philip Marlowe?"

Grace sighed. Stewart was the son of Randall McFigg, who ran a butcher shop and the local Knights of Columbus. Stewart had got it into his head in second grade that Grace McGlone—the only other student at Janesville Elementary with an Irish last name—was destined to be his bride, and he'd followed her around since. This became burdensome for Grace in fourth grade, the year Randall McFigg accidentally dropped a giant meat cleaver, blade first, onto his son's left ankle. Certain tendons in Stewart's ankle were severed beyond repair, but, after his foot healed as best it could, he donned an extra-wide green shoe (designed for him by a Chicago specialist) and continued his pursuit. For her part, Grace spent all of middle school blushing and ducking out of the cafeteria any time she heard Stewart's freaky shoe clumping in her direction. She told Stewart that her mother was fiercely Baptist and his father frighteningly Catholic, and so long-term romance between them was doomed, but Stewart persisted. In sixth grade, on Valentine's Day, he delivered to Grace in front of the class a handmade card that pictured the two of them living in a green fairy-tale castle shaped like a giant orthopedic boot. Stewart called the castle McShoe and promised Grace on bended knee that he would build it for her in the woods near the high school. In response, Grace delivered a stinging public rebuke of Stewart, in which she blamed him for all the freckles beginning to plague her body, claiming that the years of blushing brought on by his advances had triggered the speckling of her skin.

Appalled at his crime, Stewart had more or less left Grace alone since. While the other boys spent junior high cutting their teeth on soccer and football, Stewart built forts in Uncle Treemus, hoping that one such construction might impress Grace and turn her heart. At first, his forts rarely grew beyond basic floors between branches (which older kids commandeered for horseplay), but all the climbing had swelled his biceps and forearms to such mighty proportions that by ninth grade he'd become the stuff of local lore.

"What do you want, Stewart?" Grace glanced at the road to the Oval Office. Stewart or no Stewart, she was sentry to her best friend's orgasms.

"I'm building a new fort. A real masterpiece." Stewart pointed at branches above them, through which Grace could see Orion. "Wanna check it out?"

"I'm busy."

"Oh. Busy doing what?"

"None of your business, Stewart McFigg."

"Oh. I'm sorry."

Grace stared down at the floodlit field, at twenty-two scrambling athletes. She blushed, because Stewart's bare, brawny arm was six inches away, and she found herself thinking of licking his biceps and tasting what Perry promised was the worthwhile, salty flavor of boys.

"Hey, Grace?"

"What is it now?"

Stewart rolled his knuckles on the plank. "Can I ask a question?"

She tossed her eyes, lit a new cigarette. "All right, Stewart."

"Really?"

Grace longed to kiss a man, hopefully an impolite one. "Yes, Stewart."

"Okay. Cool." Stewart tucked his hair back. "Well, I see you up here lately in Uncle Treemus. And I was wondering . . ."

"Yes?"

"Well, I was wondering what you think about. You know, when you're up here, all alone."

Grace regarded the boy. She'd expected a question about algebra or the fall formal dance, and instead here was Stewart McFigg, caring about what mattered. She knit her eyebrows together, looked at her lap. The truth was, she spent her nights in Uncle Treemus pondering heaven. She wondered if her dad had made it there, and if so, whether he'd driven through the gates at the speed of light in some angelic eighteen-wheeler. Grace wanted to know if the God her mother always babbled about would welcome a fire-haired gypsy like the Max McGlone that Grace studied in Regina's photo albums. In all those pictures, Grace saw a glint in her father's eyes, a sheen on his teeth when he laughed. She guessed that this glint, this bright knife-edge in his character, had gotten her father killed, for it lit in Grace's mind the winking wonders she knew that he'd loved: silver coins thrown across a gambling table, ice flashing in a glass of vodka, the polish of women's nails, the hooks and eyes of their brassieres coming undone. An impulse for some such vice had surely lured her father to his roadhouse doom, but what troubled and thrilled Grace was her certitude that a glint similar to her father's, a sharp, dangerous sliver of some instinct to run wild, lay wedged in her own heart, waiting to prick her into action at some fateful moment. Grace had watched for evidence of a kindred danger in her mother's demeanor, but had come to the disappointing conclusion that Regina was a woman who'd never had, or else lost, or else buried for the Baptists, any bite inside her soul.

Grace had no one with whom to share such musings. Perry

played her stereo too loudly and fretted about pregnancy too much for Grace to broach the topics of souls or destiny. Neither did Grace have the skill to voice such matters before Regina. And, sitting tongue-tied beside the lame-footed suitor of her youth, Grace didn't know any boys who would understand either. So, fourteen and frustrated, she scowled at Stewart McFigg.

"Nothing," she snapped. "I think about nothing at all."

* * *

It was almost nine months later, in the summer of 1992, that the touchstone days of Grace's young life unfolded. For in June of that year, the announcement of two looming events sent Janesville into a tizzy. The first event, declared on Memorial Day in the *Janesville Bullet,* was the wedding of twenty-one-year-old Color Danning to a Rhinelander senator's son.

Color had been Janesville's favorite oddity for years. Since birth, she'd had hair of the finest silver hue, and like her mother's striking white locks, Color's fell as far as her hips. Her spooky, light gray eyes looked like cloudy cataracts, but her vision, like all of her senses, was giftedly exact. From a mile away, the girl could smell brush fires at their discarded-match inception, hear custody squabbles in the living rooms of soon-to-be separated neighbors, or chart the approach of a pair of mosquitoes. Somehow Color's looks and senses hadn't consigned her to adolescent freakdom. She advised the police on the finding of lost cats or wayward husbands, but she'd also been a loyal Brownie, a popular cheerleader, a happy prom queen, and a mediocre field hockey player.

Her clairvoyance didn't steer Color toward personal gain until one night when she was seventeen. She was babysitting Perry and Grace, playing Yahtzee with them on the Dannings' front lawn, when she sat bolt upright and said, "Here comes a guy." Perry and Grace looked up the street and, seeing nobody, forgot the remark until three years later, when Charles Jackson Tate the Second knocked on the Dannings' door while Color, Perry, and Grace were baking cookies. When Color answered the door, a young man handed her a flyer encouraging voters to support the reelection of his father, Senator Charles Jackson Tate the First. Color sighed with contentment, accepted the flyer, turned to Perry and Grace, and, jutting her thumb at the doorway, said, "Here's that guy I was telling you about."

So Color and Charles the Second were set to marry on July 5, on the shore of Lake Loomis, just outside town. This thrilled Janesvillers, who expected statewide media coverage, and it thrilled Grace, because Color had chosen Grace and Perry as the witnesses to stand up at her wedding, claiming that the girls had been with her and Charles ever since their courtship began during that front-lawn Yahtzee game.

Danielle Danning added her own thrilling touch to the proceedings. In the first week of June, she bestowed on Perry and Grace two brand-new cream-colored dresses that she'd made. Danielle had fashioned the dresses from gesso painting canvases and then assaulted these frocks with fabric softener until they were pliable and smooth to the skin. The expressionist told the girls these were the dresses they'd wear for Color's nuptials. She insisted that, for the month preceding the wedding, the girls wear the dresses each day and never wash them. In this manner, Danielle explained, all the hues, stains, and moments of their lives would be made manifest on the dresses, so that by Color's wedding, Perry and Grace would be living works of art, walking witnesses to the grit and glory of what it means to be a woman.

For two more conventional girls, such a duty might have seemed distasteful, but Perry and Grace adored their dresses and donned them immediately. School was out, and the two friends tramped around Janesville, wiping excess mascara and rouge on their bodices. Grass stains took shape on their buttocks, and after two weeks of lazy lunches at Mackidew's Diner, mustard and Tabasco and dessert fudge striped their ribs. On little girls or grown women, the gesso dresses might have looked more and more slovenly and absurd, but the summer sun was out, and Perry and Grace were sixteen and fifteen, respectively. Raven-haired and willful, Perry strode past the Fracas Pub in the center of town, a tease of a smile on her face, while beside her loped the long-legged Grace, smoothing the canvas between her breasts and hips. The windows of the Fracas misted with the breath of men staring out at these messy, marvelous girls, and, watching from her flower shop stoop, sixty-year-old Melanie Bryson yearned for a time machine.

It was at this time, in the third week of June, that the second grand event of that summer was announced. A squeal burst from Regina McGlone's throat one night as she dusted her mantel. Grace hurried downstairs to find her mother passed out cold on the floor by the hearth while the radio repeated for emphasis the fact that the Reverend Bertram Block would preach in Janesville on July 3 as a stop on his annual God's Will tour. Originally, the reverend had booked a Milwaukee venue, but at the last minute he'd told his tour directors that God was calling him to sow the Word in a more rural Wisconsin town. A partial conduit of God's in this circumstance may have been Senator Charles Jackson Tate of Rhinelander, Wisconsin, who, along with being a fellow Baptist, a former college roommate, and a financial supporter of Bertram Block's, was also scheduled to be in Janesville in early July. Chuck Tate didn't approve of his only son marrying the daughter of an artsy, heathen witch with hair to her ass, but he loved his boy, and he hoped that if Bertram was at least present at the nuptials, some secondhand graces of the Holy Spirit might settle on Chuck Junior and his bride with the stupid name. So the senator phoned the man of God and the two old friends set their schedules.

By the afternoon of July 2, both the preacher and the politician had arrived. They booked rooms at the Bryson Inn, then met for dinner at Mackidew's Diner. Half of Janesville decided to brave Hollis Mackidew's cuisine that evening, and others loitered on the sidewalk outside, sneaking looks through the window. Grace and Perry, in their work-in-progress bridesmaids' gowns, were two of the latter.

"What's the senator eating?" asked Perry. Grace had her nose to the glass, while Perry, newly split from Drew Barrister, slouched against the window and watched the avenue for boys.

"Pot roast."

Through the window, Grace frowned at her mother and three other women from Janesville Baptist who stood hovering over the booth where the celebrity men dined. Unless the setting sun was casting spells in the glass, Grace swore her mother was blushing at Bertram Block.

Perry sucked a cigarette. "What about Reverend Memphis?"

"Locusts and wild honey."

"Huh?"

"Fried chicken, I think." Grace studied Bertram Block. He did have broad shoulders, and his trademark handkerchief sprouted from his left breast pocket. His hair was as thick and white as Perry's mom's, but his countenance tonight bore none of the weight of his radio voice. His face, as he spoke to the senator and nodded at Kevin the waiter, seemed to Grace like those of her friends' fathers, a face concerned with bills and fertilizers. Grace had expected a missionary Gulliver, a Bible-beating Paul Bunyan who would eat an entire fatted calf at one sitting to keep up his Satan-bashing strength. Grace noticed, though, that despite the dandruff on the reverend's collar, Regina was still fawning over him, refilling his iced tea glass with a pitcher from the waiter's sideboard. She refilled the senator's glass too.

That's Kevin's job, thought Grace darkly. She mashed her face against the glass and bulged her cheeks, hoping to catch her mother's eyes and startle her, but Regina stayed focused on the men. Grace recalled the radio saying that the Reverend Block left his children and his wife, Annabeth, in Memphis when he toured, and she knew also that Senator Tate's wife had drowned ten years back during some yachting brouhaha on Lake Michigan. In the midst of this reflection, an image rushed to Grace's mind: her father's flaming red hair, the animal shine of his smile. Suddenly, the glinting sliver of Max McGlone's spirit quivered in Grace's heart like a divining rod.

"Hey, Perry. I know what let's do."

"What's that, McGlone?"

Grace grinned at her canvas-clad sister. "Let's go to the Fracas and fetch these two heroes some P&V."

Perry raised her eyebrows. P&V, short for Piss and Vinegar, was a homemade mystery beer brewed by Jon Fracatto, the owner and proprietor of the Fracas Pub. P&V, whose ingredients were known only to Jon himself, was stronger than a caffeinated Trappist ale, and after just one bottle of the stuff, men were known to kiss their wives' toes or choose to raise llamas or accuse moonlight of whispering. To boot, P&V was delicious, and tasted not the least bit alcoholic. It cost twenty dollars for a twenty-ounce bottle, it was sold only at the Fracas Pub, and then only at Jon Fracatto's discretion. Jon kept a log of all Janesville residents and how many P&Vs they'd purchased. His commonsense limit was to allow each person just ten bottles in a lifetime, roughly two bottles per adult decade. Otherwise, Jon claimed, the natural order of the universe would get disturbed.

Janesvillers reserved P&V for milestone anniversaries or the enduring of Christmas with in-laws. Imbibing the stuff was risky (Manny Clausen had won a marathon after downing a bottle, whereas Wilbur Wix had slept for three weeks, missing Mardi Gras), but in every case, the imbiber ended by considering the experience salutary, or at least meant to be. Exhausted parents might rub the brew on the gums of their bawling, teething babies, but outside of that, P&V was even more off-limits to children than normal alcohol. This meant that teenagers sought the drink with unquenchable fervor. A few nights each year, usually during high winds or heat lightning, whispers went around the Oval Office that someone had swiped P&V from his parents' strongbox and was passing the magic hooch around. A real bottle of Jon Fracatto's creation never materialized in the branches of Uncle Treemus, but often an industrious teen would peel the label off his malt liquor, pour some Pixy Stix into the swill, and share with his friends some imaginary epiphany.

"Mr. Fracatto won't go for this," said Perry. She and Grace walked, arms linked, down the sidewalk.

"We'll see." Grace pushed open the pub door and dragged Perry inside. The Fracas was done in wood, with sawdust on the floor, and though it wasn't a men's club, the clientele that evening, and almost always, was woman-free. Gerry Hilliard and Ike Wappis sat at a corner table, hand-rolling cigarettes and hating the New York Yankees. Leaning his skull against the cigarette machine was Todd Wilcox, who needed one double Dewar's per rotation of the earth. Pete Poole and Joe Manson played dartboard cricket, and camped on bar stools were three scruffy men Grace didn't know.

"Mr. Fracatto?" Grace stood at the end of the bar and waved the proprietor over.

Jon Fracatto was a bald lifelong bachelor in a tank top and a grimy chef's apron. A strong forty, he hefted barbells each morning in the pub basement, where he lived and slept. His voice was graveled, and his stomach muscles cut across his torso in taut, defined slats that Jon hid behind his apron. As far as Fracas regulars knew, Jon had never cooked a meal in his life (he subsisted on cellophane-wrapped German sausages that his aunt sent from Milwaukee), but the apron suggested he was ready for action.

"Yeah?" Jon chewed a toothpick and frowned at Grace and Perry. He had little time for girls.

"Two bottles of P&V, please." Grace stood with her shoulders back. She refrained from swaying her hips.

Jon shook his head. "Nothing doing."

The three men at the bar were watching the girls. The burliest man had hair like muddy hay and he threw winks at Perry. The second stranger, a squat block of a man whose mouth hung not quite closed, was looking at Grace's legs. The third man purred and said, "Nice dresses."

"Go screw yourselves," said Perry.

The strangers hooted. "We will," said one, "if you gals give us a hand."

Perry offered the guy her middle finger. "Fuck off, hicks."

"Hicks?" The burly stranger got off his stool and stepped toward Perry. At this, Pete Poole and Joe Manson, who'd been listening and who'd both wrestled in their James Madison days, quit their darts and came to the bar. Grace wondered if she was about to witness the kind of clash that had cost her father his life. Jon Fracatto, however, faced the three strangers and pointed his left hand at them like a wizard. The man moving toward Perry paused and took in Jon's hand, which featured a scar-blackened thumb and three hideously stubbed fingers.

"Leave my pub," said Jon.

"Now, wait a minute," said the former winker.

Jon came closer to the men and set his left hand on the bar like a voodoo talisman. Jon was under five nine, but he'd killed twelve men in Vietnam, and the grenade that shredded his hand had also embedded gnarled shrapnel in his jaw.

"Leave my pub and leave my town," said Jon quietly. "Do it now."

The three men studied Jon's jaw and hand, saw all they needed to. The purring man laid a twenty on the bar, and the strangers left.

Perry rocked on her heels. "Thanks, Mr. Fracatto. They were creepy."

"Now, about those P&Vs," said Grace.

Jon reached below the bar and hauled up a leather-bound parchment-paper ledger. Clawing through it, he came to pages that bore the heading JANESVILLE BIRTHDAYS.

"Periwinkle Danning," read Jon, "born September 7, 1975, currently sixteen years old." He flipped pages. "Grace Emily McGlone, born November 10, 1976, currently fifteen years old."

"The drinks aren't for us," explained Grace. "We want to give them to Bertram Block and Senator Tate, over at Mackidew's. You know, P&V, the true nectar of Janesville, presented to our distinguished visitors by two sweethearts of the local corn."

Perry curtsied extravagantly. Grace followed suit.

Jon crossed his arms on his chest, eyeing the girls. Normally, he would've refused them even entrance to his pub, but he'd watched them tramping around town recently, and he had a fondness for their dresses. Or perhaps Jon thought wistfully of the affair he'd shared just after Watergate with Danielle Danning, who was replete with lovers and who eschewed matrimony. It was common Janesville knowledge that the Danning children all had different, undisclosed sires, and there was more than a fair chance, Jon knew, that Perry was his flesh-and-blood daughter. So, softened by the girls' earnestness and the dying shafts of sun in the pub door's windowpane, Jon fetched two bottles of P&V from the basement. The bottles, fashioned from blue glass and corked with reusable hinge stoppers, bore a few cobwebs and no labels. Jon set the bottles on the bar.

Grace grinned and reached forward. "Now we're talking."

"Tallyho," said Perry.

Jon held up his wrecked hand in warning. "As a onetime exception in honor of Color's wedding, these P&Vs are gratis. But don't come around here again till you're of age."

"We won't, sir." Grace petted the bottles, cradled one in the crook of each arm.

Jon placed his black thumb on her forearm. "And if the out-of-towners refuse these, you take proper care of them."

Grace nodded, shivering at the publican's rough touch, wondering if his final word, *them,* meant the potions or the men.

* * *

The next morning, Perry picked blackberries in the woods behind her house, while Grace sat sulking on the lawn, lacing grass blades around her toes. It was a sweltering morning, ninety degrees before noon, and both girls wore their gesso dresses. Beside Grace sat a cocktail bucket full of ice cubes, and every few minutes the two friends ate ice and rubbed it on their necks and arms.

"I can't believe they turned us down," said Grace.

Perry stood chomping ice, spitting wet pebbles of it on Grace, who pinched Perry's calf and sent her laughing back to the bushes.

"Since when do men say no to liquor?" complained Grace.

Perry shrugged, watching for thorns and nettles, and collected berries in her hem. She didn't care that Bertram Block and Charles Tate the First had declined the P&Vs the night before. Apparently, the reverend never drank, but Charles, during a campaign trail stop five years back, had bummed a tug of the brew from a voter. After just that one swig, he'd spent three days dizzily renouncing his lifelong Republicanism and asking Janesvillers where he could buy a donkey. The episode passed, but Senator Tate swore off forever the suspicious libation that had summoned it.

This all mattered little to Perry. It was July, and she was just days from standing witness to her only sister's wedding. Pete Deegle had phoned her this morning to ask her out for next Saturday. Perry had said yes, then showered, shaved her legs, and called Grace over for berry picking and ice chewing. These were the things that made sense to Perry: fingertips stained purple, too much sun, sharing your tongue with a boy. The Dannings didn't have religion or politics in their house, so Perry, on a summer morning, wasn't pondering Reverend Block or Senator Tate. She was embracing the earth, its palette of hues, its facts and smells.

"Did Mrs. Yahweh confiscate your booze?"

Grace had ringed the toes of her left foot with grass. "She stashed the bottles in my dad's old liquor cabinet, but I jimmied the lock. Anytime we want them, there are two P&Vs buried beside our backyard well." Grace wiggled the toes of her right foot and began adorning those.

"Maybe we should return them to the Fracas." Her hem pregnant with blackberries, Perry scampered back to Grace and sat behind her. Perry wedged her crotch close to Grace's buttocks and splayed one leg to each side of Grace, as if they rode tandem on a sled. "That way, you could see Mr. Fracatto again."

Grace studied her right pinky toe. Annoyingly, Stewart McFigg popped into her head, complimented her weave-work. "Why would I want to see Mr. Fracatto?"

Perry leaned to Grace's ear. "So he can bed you, you little whore."

Grace laughed. "Tallyho."

Perry's fingers came around to Grace's mouth and placed a fat blackberry between her lips. "Bite," instructed Perry.

Grace bit the tart berry, ate it. Perry's juicy fingers went away. Grace felt the fingers tracing on her back.

"Hey, what're you drawing?"

Perry giggled. "You want to suck on Jon Fracatto's thumb."

"I do not."

"You want to swallow his manhood."

Grace's cheeks flushed. "What're you *drawing*?"

Perry pinched berries till they burst, applied the dregs to Grace's back in lines and whorls.

"I wonder if Pete Deegle will try to bed me," said Perry.

Grace thought of her father. She wished he were a series of intimate memories, a long chronicle of hugs and scoldings. Instead, Max McGlone was merely pictures, a celebrity in Grace's mind, a famous actor who took roles in thrillers and road movies. He was the stunt driver who stole truckloads of plutonium from terrorists, the James Bond–style rogue who trysted with lovelies but, down deep, cleaved to country or wife or *something*.

"I hope Pete Deegle tries to bed me," chatted Perry.

That night, Regina McGlone drove herself and Grace out to Lake Loomis, where Bertram Block was preaching after sundown. Regina was thrilled not only to be seeing the reverend testify but also because her daughter had consented to attend. True, Grace was still wearing her filthy smock of a dress, which she'd refused to have washed. But Regina believed that God worked in mysterious ways, and if He'd converted hardscrabble fishermen two millennia back, He could shake sense now into a lazy teenage girl.

"Perry didn't want to come?" asked Regina.

Grace shook her head. As the McGlone station wagon bumped along the pitted dirt lane to Lake Loomis, Grace's ruby hair flounced on her shoulders. Reaching out a hand, Regina stroked her daughter's locks.

"So, will you let me trim this jungle soon?"

Grace moved her head toward the window, out of range. "Mother."

Regina sighed, brought her hand back to steering.

In her heart, where she kept her mother-daughter meter, Grace felt a click of guilt. "Maybe I'm like Samson," she ventured. "Maybe my hair is my strength, and should never be cut."

Regina gasped, pointed. "Oh, Grace. Look."

A quarter mile up the road, pitched on the hillock at the head of Lake Loomis, was an enormous, cream-colored tent. It covered the area of a football field, and charged from within by lamps on telephone-pole–size posts, its walls and roof glowed as if they were made of light. Parked on the grass all around were hundreds of cars and a bright, gilded ghost of the tent spangled in the calm lake water. To Regina's mind—given the small array of stars that night and the sliver-thin moon—the tent glimmered in the darkness like a divine homestead.

"Damn," said Grace.

"Don't say that word," said Regina, but her voice was a whisper, her eyes feasting out the window.

They parked in the field of cars and approached the tent. Attached to the glowing structure at one end was a large white

RV with the words GOD'S WILL branded across the side in black script. Regina pointed the RV out to Grace. "The reverend's private trailer," she marveled. "His sanctuary."

Inside, the tent was rollicking. A good thousand souls had arrived already, and more were streaming in, all clamoring to get a seat near the giant stage at the tent end closest to the RV. Regina flitted about with a blush to her cheeks. She hugged friends from Janesville Baptist, and greeted customers of Thou Shalt Read. So spry was her mood that she forgot to make excuses for Grace's dress.

As for Grace, she had to admit she was impressed. The sea of cars outside boasted license plates from Iowa, Illinois, even the Dakotas. Grace had agreed to attend the revival mostly because two nights from now, this tent would host the reception of Color Danning and Charles Tate the Second. Senator Tate had cajoled Danielle Danning into letting him throw a much more formal post-vows party than had been planned (Danielle had envisioned a casual Loomis Forest night where guests would stroll barefoot and gnaw wild mushrooms), and Grace wanted a peek at the big top under which she'd soon taste duck à l'orange and Pouilly-Fuissé. She figured that roughly where the stage currently existed was where the dance floor would be, where she and Perry would scandalize the adults come reception night. The two girls had choreographed a body-grinding duet they intended to perform belly-to-belly in their gesso dresses just as the cake was being cut.

Yet tonight Grace felt content to walk amid thronging Protestants. Neighbors and strangers fussed by, all claiming seats and wearing white. Grace liked how their adult bodies, ripe with talcum and aftershave, brushed past her, fervent and oblivious.

Gregory Sleech, the pastor of Janesville Baptist, kept ambling onto the stage, checking the microphones like a rock concert roadie, while his wife, Miriam, worked the crowd in a lilac gown. The day's humidity had not abated, and sweat shone on every brow. Tables bearing punch bowls and clear plastic cups lined the tent wall opposite the stage. The bowls were filled with iced water and sugared lemon slices, and men and women drank from their cups with proper, dainty greed.

At eight o'clock, amid deafening hurrahs, Bertram Block emerged from his trailer, took the stage and microphone. He pulled his handkerchief from his pocket and waved it. "Whom will you serve?" he shouted. "Before whom will you shudder?"

"The Lord," hollered the crowd. Grace stood by the punch bowls, leaning on a tent post, watching the believers. Regina was somewhere in this mass, lost to her daughter's sight, but Grace, just months from sixteen, liked it that way.

"Will you serve a golden idol?" boomed the reverend. "Will you serve a blind, dumb thing?"

The tent-folk shouted that they wouldn't. From eighty yards away, Grace studied Bertram Block, his striding to and fro. Last night in Mackidew's, she'd met his amber eyes up close, and they'd surprised her. Grace had figured that a preacher as tall as the Reverend Block—nearly six and a half feet—would have eyes to match his stature and voice: fierce, roving eyes, deep like the mouths of twin battle cannons. What Grace had seen instead, as she'd offered him a P&V, were two simple brown orbs, as soft as syrup dollops.

"Will you love a graven image?" called Bertram Block. "Will you hail the created before the Creator?"

"No," replied the mob.

The reverend made his right arm a staff over the congregation, then spread the fingers of his hand, and the crowd hushed. With his left hand, he brought the microphone to his lips. "The answer is yes," he whispered, "for we are sinners, all."

Grace slipped out of the tent. Having heard Bertram Block preach countless times on the radio, she was familiar with the arcs of his sermons, so she knew that the "we are sinners, all" line was his intro for a lecture on hell or, as the Reverend Block called it, the fire pit of Gehenna. Months back, while dusting the mantel, Grace had heard Bertram explain this Old Testament reference—Gehenna was some nasty valley in Judah—but as a child she'd always imagined an actual creature named Gehenna who lived in an underworld fire pit. Gehenna, in Grace's mind, had the body and swelled head of a giant, angry chicken. What Grace feared most about this beast was its idiocy. All Gehenna did, day after day, was strut around and sound off a livid, squawking gibberish. The human souls damned to Gehenna's company couldn't tune this drivel out. They soon got so irritated that they, too, began strutting and screeching. They tried to drown out the demon fowl, but couldn't, so they ended up chirping and shrieking for eternity.

On a beautiful summer night, though, Grace didn't want to hear about Gehenna. Fortunately, she'd planned to skip this part of the sermon. She weaved through the flock of cars to her mother's station wagon and found under the shotgun seat the bottle of P&V she'd stashed there. She felt guilty drinking it behind Perry's back, but something told Grace her first experience with this cryptic potion should be a solo act. So she scuttled down to the lakeshore, kicked off her sandals, waded in to her shins, and popped the cork.

For a while, as she drank, Grace noticed nothing special. She stood in the lake, her dress hem drenched. Her calves felt slick, and in the shine from the tent, the water around her was a wide plate of light. Gradually, Grace became aware of her heart in her chest and her head blooming warm with some new current.

"Tallyho," giggled Grace.

She splashed out of the water. Mud massaged the arches of her feet, the buzzing of cicadas tickled her ears, and the stars seemed to Grace like candies she might reach for and pluck down and eat. A sultry sweat was in her hair, beading between her breasts, trickling down her arms. Grace felt her forehead.

"Wow." Her temples were hot, but she felt no fever. Some new energy was loose in her, seeking a home, or outlet, or point of devotion. A hymn began in the tent behind Grace. She finished off the P&V, dropped the bottle, stood trembling. She felt electric, tuned in.

" 'How sweet the sound . . .' " sang the tent.

Grace reentered the big top. The believers were on their feet, a clapping, singing legion.

"Jesus," whispered Grace, gaping around. The P&V had somehow empowered her eyes, for each person appeared in unique, startling relief. Grace had never noticed so acutely the sad hunch with which Melanie Bryson carried her shoulders. Stan Gurtenberg, the retired mail carrier, was a wilting weed of a man, with a cane and arthritic ankles, and even Miriam Sleech cut a melancholy figure: she stood in her lilac gown, singing, her hands clasped before her heart, but her alto strains made little mark on the greater chorus, and her open mouth showed teeth black with fillings. Grace was filled with a sudden sympathy for her neighbors, and a vision of her father flooded her mind. Max McGlone lay dead in his coffin, his cheeks gray, his lips stitched closed with blue thread.

Grace groaned, tried to blink this specter away. Out of nowhere, the sound of Stewart McFigg's addled foot danced in her brain. Dizzy, Grace reached out a hand, grasped a tent post, only to have Mr. Francis Pyle, who'd lost his wife to Hodgkin's last autumn, nod at her serenely as he shuffled toward the punch.

"Jesus," said Grace again.

She closed her eyes, her soul brimming with a sadness, a sky-wide empathy that the P&V had unlocked. A sensor had wakened in her heart. The dormant shard of her father's bravado seemed now a needle gauge within her that jumped at every human frailty she witnessed. The Baptists around her rang out their hymn. They sang of the Lord's might, while Grace, eyes shut, clutched her stomach, wondering if she might retch, wondering why weakness rather than might was in charge of her knees.

"Open your eyes," boomed a voice.

Grace obeyed. She saw, through a tunnel of waving arms, the Reverend Block onstage. His right hand was on the forehead of Abigail Drake, a formerly agnostic mother of three, who knelt before the preacher, head bowed.

"Open your eyes and receive the Lord," intoned Bertram Block.

"Amen," said Abigail. The preacher slapped her brow.

"Amen," roared the congregation.

People bustled toward the stage. Stanley Quimby, a heavyset mute, lumbered down the aisle, and behind him was Pauper

Jeckett, who'd torched his sister-in-law's prize begonias. Kim Lalohsa, the healthy, cheeky Democrat, hurried forward and knelt before the preacher. Grace understood. These were the altar calls she'd heard about, the moments when anyone moved by the Spirit was supposed to rush pell-mell for a laying on of hands. What she didn't understand was why she, too, was suddenly galvanized by Bertram Block. He was the man she'd heard yammer year after year about Gehenna, yet tonight he was a force before her, a flesh-and-blood man, in whose presence she wanted to bask. His height, his suit, his jaw, his white hair, all seemed like special male credentials.

"Receive the Lord," yelled Bertram. He slapped Kim Lalohsa's forehead.

Grace stood riveted. She'd forgotten her sandals at the water's edge, and her calves were flecked with mud. The ground beneath her trembled with the stamping crowd, their noise clobbered her ears, P&V swirled in her belly, and in the middle of all was the giant preacher, his hand gripping men's and women's foreheads. As Grace watched, the weakness in her knees became a strength, a courage in her thighs. This man was wielding power, his own or someone else's, and Grace felt a dizzy need to get close to him, to stare into his maple eyes, to let him touch her too.

"Hallelujah," thundered the crowd.

The altar calls were ending. As the Baptists swayed and chanted, the reverend was waving good-bye, leaving the stage, heading for his trailer. The crowd—a frenzied body—surged in his direction.

"Wait," whispered Grace. She sprang forth and dodged

between her stirred-up neighbors. As she hurried toward the trailer, arms flailed against her like switches of wood in a forest.

"Wait." Grace pressed onward. She felt in need, charged with P&V. Breaking through a wall of adults, she caught Bertram Block's arm as he reached his trailer door.

"Wait," she told him.

Bertram turned, his body hot from performing. He beheld what he so often beheld on such nights, a rabble of fans raging around his RV, crying out for autographs, for healings, for God's Will. There were Bibles thrust forward for him to touch, and arms in Ace bandages. There were bonnets and beards, and shoutings of his name. In the midst of this din was a glorious young woman in a chaos-colored dress. She gripped his arm, a fervor in her eyes, and sly Bertram Block did what he so often did on such nights. He pulled his trusty handkerchief from his pocket, held it up high, tossed it far into the mob. Anxious for a trophy, the crowd watched the handkerchief sail, and fell upon it. Meanwhile, Bertram, in the instant that eyes were averted, grabbed the girl's wrist, tugged her into his trailer, and shut and locked the door.

"Hey." Grace was alone in the dark with a man. Her eyes, used to the tent lights, could see nothing.

"Hey," she said again. The darkness cleared its throat.

What happened next happened quickly. Still balmy with P&V, Grace found herself pushed onto a water bed, her dress shoved up around her shoulders. From outside came a frenzy of singing, while hands made Grace's bra and underwear vanish.

"Wait," she said, but the hands didn't wait. They clutched her breasts, petted her ass, and a strong skull worked between her legs. Grace gasped as a tongue came alive at the meeting of her thighs.

You're married, she thought, but she didn't punch the preacher. She breathed hard, in and out, and the water bed slushed. She could make out a stove, and a daddy longlegs on the ceiling. She gripped the bedsheets. A thrill and a thrumming sprang up in her lap.

"Oh," panted Grace.

She strained her neck, tried to look at the man wolfing his face into her, but her dress, a mound at her throat, blocked her view.

"Oh God," she moaned.

Bertram Block snorted, kept at her. Grace closed her eyes, breathing fast. A power was brewing in her loins, a color she couldn't name but wanted to. She clenched her teeth, men rushing through her mind. Jon Fracatto became the face in her thighs, then the Danning boys took their turns, and, finally, Stewart McFigg had his shy, strong way with her.

"Oh. Oh my God." Grace covered her mouth with one hand.

Come on, Stewart, she thought, grinding her hips. *Come on, boy.*

Without warning, Bertram reared back on his knees. He unlashed his pants, downed them, laid his body on Grace's. She cried out as a jowl grazed her ear, and, down in her crotch, a new, urgent muscle pinched, joining its way inside her. The singing was fading, while a hot mouth met Grace's ear. "God's will," it whispered. "God's will."

Grace gripped the body upon her, accepted it. She huffed, held a rib cage between her palms, gave herself to the driving in her lap. She dug her nails into the preacher's buttocks, and a trembling gathered in her lungs. As she let out a moan, the unnamed color between her legs peaked and released. The man cried out, too, and his body tensed, thrust once more, and shuddered. When the shuddering passed, the preacher slid off the girl.

"Oh." Grace lay floating. "Wow. Oh."

Bertram Block was naked from the waist down but still wore his suitcoat and tie. He rolled away from Grace, making waves, and wrapped his bottom half in sheets. He turned his face to the wall.

"Wait ten minutes till the crowd disperses." His voice was small.

Grace blinked. Little convulsions seized on and off in her groin. She watched the spider on the ceiling, wondered if this man loved her. "Um . . . What?"

"Come on, now." He sounded impatient. "Pull your dress down. Peek to see that the coast is clear, then slip out and go home."

She frowned. Up by her chest, she found her hem, still damp from the lake, and pulled it over her knees. When she sat up, she saw a stain on the white sheet beneath her.

"I bled," she guessed aloud. She felt sore inside too.

"Go." The preacher recoiled from her, curled into a ball. Grace frowned again, confused. She touched his shoulder. After all, she'd moved toward him in the crowd, and he'd brought her through the door.

"No." The man in the suitcoat removed her hand, pushed it away.

"Go home," he said.

* * *

The next morning, Grace sat cross-legged in her backyard, by the well that bordered the Killians' cornfield. She'd had a shower an hour before, then dressed in her rust-colored blouse, blue jeans, and sneakers, and come out to think in the grass and sun-dry her hair. Her mind was clear of P&V now, though she sat on the spot where the second bottle of it was buried. In her lap lay her folded gesso dress, the only real clothing she'd worn for the last month. Grace stared at the well wall's rough, mortared stones as tears dripped down her cheeks.

A sparrow spoke, and Morton, the Killians' beagle, howled in response. Grace sniffled, wiped her nose. The night before, when she'd slunk away from the RV, she'd found her mother by the station wagon, chatting with Miriam Sleech.

"Grace!" Regina had hugged her daughter. "Wasn't that fantastic?"

Grace's mouth had opened, formed no words. She'd stared at her mother and the minister's wife, both of whom wore rosy expressions. For one loopy, bacchic moment, Grace had wondered if these women had actually planned her deflowering.

"That was the reverend's best testimony yet," Miriam had said.

Grace reached out now, touched the well wall, which she'd always loved. Its stones were football-size, gray and warm in the sun. She sniffled again, blinked tears away. Last night, in less than an hour, she'd lost her sandals, her bra, her panties, and her maidenhood, but this well had been here for a century, a pillar in the earth, a help to her family and others.

"Hello, Grace."

Grace turned to see the Killians' cornstalks rustling. When they parted, Color Danning emerged from the maize.

"Color?" Grace wiped her eyes, sat up straight, tried to look composed.

The young bride-to-be knelt before Grace. Color wore a plain brown dress that could have been the frock of an abbess. Her silver hair, parted down the middle, fell in two clean curtains on either side of her head, and her misty gray eyes focused on Grace.

"We were about to leave for the wedding rehearsal when I heard you crying."

"From your mother's house?" asked Grace, but she immediately lowered her eyes. She knew better than to question Color's faculties, despite the Dannings' house being two miles away.

"I sent the others ahead to Lake Loomis and walked over." Color took Grace's hand.

Grace teared up again. "D-do you know what happened to me last night?"

Color glanced at the dress in Grace's lap. "I have some guesses."

Grace sniffled. "Um . . . Yeah. Well." A breeze rippled over the Killians' corn, smelling like harvest. Color squeezed Grace's hand.

"I—I can't be your bridesmaid," stammered Grace. "The person who . . . well, he'll be at your wedding, so—"

"It's all right, honey." Color brushed tears from Grace's cheeks. "Don't worry. It's fine."

Angry, confused, fifteen, Grace poked at the dress in her lap. Drawn in dried berry juice on the gesso that had covered Grace's back were two intertwined figures, one a man, the other a woman. The action of these beings was indistinct. Among grass, coffee, and mustard stains, they were wrestling or making love or biting each other's heels. Perry had fashioned the couple in broad strokes so that Grace wouldn't be chastised by Regina, but Grace wondered now, as she stared at the writhing pair, whether Perry didn't possess some prescient power similar to Color's.

"I can't be there." Grace cleared her throat. She'd stopped crying. "I can't be there, and I can't tell people why."

"All right."

"I can't tell Perry, or my mother, or yours. I can't tell them about last night, ever, and neither can you."

Color inclined her head, a promise.

Grace glared at the gesso dress. "And I can't wear this... thing anymore."

"Let's get rid of it, then." Color stood, pulled Grace up. The gray-eyed abbess stepped to the well wall and peeked over. "Toss it in. Lay it to rest."

Grace leaned over the well stones, stared into the black.

"Come on. Down the hatch she goes."

Grace held the dress over the well. She hesitated, looked below at the darkness she'd spent her girlhood fearing, pondering. She didn't want to gum up the earth, to clog whatever nether-spring brought water to her mother.

"Hey." Color nudged Grace's shoulder. "You're Grace McGlone. No dress and nobody's got nothing on you."

Grace nodded. The empathy that the P&V had roused within her kindled, and for one moment, as Morton the beagle brayed nearby, Grace aimed that empathy at herself. She shivered, threw back her shoulders, and let the dress fall.

"Tallyho," she whispered.

That night, Grace walked to the Oval Office, to climb Uncle Treemus and watch the fireworks that the Janesville Fire

Department launched each Fourth of July from the football field. She'd been forced to get there on foot, because Perry—furious with Grace for backing out of Color's wedding—had refused to speak to her, let alone give her a ride. Grace climbed high in the vast, ranging oak tree, and lay on her favorite platform, reading *The Big Sleep* by flashlight, while lime and strawberry explosions shook the firmament. In the oaks around Uncle Treemus, Grace's schoolmates kissed and drank and howled at the sky, but Grace cleaved close to Philip Marlowe, to his calm and wit amid shenanigans. She was upset about Perry, but she'd outlasted her friend's tantrums before, and she was content tonight to forget her. When thoughts of her father came, Grace shut him out, too, by reading aloud to herself.

It was only when a particularly bold orange firework blossomed that Grace glanced up and spied, in the highest boughs of Uncle Treemus, the silhouette of Stewart McFigg. He was sitting on a plank outside what looked to be his most complete tree house yet (it had a full roof and, if she wasn't mistaken, a chimney), and as he gripped the branch above him, his biceps bulged in the night. He looked to Grace like a sturdy frontier homeowner taking his ease. She left her book and flashlight and climbed to his height.

"Hey, Stewart."

Stewart jumped, his hands tensing on the bough they held. When he saw the visitor on his plank, his face melted from shock to bliss.

"Ha," said Grace. "Got you."

"Grace." Stewart tried to straighten his vest. "Grace, I'm so glad you've come."

"Easy, McFigg. I was in the neighborhood."

Stewart hauled himself to his feet. Above the football field, a yellow spider of light crackled.

"Happy Fourth of July."

"Happy Fourth, Stewart."

"Hey . . . where's that crazy dress you've always got on lately?"

Grace crossed her arms. "I couldn't very well climb up here in a dress, could I, genius?"

"Oh. I guess not."

The boughs holding the tree house swayed slightly. Grace took a step to balance herself, and Stewart's hand shot to her shoulder, held her.

"Careful. Watch your step out here on the porch."

She shrugged his hand off. "The *porch*? Give me a break."

Stewart blushed. His hands dug for his pockets. "Sorry I grabbed you."

Grace gazed at his orthopedic boot. She figured two full pairs of her sneakers could fit inside it. "Well . . ." She nodded at the tree house. "Do I get a tour?"

Stewart raised his chin and beamed. "Sure." He wiped his hand on his jeans and held it out to Grace, who gave him her palm.

The tree house was a masterpiece indeed. Stewart had built three attached rooms. One, which held a mess of blankets and pillows, was a sleeping nook. A small second alcove held a camping stove, above which Stewart had cut a chimney. The spacious main chamber, though, was most impressive. It was large enough for four men to stand in, and the floor was covered with a bearskin rug Grace recalled seeing on sale at Pyle's Thrift Emporium. In one corner stood a crude but solid bookcase laden with Marvel Comics, boxes of caramels, and, to Grace's surprise, a Bible. Hanging in another corner was a battery-powered lantern, and below this stood a chair whose back was an old window shutter. A third corner featured the spine of Uncle Treemus himself, the tough, bark-covered buttress around which Stewart had stacked all three rooms. Nailed into this bark was a crucifix.

Grace stared at the cross, at its black-eyed Jesus. "So, what happens up here?" She sat on the rug. "You come up here and eat candy and pray Catholic prayers?"

Stewart joined her on the bearskin, but kept his eyes focused out the single, pane-free window, where red and purple galaxies burst into being.

"Sometimes. Or I try to do homework. Mostly I read my comics."

Grace glanced at his arms, which looked twice as dense as any Janesville man's. She imagined Stewart's fist balling, crushing into Bertram Block's gray matter. "What comics are those?"

"Oh." Because of his boot, Stewart sat with his feet splayed, like a boy at the beach. "Mostly I read ones about this guy, the Thing."

"Who's he?"

"He's this guy. He's made of stones, but he's also, like, a scientist."

Grace stared at the bookshelf. Draped over one ledge was a comic whose cover showed the man made of stones. In a lab coat, he was running from men with guns. Over his shoulder he carried a buxom blonde in a tight blue sweater.

"Is he good or evil?"

"Good. Well . . . he can be somewhat evil if the situation calls. He's a bit of both, you know. He's, like, thorough inside."

"Thorough." Grace thought of her gesso dress, buried, muddy, gone. "You mean complex?"

"Yeah, complex. You want a caramel?"

"All right."

They had caramels, two each. While they chewed, fireworks and people whistled far below them.

"Hey," said Stewart, "isn't Color's wedding tomorrow?"

"I don't want to talk about that."

"Oh. Okay, Grace."

A breeze came up, and the tree house shifted.

She put her palms flat on the floor. "Wow."

"Don't be scared." Stewart tongued the confection in his teeth. "It's like being belowdecks on a boat."

"I'm not *scared*." The wind lifted higher, though, and her stomach went hollow. It was warm in the tree house too. Grace felt sweat beneath her blouse, recalled the preacher's hands on her belly.

"It couldn't fall, though, right?"

He smiled, quick and patient. "We won't fall. Don't worry."

"I'm not *worried*. I'm just saying."

Stewart smoothed a bump in the rug. "I built this place good."

She shrugged. The breeze quit, and the tree house steadied. Grace petted the rug, tapped the claws on one of the bear paws.

"Yeah, I guess this place is cool, Stewart."

"Thanks."

Outside, a finale of light happened. The crowd whooped.

"So, don't kids come up here? You know, steal your stuff?"

"Most kids won't climb this high. Plus . . ."

"Plus what?"

Stewart grinned a little. He crooked his right arm, made a muscle. "People don't screw with me anymore."

Grace figured that Stewart's crippled foot, without the boot on, was probably tough and swollen.

"Sorry I bitched you out that time in sixth grade, Stewart."

"That's all right."

"You're not a total loss, I guess."

"Oh. Thanks."

The night before was pulsing in her groin, confusing her. She wondered if this confusion was adulthood. Stewart was two feet away, and Grace had run out of words. She hadn't climbed with an agenda, but she focused on the biceps before her and, guts burning, made up her mind.

"By the way, Grace, you can come up here anytime you want. You can even borrow issues of *The Thing*. Just tell me which ones."

Grace crawled over, laid herself on top of Stewart.

"Yikes," said Stewart.

She worked her tongue awkwardly into his mouth. She put her hand on his thigh, but Stewart batted it away, urged Grace off of him.

"Whoa, Nelly," he panted. "Hey, now."

"What?"

He was on his feet, his face flushed. "I didn't mean to swat you, Grace, but . . ."

Grace tugged Stewart's pant leg, tried to usher him down to

her. She was nervous, too, but figured she had no choice. She figured, given her roll in the RV, that this was what a man and woman did when close and alone in the night.

"Come on, Stewart." Grace pulled off her blouse. "Lie down.... Bed me."

Stewart backed against his bookshelf. "Oh. No, thank you." He licked his lips, his eyes on her floral-patterned bra. "I mean, we can't."

Grace noticed a fold in her stomach skin. She panicked. "Am I fat?"

"No. God, no. You're beautiful. That's a really pretty brassiere."

She felt stupid. She stared at the comic book cover, the freckle-free blonde. "Then what's wrong?"

Stewart pushed hair from his eyes. His boot and sneaker were rooted in place. "We're Christians."

No wind was rocking the tree house now.

"I'm Catholic. You're Baptist." He shrugged his shoulders. "We're trying for heaven."

Grace frowned. On the floor beneath her and this boy was an animal hide, the kind people made love on in movies.

"We're Christians, and we're not married." Stewart tossed his chin toward the crucifix. "So . . . you know. No humping."

Grace thought of Bertram Block, his awful mint breath, the lock of his hips against hers. "And you really believe that?"

"Yes, Grace."

"You'll never . . . hump, till you're married?"

"No."

She wound bear hairs around her fingers. Perry, at Grace's last count, had slept with four upperclassmen. "Why?"

"I told you," explained Stewart. "I'm trying for heaven. Just like you."

Trying for heaven, thought Grace. *Trying for heaven.* She stared at this maimed boy in his sleeveless vest, his back stiff to the bookshelf. He was serious. He wasn't going to touch her.

"Do you *want* to hump me, though? I mean, do you wish you could?"

"Oh, sure. I'm not homosexual. I'd love it if we humped. Like I said, your brassiere's really great."

"Thanks."

"The flowers on it look nice."

"Thanks."

"But we're Christians."

She nodded slowly. Stewart, all by himself, had built this little house she was in. "Right," she said.

There was a long pause. Stewart stepped out onto the porch. Grace tugged her blouse back on and followed him. Stewart was staring up, fidgeting his fingers on his thighs.

"Well," said Grace. The stars were immaculate, everywhere. The scent of burnt sulfur, a ghost of the fireworks, hung around Uncle Treemus.

"Are we in love?" Stewart sounded worried. He looked at Grace. "Should I take you to a dance?"

"No."

"I . . . It's just that I can't dance, Grace. You know, my foot . . ."

"We aren't in love, Stewart. We aren't a couple." She felt armed with something new, knowledge maybe.

Stewart looked frustrated, like he might cry. "But I care about you. . . ."

"Thank you, Stewart," said Grace, and she climbed down to the ground, alone.

* * *

During the rest of that summer and into the fall, Grace discovered she had no friends. Perry, who'd always been her constant companion, made good on the silent treatment that began with Color's wedding. She shunned Grace's company entirely, and, to Perry's shock, Grace didn't care. This sudden continental divide between them surprised Grace, too, but she believed she had a new perspective on her former friend, and that perspective told her Perry was a catty, sentimental slut. This opinion formed in Grace's mind not with scheming jealousies or hopes for feuding, but with a simple observation of fact. Perry pretty much bad-mouthed every student at James Madison, except whichever athlete was currently nailing her, and whenever she moved on to a new stud, she lumped her former beau in with the contemptible masses. As for sentimentality, Grace thought it unhealthy that the only time Perry called a truce and phoned her anymore was after midnight on weekends, when Grace would lift the receiver and hear boys hooting in the party-loud background as Perry sniffled and sobbed and said, "I just blew so-and-so and now he's acting all distant and shit."

Grace tired of these calls and stopped answering them. Instead, she quit smoking and paid attention in school, got herself jazzed on *The Great Gatsby,* Willa Cather, *Travels with Charlie*. To her amazement and her mother's tearful relief, Grace also started spending afternoons at Thou Shalt Read. She sometimes worked the cash register or stocked books, but most often she climbed the ladder to the store's attic, where, beneath a square skylight, she would settle into a green beanbag chair and read the works of Christian writers. She didn't know exactly why she was burning through these texts, but she liked that Stewart had said she was trying for heaven, and she loved that when she read Luther, Calvin, Augustine, C. S. Lewis, she didn't feel sixteen anymore.

The next spring, she sprinted on the track team, and she craved Pepsi constantly, and when she curled reading in the beanbag, she kept her hair back in complicated scarlet braids, while her feet rubbed and groomed each other, like sisters. So, she was young—but when she pored over Thomas Aquinas and the New Testament, she felt a timeless part of herself taking in the words and stories, a realm within her where wisdom, maybe even glory, might someday make a home. Bertram Block, too, had thrust his way into this realm with his voice and his body, but Grace, as she turned seventeen, realized what bothered her most about her tussle with the preacher. He'd wowed the crowds at Lake Loomis, but he was missing whatever kept Stewart from screwing Grace in Uncle Treemus. Grace decided that the thing Bertram Block was missing—the secret that freaky old Stewart possessed—was honor.

Grace began spying that honor around her, peeling her eyes for it. She saw it in her mother's fingers as they taped broken book spines. She smelled it in the gravies and soups prepared in her school cafeteria by Gunther Hodge, who was fifty and slow-minded and teased, but who fed even the students who mocked him most. Grace saw honor, too, in freshman Jessica Linson, who could sprint a quarter mile in fifty-four seconds, but who, after each race, hustled to the high-jump pit to cheer for her older, talentless sister, Ida. Something in these people's habits moved Grace, refueled the loopy compassion that the P&V had poured into her heart. For her own part, Grace decided that she'd try to be like Stewart McFigg from now on. Yes, she prayed for trim hips, and, yes, she got a lurch between her legs when she bumped into Crimson Danning at Todd's Supermarket, but, in hopes of honor, she would save those hips and that lurch for her spouse. *If wisdom could be got through sex, well, amen, brother,* thought Grace. *But I'll be damned,* she thought, *if I go all the way again with some adulterous soapbox schmuck with Certs on his breath. And I'm not giving it up for the Drew Barristers of this world, either.*

In short, Grace McGlone became a believer. She didn't announce this, didn't attend church with Regina. Instead, over the winter of her junior year, she paid visits to the Reverend Gregory Sleech. She told him in confidence what she felt. She felt that her father was still alive somewhere, still looking out for her. She felt bad for lies she'd told, and for having stood guard for a certain friend's Oval Office rendezvous. Finally Grace admitted that she believed, after reading the Gospels, that if there was one fellow who'd ever walked with honor, it was Jesus.

Hearing all this, Gregory Sleech smiled, and in a private August ceremony at Lake Loomis with only his wife, Miriam, standing witness, he baptized Grace. It was the summer before Grace turned eighteen, and, wearing cutoff jean shorts and her old rust-colored blouse, she'd ridden her bicycle to the lake, a white dress stuffed in her backpack. She had by then an after-school job at Carlson's Car Wash, and she'd used fifty dollars of her wages to buy the secondhand dress at Pyle's Thrift Emporium. Once she'd pedaled out to Lake Loomis, Grace changed into this dress in the woods, and after the Reverend Sleech dunked her in the lake, Grace changed in the woods again, then wrung the dress out and shoved it in her pack. She biked to the Oval Office, and after yelling up to make sure Stewart wasn't in Uncle Treemus, she climbed to the tree house and left the damp baptismal gown hanging on the bookshelf, hoping the ill-footed lord of the manor would know it was a gesture of gratitude.

After that, eight years eased by for Grace McGlone. She attended the University of Wisconsin at Madison, where she took ethics, theology, literature. During her summers off, she lived home in Janesville, where she read in the beanbag and worked at Carlson's. Paul Carlson gave Grace minimum wage and only Sundays off, but Grace loved the car wash, loved the simple beautification to which customers surrendered their vehicles. Carlson's had used the same clack-track scrub tunnel for decades, and it was Grace's job to make sure the detergent vats stayed filled with their clear, yellow-smelling liquid. She also tended the black washing tentacles, replacing them when they frayed, and she kept the gears of the clack-track clean, and she wiped down each car when it emerged from the tunnel. Grace enjoyed these tasks because they seemed basic and good, and they left her mind free to laze or romp the universe. She got decent tips at Carlson's, and Chubb Gesthoffen, who could double-coat hand-wax a car in twenty minutes, worked beside her. Chubb was thirty, and married with babies, and though he never came on to Grace, he nicknamed her "little banshee" and bet her a hundred bucks each day that she wouldn't walk through the scrub tunnel in just her Carlson's T-shirt and jeans.

So Grace's early twenties were a calm, burgeoning season. She drank beers and dated some boys at the university, but mostly she studied and prayed and tried for heaven. When she graduated Madison, she spent the next few years working at Carlson's full-time, making ten dollars an hour. She babysat sometimes for Chubb and Karen Gesthoffen, and lunched with her mother at Mackidew's Diner, and read every so-called great book from Sophocles to Sartre to Shel Silverstein. Occasionally, Grace saw a film or took a walk with Stewart McFigg, who was now building houses, on earth, for a living. Grace could still picture sinking her teeth into his gargantuan muscles, and she knew that on certain nights, he was working himself up to kissing her. But Grace always turned away or faked a cough at the moment of truth, leaving Stewart to stammer about the weather, or drywalling, or home zoning rights. For in those days, Grace was hot with distraction. All her elements—her heart, her thighs, her prayers—were holding out for some looming adventure, some quest that Grace felt was somehow imminent, and somehow grander than anyone or anything in Janesville could deliver.

What this adventure would be, Grace didn't know, but the balls of her feet ached, and she believed God wanted some motion from her, some propelling drive out into the world. Grace believed that this action, this drive, might be required at any second, so she tore through Scripture and lingerie catalogs, ran five miles every evening to stay in shape, and always kept her ATM card tucked on her person. At all times, she felt her youth within her like a recipe, for stirring in her heart were her father's lust for the road, and the abandon of P&V, and Bertram Block's thrusting, and Philip Marlowe's intrigue. Since so many of these ingredients were men, Grace felt convinced that another man was coming, the one that all these had been pointing toward. After midnight sometimes, when she couldn't sleep, she'd stare out her bedroom window at the darkness beyond the Killians' corn and dream that the blackness of night itself might engender its own limbs and muscles, might sculpt itself into a mystery man whose lot was to come and claim and challenge her. It escaped Grace that there might be something missionary and myopic—and thus potentially dangerous—about the singularity with which she hoped for such a mystery man. To her own thinking, Grace was just like any single hopeful twenty-six-year-old American woman: highly sexed, ready to go, on the lookout for a guy or some other divine opportunity.

So that's where things were in the life of Grace McGlone one May morning when she showed up at Carlson's Car Wash. As usual, she got there at seven, filled the detergent vats, then sat beside Chubb on what they called the sunrise bench. This was a plank set across old tar barrels in front of Paul Carlson's office (Paul didn't come in till noon), and Grace and Chubb sat there each morning and watched across Main Street as the sun bloomed pink, then white, then gold, over the Bryson Inn. Melanie Bryson drove her Cadillac over to Carlson's every morning at seven-thirty for a wash, and that signaled the start of Grace and Chubb's workday.

On this day, as the two workmates sat beneath the climbing sun, Main Street was deserted except for a red Chevy pickup with Illinois plates. Grace and Chubb watched the truck pull into the Mobil station beside the Bryson Inn. A tall man with dark hair jumped out of the pickup, which he left running. The man wore a denim jacket, and before going into the Mobil mart, he pulled a squat silver suitcase from his truck and took it in with him.

"Check it out, little banshee." Chubb pointed. "Guy leaves

his truck running, but can't let go his briefcase for five minutes. What he's got in there, nuclear launch codes?"

When the Illinois stranger reemerged from the Mobil mart, he held both his silver case and a new U.S. road atlas. He leaned against his puttering engine, opened the atlas, and studied it, his boot tapping the pavement.

"He's heading north to Ontario," guessed Chubb. "He's had enough of Uncle Sam, but he fears the future. Thus the tapping foot."

Grace didn't speak. The stranger was handsome in a hulking, criminal way, with a thick jaw and what looked like bruised, inflamed knuckles. His face, as he stared at the atlas, was as set and determined as a law. Grace felt something give in her stomach, in her groin. Then a voice within Grace—a voice as loud as a clarion—blared a single word: *him*.

"Maybe the poor bastard's just lost," said Chubb.

Grace's eyes hadn't left the man across the street. Something momentous, something she'd waited a lifetime for, was unfolding. "Hey, Chubb?"

"Yeah?"

"You still dare me to walk through the scrub tunnel?"

"Sure, banshee." Chubb laughed, unserious. "A bet's a bet."

Grace walked to the mouth of the tunnel. She wore blue jeans, brown work boots, a white Carlson's T-shirt. In her left boot was her ATM card, and in her bank account was the eight thousand dollars she'd saved.

"Grace?" called Chubb. "Where you going?"

On a wild, sure whim, Grace pressed the red button on the wall. The clack-track whirred, and the car wash shook to life. Grace could make out—through the tunnel of waving black tentacles—the Illinois man leaning against his truck, focused on his map. He was maybe one hundred yards away. Grace drew a breath. *If he's still there when I come out,* she told herself, *I'll go to him.*

Chubb hurried up beside Grace. "Hold on now, banshee. You're not actually going *in* there?"

She strode forward between the gutters of the clack-track. The first spray of water misted her skin.

"Grace, wait!" begged Chubb. "You'll get hurt. . . ."

Grace walked on. Jet streams of soap lashed her body. She closed her eyes, kept her feet moving, one primly before the other, like a high-wire walker or a princess.

"Grace," called Chubb.

The tentacles had Grace now. They slapped and scrubbed her, washing her hair, thwapping her limbs and clothes. The foaming scrub wheels beat at her elbows, burnished her breasts and her boots. Grace breathed through her nose and stepped on. A faraway voice called her name, but two walls of rinse water drowned the voice out. Moments later, gushes of air blasted Grace, and hanging strips of warm linen lapped her body. Grace liked the tickling, the heat, the wealth of attention, and then she was out of the tunnel, free.

She opened her eyes. A brilliant May sun greeted her, and she stood drenched, panting, feeling funky. Her hair and every part of her dripped water, and her clothes were sucked close to her body, a second skin. Her feet squished in her boots, but she could feel her ATM card hard and square against her ankle.

Chubb ran up. "Grace! Jesus Christ, Grace, you're a crazy little banshee, no kidding about it!"

Grace stared at the Mobil station. The Illinois stranger was there. He was looking at her. Her heart tremoring, Grace walked across Main Street.

"Grace?" called Chubb, but Melanie Bryson's Cadillac pulled in, and Chubb had to tend to business.

Grace strode straight to the man in the denim jacket. She stopped a few feet from him, her hands on her hips, showing herself off. At first his eyes creased, suspicious, but when Grace didn't talk or leave, just met his gaze, the stranger let his eyes dance up and down her soaked and sunlit body. Finally he grinned.

"Ma'am, unless I miss my guess, you just strolled unprotected through an automatic freaking car wash."

Grace nodded. She thought of the Bible on her bedside nightstand, the pork chops Regina was planning for dinner. Slowly she unbraided her hair, let it crash slick and brilliant over her shoulders. She wrung the hem of her shirt as fetchingly as she could and smiled at the stranger, whose foot was no longer tapping.

"I'm having a weird morning," admitted the man.

Grace studied him. His hair and eyes were the color of gun bluing. He was over six feet tall, and his left hand featured two grotesquely large, sharp knuckles, both marked with dried blood. This man had punched someone or something within the last hour.

"What's in the suitcase?" she said.

"Trouble."

Grace stuck out her hand, like a fellow at an Elks Club. The stranger shook.

"I'm Grace McGlone."

"Henry Dante."

Grace wondered if sparks were ever real. She wondered if

tiny bright molecules ever popped and snapped in the air between people, and people just never took the hint.

"Where you headed, Henry Dante?"

The stranger grinned again, a grin full of luck and death.

"West," he said.

Grace squeezed water from her pant legs. She wiped her hands on her thighs, hurried around, and hopped in the shotgun side of the pickup. When the stranger got behind the wheel and placed the suitcase between them, Grace said, "Tallyho."

CHAPTER THREE

Mission

LIKE A MAN TAKING MEDICINE, HONEY POBRINKIS spooned red wine into his mouth. "You saw the truck's license plate, Floyd?"

Floyd Webber nodded. "Red 1989 Chevy pickup. Illinois tags, reading S-H-P-R-D-S."

It was four o'clock on a May afternoon in Chicago. Roger Pobrinkis and Floyd, having spent the previous six hours hitch-hiking their way back from Charles Chalk's farm, now stood inside Ferryman's restaurant, which was devoid of patrons at the moment. Each man was severely battered and bruised. Roger's right eye was black, and Floyd's left eye was black. The skin of Roger's forehead had been torn by the butt of a handgun, while Floyd's nose, cracked and stuffed with dried blood, whistled as he breathed. Both men's right cheeks were emblazoned with two deep red notches, as if a branding iron had sizzled their faces. The partners stood before their boss, Honey, who sat, as he did all day on most days, at a corner table near the bar, eating a bowl of blueberries with merlot and sugar. Honey's teeth, permanently stained by what he ate, were almost as blue as his henchmen's bruises.

"Shepherds," said Honey. "Hmm."

Floyd looked around, confused. "What shepherds?"

"The license plate, fuckbone." Roger was pressing a towel to his wounded eye. The towel held chunks of ice. "The letters you saw stand for *shepherds*. It was Charles's truck Henry was driving."

Floyd blinked, then grinned. "I get it. *Shepherds*. Like, because Charles had sheep. Cool."

Roger studied his uncle. He couldn't tell yet whether his botching of the morning's work would cost him his left pinky finger or perhaps his life. Knowing enough not to apologize, Roger merely stood, keeping ice on his eye, holding his gaze straight ahead. His porkpie hat sat on his black-and-blue head. At the University of Chicago, during the semester that'd just ended, Roger had taken a history course called Fierce Leaders. The syllabus had focused on Napoléon, Hitler, Stalin, Pinochet—men who'd exercised mammoth control over others and done so with a violence that seemed to Roger always calculated, never giddy.

"We think Charles and his wife took the Buick," said Roger.

"Oh, man." Floyd shook his head in disbelief. "Oh, man, boss. First a hawk gives head to your windshield, then Charles shanghais your ride? When I get my hands on that old fossil Charles—"

"Floyd . . ." began Honey.

"When I get through with Charles, that geezer—"

"Floyd!" Honey set his spoon down. "Forget Charles. Forget the Buick. Our only concerns are a 1989 red Chevy pickup, the driver of that pickup, and what that driver's carrying."

"Well," said Floyd, "that's easy. Henry's the driver, and he's carrying the Planets. You know, the diamonds."

"Jesus Brain Surgery Christ." Roger glared at Floyd. "You know, it amazes me sometimes that you can even walk upright."

"Oh, man. Fuck you. I tolled the bell."

Honey stared into his bowl. In public, all he ever ate was fruit and wine. Late each night, though, when the restaurant was empty, even of staff, he cooked himself a bloodred slab of prime rib.

"Henry's not stupid, though," Roger told his uncle. "He'll have changed cars by now, or swiped some other car's plates."

Honey closed his eyes. He gnawed his front teeth over his blue bottom lip, imagining the Planets snug in their case at Henry's side. "Did I ever tell you about the night I met Henry Dante?"

Roger and Floyd shook their heads. Floyd drew his butterfly switchblade from his boot, stood polishing it with his T-shirt hem.

Honey opened his eyes. "I was in this Rainbow Beach pool hall, eight years back—"

"Was it Lotta Green Billiards?" asked Floyd. "Down on Yates?"

"I was in this pool hall, and some little Irish mick was shooting eight ball against Henry. I didn't know either guy, I was just waiting to meet Frankie Bales."

"Yep." Floyd's nose whistled. "Must've been the Lotta. Frankie loves their tables."

Roger clipped Floyd's shoulder with his own.

"So Henry and the mick are shooting eight ball, and I'm watching, and so is this platinum blond lovely who's got cutoff jean shorts and legs as long as summertime. Anyway, the mick's lining up a bank shot, when his face fists up all red, and he's staring at the knockout woman, and you can see he's getting salty. He marches up to Miss Platinum and gives her the end of his pool cue in her gut, twice, hard."

"Ouchie." Floyd blew on his butterfly, admired its bone handle.

"Put that away," said Honey.

"Oh. Yes, sir. Sorry."

Honey rubbed the sugar on the rim of his bowl. As he spoke, he brought pinches of the sugar to his tongue. "So Henry sidles up to the mick, who's short but has that pit bull Dublin look, and Henry says, what gives, hitting a lady. Madam Platinum's doubled up and holding her belly and crying but trying to hide it, and the mick turns his bulldog mick face to Henry and says, this is my wife and it's none of your business and fuck you very much, now let's play pool. Henry stands his ground, though, cool as milk, and says, why'd you hit your wife, sir. Badass Saint Patrick sees that Henry's serious and by now I don't care if Frankie Bales turns up or not, this is a good show."

"And did Henry pound the husband?" blurted Floyd.

"So the mick tells Henry, listen, she's been eyeing the bartender, throwing him fuck-me looks, and she's got on her red leather fuck-me boots, which she knows she shouldn't wear outside the house, and she just blew a kiss to the bouncer.

Henry nods, like he's third circuit court judge, and he taps platinum wifey on the shoulder, saying, excuse me, ma'am, can I ask you some questions. The mick says, no for fuck's sake, you can't ask her jack, but Henry holds a finger in the guy's face, and the lovely looks at Henry like okay, go ahead. Henry says, is this your husband I'm playing pool against here, and she nods. Henry says, have you ever cheated on him and don't lie or I'll know. She looks in Henry's eyes, shakes her head no. The mick's got his arms crossed, and Henry says, ma'am, I've got two more questions."

Honey's bowl was wiped clean, his hands folded before him on the table. Even Floyd knew not to interrupt now.

"Henry points to the bouncer—it was Dale Derry, I think, or some other chump with sideburns—and Henry says, did you blow that man a kiss, and the woman says no. Finally, Henry pats her shoulder and says, last question, where'd you get those boots. And little miss cutoffs sniffles and says, from my sister Maureen for Christmas. Henry studies her face, then turns to the mick and says, you can hit me first if you want, mister. The mick says why and Henry says, because I'm about to hit you, on account of you're a domestically violent coward. The mick turns about the shade of the fuck-me boots and lays one roundhouse on Henry's chin and that was that."

"What was what?" said Floyd.

Honey shrugged. "Henry rearranged the guy's atoms. With maybe four punches, he cracked the mick's jaw and a couple ribs, made a Bolognese sauce out of his nose. Then he walked outside and I walked out after him."

"Huh," said Floyd. "Good story. I'll tell you what else about

Lotta Green Billiards, though. They serve some piss-water, shitty drinks. Me, I boycott the place."

Honey edged his bowl forward to show he was finished. When he cleared his throat, Floyd said, "Oh," and picked up the bowl, walked it to the bar, and returned to Roger's side.

"I followed Henry out of that place and hired him. Now, why did I do that?"

Roger remained quiet. Floyd raised his hand like a schoolboy.

"Because Henry pounded the husband. Henry's got those devil's horn knuckles, you know? What a specimen that fucker is. He totally coldcocked me this morning."

Honey tsked his tongue. "I hired him because he *listened* to the mick *and* the wife. Then he let the mick swing first." Honey stood, walked over, pressed a finger to Floyd's black eye, then to Roger's, testing their wounds. Floyd winced, but Roger didn't.

"You see, Henry acted with discretion. He gave both parties a sporting chance. In fact, that's a phrase you'll hear Henry use if you listen. 'Sporting chance,' you'll hear him say. Sporting chance."

Honey took his nephew's face fully in his hands. He stared in Roger's eyes, coddled his cheeks back and forth, as if kneading dough.

"The moral of the story," said Honey, "is Henry won't change cars. He won't switch the license plates off the truck. He won't do those things because, in his heart, Henry is a very dangerous thing."

"A diamond thief," volunteered Floyd.

"No." Honey's hands dropped to his sides. "No, Henry's a gentleman. Moreover, he's a gentleman with a soft spot for women in distress. Especially beautiful women. Like, for instance, Helena Pressman." Honey searched Roger's eyes. "You knew that, though, didn't you, Roger? About Henry's soft spot for women in distress? You knew that and took it into account before doing anything stupid this morning, didn't you?"

Roger didn't speak. He thought of his Fierce Leaders course, of hard men and the Fifth Amendment. He also thought of Robin Areena, the Ferryman barmaid he'd once lost his temper with and slapped in front of Honey and a barful of patrons.

Floyd touched his nose. "All due respect, boss, Henry didn't seem like a gentleman when he was kicking me in the spleen. I mean, the guy coldcocked me."

"You're lucky he didn't tear your teeth out," snapped Honey, "or put a bullet in your shit-for-brains head. He could've. But, like I said, he's a gentleman, and he knows the Planets aren't really his, and by leaving you two alive, he's giving us a sporting chance to find him."

"How do we do that?" Floyd adjusted his tank-top straps.

Honey walked to the window, looked out at the afternoon. Across the vacant lot beside Ferryman's was an abandoned meat-packing warehouse made of brick. Sometimes late at night, as he ate his prime rib, Honey would stand by this window and watch the warehouse, and in his mind loomed the hundreds of thousands of cattle that'd been slaughtered there over the decades as Chicago grew up, tough and hungry. He wondered whether anything remained of those animals now, whether bits of their hooves lay mixed in with the street dust, whether their fat, sad-eyed spirits herded in the air around Ferryman's.

Honey shook his head. He didn't like such thoughts, such

fanciful musings. What he liked were diamonds: cold, crystalline diamonds, their meaning and value clear to him and everybody. He turned from the window. "I still know a few cops in this country. One vanity-plate pickup shouldn't be too hard of a mark."

When Floyd laid his finger to his nose and pressed just right, the fluting in his nostrils stopped. "Hey, boss, you know what? It's too bad you didn't get a glimmer last night that *Henry* was going to swipe the Planets. I mean, here you knew that Charles would up and pull a fast one, but your glimmer didn't, like, *expand* itself to cover the move Henry made today. Isn't that ironic or something?"

"Well, Floyd, I suspect more than one person did something unforeseeable this morning." Honey glanced at his nephew. "I can't predict every idiotic decision perpetrated by *Homo sapiens*."

Enough, thought Roger. He straightened his shoulders. "I'll need a new gun, Uncle Honey. Henry took mine."

"So you said. Wait here."

Honey walked to the pantry, then descended the flight of stairs into Ferryman's basement. To one side was a wine cellar, to another was an office, and directly before Honey was a giant silver cube, the high-security walk-in vault that no one but he ever entered. Honey worked the electronic combination and moved into his lair.

The vault was as large as a cage for three lions. The walls were two-foot-thick steel, but the inside looked like an aristocrat's study. A fine mauve carpet covered the floor, and upon this carpet stood a leather reading chair and lamp, plus a shelf holding books and some rare vintage wines. Before the nightly dinner rush, Honey liked to squirrel himself away in this vault, to sit in the leather chair and gaze at the diamond and gun collections he'd mounted in cases on the walls. Often he read Thoreau or James Fenimore Cooper, and pretended he was Theodore Roosevelt or some other warrior, retreating into the company of good wine and wisdom.

On this afternoon, though, Honey did not sit and ponder. He moved to the gun case, opened it, looked over his weaponry. Arranged on hooks was an assortment that ranged from Glocks to Winchesters. This was the only stash of guns on the premises. Honey thought it unsafe to keep firearms behind the bar or in other nooks where an employee or customer might grab them. The exception to this rule was the gun that never left Honey's person, the ace he kept quite literally up his sleeve.

This ace had been a gift from Charles Chalk, who, with his keen eyes, had possessed more than a talent for procuring diamonds. Out on his farm, Charles and his dexterous fingers had also dabbled in gadgetry. The loft of the Chalk barn was a Bat Cave filled with metal contraptions, lethal inventions that Charles designed and offered Honey. The loony farmer had once tried to create a razor that could pop a secret blade and slash its user's throat. He'd also promised Honey he could outfit the Buick with a passenger-side ejector seat. Honey had always refused the gizmos, until seven years ago, when Charles perfected a small four-bullet handgun that could be concealed under a suitcoat on a forearm band. The proper flexing of arm muscles triggered the spring-loaded gun to pop out your sleeve and into your palm.

Honey had taken a fancy to the gun. It put him in mind of

ghost-town stories, poker table showdowns. He'd practiced with it in his vault, become adept at drawing it. After Jack Deck made his failed attempt on Honey's life, the paranoid Pobrinkis wore the gun every day. He'd kept it on his arm for five years now, until it had become as natural to him as a watch, and none of his henchmen or wives had ever seen it. It tickled Honey to have a secret, dangerous piece of craftsmanship, and it was not without some top-dog pride that he now selected from the case a lowly Smith & Wesson to give Roger.

Reemerging upstairs, Honey tossed the six-shooter at his nephew.

"Go get me my Planets. No more fuck-ups."

Roger inspected the gun, frowned, tucked it in his holster.

"Right on. The game is totally afoot." Floyd rubbed his mangled jaw. "I wouldn't want to be Henry Dante about now. I've got an ass to grind with that guy."

"An axe," said Roger.

"What?"

"An *axe*. You've got an *axe* to grind with Henry. That's what you were trying to say."

Floyd crossed his arms. "I'm saying, Henry coldcocked me, and when I get my hands on him, I'll grind his ass. You know, like kick his ass. That's what I'm saying." Floyd's nose blew a long, high note, like a referee's whistle.

"Picture an axe," said Roger patiently. "It's a tool, a potentially lethal weapon. But for it to cut well, you have to keep it sharp. So you *grind* it to sharpen it."

"Yeah, right. Like I'm going to go after Henry with only an axe. He'd see me coming a mile away."

Roger sighed.

"I just don't see what an axe has to do with anything."

"It has to do with you being a moron."

"Oh, man. Fuck you. I tolled—"

"Shut your mouths." Honey licked his lips, which were the color of corpses. "Both of you, shut your mouths, and go find my diamonds."

Roger and Floyd glared at each other.

"Yes, sir," said Roger.

"And bring me Henry Dante. Alive."

CHAPTER FOUR

Vows

THIS TRUCK ISN'T MINE, THESE DIAMONDS AREN'T mine, and this Grace beside me, this suddenly here, utterly soaked woman, she's not mine, either. But God, she's lovely.

"You're lovely," I say.

"Uh-huh." The redhead rolls her eyes. She's riding shotgun in wet blue jeans, a wet white T-shirt, brown leather boots. A few exits back, she walked through a car wash to get to me.

"Well, what'm I supposed to say?" I'm driving on Route 90 in Wisconsin. The morning sun's out, and I see signs for strange towns. Baraboo. Hustler.

"Stop off at this exit," says Grace.

"Why?"

She smiles. Her teeth are thirty-two perfect reasons to shut up and obey.

"Well, Henry Dante, if I'm hitching west with you, I'll need to buy some things."

So I pull off. This Grace, she directs me to a white concrete superstore, where she runs inside alone. I wait in the truck, cursing the weakness of man, knowing I should bolt.

"Dammit," I say. Stashed below my seat is the gun I took from Roger. I took his pride, too, and he'll want both things back. He and Honey will come for me soon enough. So I ask myself the right questions. *Why'd you grab the diamonds, Dante? Why'd you pick up the woman?*

The thing is, there are bold moments sometimes, moments that scare you and call to you all at once. When I was young, my parents' house was as ramshackle as their marriage, but we lived close to the Plainfield Drive-in, and late on summer nights, while my mother and father fucked or fought in their bedroom, I crawled up through our attic to the batshit-caked roof. I stared at the drive-in from there, saw giant, glowing humans, and bats flapped close. When I huddled on high like that, my blood raced. The bats thrilled past my ears, and Karen Allen's cleavage was in tight trouble on the screen, and common sense softened in my head. I had longings, made impossible decisions to run away. I would become a Portuguese matador, or scale three Himalayas in a week, or discover the formula for cold fusion but share it only with leggy Southern belles.

"Dammit," I say again, staring at the superstore.

It wasn't just the drive-in that ripped the world open for me, made me want to explode, break out. One time when I was thirteen, walking in the woods near my house, I found a frog that seemed to have a six-foot tail. As it turned out, the frog was being swallowed by a snake, and the snake's mouth, stretched wide, was taking its deadly, horrible time. I stood frozen, my arm hairs tingling. What I was seeing might have repulsed other kids, but to me, it presented possibilities. At that moment, the frog and snake weren't just themselves anymore, they'd become a brand-new creature, a mystical thing like a griffin, but a thing only I could recognize. Seeing that creature charged me up, made me want to become a new animal too.

What I mean is, sometimes the atoms of the world rush together, and burst out of their regular day jobs, and give you a show. They dare you to do something fresh, something right, something beautiful. That's all the explanation I've got for what's gone on this morning. That lucky, living squirrel, the Planets, Helena Pressman—they teamed up on me, got me primed to steal and flee and let a sopping wet vision into my truck.

"Dammit, dammit, dammit."

Grace comes out of the superstore. She's still in her leather work boots, but she's no longer sopping. In fact, she's in a dress now, a mustard-colored Navajo-looking buckskin thing with the price tag still on the hem. Also, she's got a new black satchel over her shoulder and it's full of who knows what. Feminine wiles, probably.

"Even lovelier," I say, when she's back beside me. We head west on the 90, but my attention's on Grace, on the tiny whorls of down along her jawbone. Her feet are out of her boots now. She spreads ten marvelous toes on the dashboard, dries them in the sun.

"They had an ATM. I took out three hundred dollars, but I've got more in my account."

I'm still checking out her feet, her everything.

"I've got eight thousand dollars," says Grace.

She bites the price tag off her dress, fidgets under my gaze. She fidgets and blushes and thinks her own thoughts. Her eyes are like chocolate, or the ground in a forest. On the other hand, how the hell do I know what her eyes are like? I'm only thirty-two.

"You just gonna keep staring at me?"

I nod. "Yes, ma'am."

"Till when?"

Till the moon splits in three, I think. *Till the Red Sox win the Series. Till we both get what we want.*

Grace tosses back her hair, which is the best red stuff I've seen. There's no radio on, no perfect song by the Eagles or the Grateful Dead playing around us. But there might as well be.

"You'd better pull over," says Grace.

Three miles later, I park at a rest stop. Grace and I pull each other into the truck bed. I tug my silver suitcase back there with us and toss it at my feet. The air mattress is already inflated, thanks to Charles Chalk. Everything happens fast and right. Off comes Grace's dress and bra and panties, ditto my shirt, jeans, and the rest, and we're at it. We claw and kiss. Grace tells me no screwing, which is fine, I guess, as long as certain mouths end up on certain things, which they do for both parties. Then there are moans, and busy tongues, and I'm tasting not just her body but her whole female swirl, her IQ, and her humor, maybe even her womb. We let out two huge yelps, and the ceremony's done. We lie naked and stunned in each other's arms, and the sun from the window's across our bellies in the shape of a gift box, the kind long roses or rifles come in.

"God," I say. "God, that was good."

Neither of us has had anything better, ever. We don't say that, but I feel it spread through my body like the truth, like the opposite of cancer. What I mean is, Bella Cavasti has been lying on a daybed in my mind for years, but she just stood up and left the room.

Grace kisses my neck, turns me on my side, and inspects my back, where my Four Horsemen tattoo stretches black and purple from my shoulders to my ass.

Grace whistles. "Whoa, mama."

"That's the Apocalypse."

"I know what it is." Grace touches the muzzle of one horse, Pestilence, I think, or else War. "When'd you get these guys?"

"High school. They've been chasing me ever since."

Grace kisses each horse, rolls me back over, saddles herself on my stomach, her knees at my kidneys.

"Why'd you ever get such a creepy tattoo?"

I close my eyes, and for a flash, I'm fifteen again, bad at math, a Chicago sophomore, bulky, glaring, slouched against lockers. I remember skulking around the Coal Mine Tattoo Parlor, craving brutal colors, wanting a wild end to things, or a wild beginning.

When I open my eyes again, though, geometry's gone, and so are my parents, who died in a car crash when I was twenty, and so is Honey Pobrinkis and me crewing for him. Instead there's this Grace, with her thighs a tent over my torso, with her freckled Wisconsin skin.

"Maybe I got my Four Horsemen for the same reason you got in this truck."

She leans down, kisses me. She likes what I just said. We share tongues until sweat and other juices of hers drip down her thighs to my ribs. I roll her onto her back and we're at it again, but she still won't let me have her the old-fashioned way. I ask what gives.

"I'm trying for heaven," says Grace. "And if you want me, so are you."

I don't understand, but she's right that I want her. So we get creative again, stroking and lapping, till we yelp the two yelps. We lie back, panting.

Her eyes snoop around the truck bed, the books and soup cans. "I was in a tree house like this once."

"Wait," I say. "So you're religious?"

"I'm a Christian. I'm trying for heaven."

I scratch my jaw. I was christened Catholic in my diaper days, but I haven't been to church since forever. The secrets I've whispered to women's thighs are the nearest I've come to confession.

"Trying for heaven," I say. It sounds like a song name.

We're both naked and it's not yet noon. Grace sits up. She stares at my bullet-wound scars. "Those are from guns. You got shot, Henry Dante."

"Three times."

Grace fingers my scars, first the one above my hip, then the one on my shoulder, then the one on my neck. Her touch is timid, a little fearful. I can feel her asking questions, and I don't blame her. They're like nasty, raised volcano mouths, my scars are, except the ripples down their sides are skin instead of lava. Grace traces her fingertips over these eruptions, then looks away. She pokes her foot at my silver suitcase, like it's a safe thing to focus on.

"If I'm going to stick around, you have to show me what's in here."

So I sit up, too, hold the case in my lap, pry it open, spill my story. I tell her about Don Canto, Honey Pobrinkis, Charles Chalk, Helena Pressman. I tell about how I'm on the lam, about some of the lives that I've smashed.

Grace stares at the Planets, absorbing. "So . . . you're a tough one. A tough motherfucker."

"Not always."

"I'm not sure I should hang with a tough motherfucker."

She hasn't dared to touch the diamonds yet. Neither have I.

"I'm not so bad," I say. "I've never greased somebody. Never killed anyone, I mean."

"But your boss. Honey Pobrinkis. *He* kills people."

I glance at the shotgun Charles mounted on the wall, the stack of shell boxes below it. I know what's coming.

"If you work for a killer . . ." Grace swallows, like she needs extra air or food to say this. "If you work for a killer, if you help him at all, you're a killer too."

I'm a foot or so taller than this woman, almost twice her weight. I could beat her bones into pudding, talk sharp to her, argue high and hard for the man I've tried to be. But I've gone all my years without skin like hers kissing mine, and everything she's said is true. Not only that, but, like I said before, the atoms of the world are in high gear this morning. They're jumping out of their grooves and ganging up on me, daring me to choose this Grace. They're prodding me to side with her instead of siding with my last seven years, where I've slept alone and never hung holiday lights.

I clear my throat. "I don't work for him anymore."

"Hmm."

"I don't."

"Is that a promise?"

I laugh, just a little. I've got seven wonders in my lap. I study Grace's ribs, try to see the beliefs they're guarding.

"Sure. Absolutely. It's a promise."

"Good."

Out the window, a van of college dudes pulls in. They park three spaces down and tumble out, all laughter and language and baseball caps. The dudes lope into some shrubs, drop their pants, piss. I scowl out the window at them.

"May I say something else?" asks Grace.

"Say whatever you'd like."

"Okay. Listen." She leans close. "You have a soul, Henry Dante."

"I know I have a soul."

Grace licks her forefinger, traces it around my navel. "Well . . . it looks like you could use some help taking care of it."

All of her body faces me, and so does something behind her eyes. I know I'm signing a declaration of dependence, but I don't mind. Maybe Grace gets off on tending bad boys, but I don't mind that either. She's coming at me straight on, no pussy politics, and that jazzes me. I'm in. "Go for it," I tell her.

"I will."

I take the case from my lap, set it between us. We gaze at the stones. The Planets look hot and special in the late-morning sun. Grace and I glance at each other, children seeking permission. Then we give in, touch the Planets. We lie beside each other, hold these worlds in our palms, pass them back and forth. We clink Mars against Mercury, like we're toasting champagne. We stack Saturn, Uranus, and Jupiter, then topple them. Light dances crazy off of each cut and facet, and Grace places Venus under her tongue like a gumdrop. She grins at me like she'll swallow if I dare her, or else buy a mansion with what's in her mouth. And just then, watching Grace, watching joy bulge her cheeks, I get it. I get why Charles grabbed for the Planets, why I took them myself, why I couldn't leave them with Floyd and Roger or haul them back to Honey. They were made for sex and sunshine, these Planets were, for stupendous moments like the one in this truck. My groin goes hard, and I pick up the Earth, lick and kiss it all over. I push Grace on her back, get my hands between her calves.

"Olmph," says Grace, surprised. She's got Venus under her tongue, I've got the wet Earth sliding up her thigh, and her eyes say a naughty yes. She's breathing heavy. I'm teasing Earth and my fingers higher, toward slick delight, when Grace sits up. She stops my hand, spits out Venus.

"Wait a minute," she breathes.

"What?"

Grace takes Earth from me, sets it firmly in the suitcase foam. She puts the other six Planets back in too.

"What's wrong?" I reach for her, but she bats my hand away.

"I just realized." Grace finds her bra. "These diamonds. They were paid for with blood money."

"Blood money?" I grin. Someone's seen her share of movies.

"They were paid for by Honey Pobrinkis, right?"

"Right."

Grace straps on her bra. "That's blood money."

I don't know what to say. My cock deflates. Grace puts her

panties back on. The panties look new and black, and they've got a stitched-on pink ladybug up around the belly.

"I don't get it."

Grace juts her chin toward the Planets. "If I'm going to stick around, we have to get rid of those. Give them away or something."

"That's crazy. They're worth forty million bucks."

She tugs her dress on.

"We could fly to Sri Lanka," I suggest. "Buy a palace. Raise elephants."

Grace crawls toward the cab like she's leaving. I grab her ankle. She kicks me hard in the chest.

"Let me go!"

"Wait." I'm still holding her foot.

Grace twists and kicks. "You can't just sex me up with blood-money diamonds! I've got morals."

"All right. *All right.* Just . . . hold on. Truce."

Grace stops struggling, sits in a cross-legged pout. She arranges her hem over her knees. "Well?"

I look at the Planets. As of yesterday, I'd never seen them, but now they're here, like destiny.

"Let me think." I pull my jeans on. "This is a lot to . . . just let me think a minute."

Grace looks around her, touches the Coleman stove, flips through a paperback called *Little Julia Rants and Raves*. "So this was Charles and Helena's truck?"

"I—yes."

"And Honey Pobrinkis won't go after them, but he'll come after you?"

"Right."

Grace returns the book to its stack. "So why not ditch this truck and get another?"

I sigh, overcome by her topics. I put my hands on Grace's shoulders, give her the dope about me. The dope about me is, no pussy politics. I can't just duck charges, switch trucks or license plates. It sounds crazy, I tell her, but everyone deserves a sporting chance, even Honey.

"Hmm." Grace gives me all of her eyes. "Can I say what I think about this?"

"Sure."

"I think you're seeking rectitude. I think that you, in a somewhat fucked-up way, want to atone for your sins."

Sins, I think. *Sins.* "I've made some mistakes, if that's what you mean."

"I also think you'd like to screw me. To fill me with bliss."

"Bingo."

"Then here's how it'll be," begins Grace.

A big, delicious pause happens. We're in America, with a half tank of gas, and I'm sick of Chicago, the predictable grid. The long claw of Honey Pobrinkis might stretch out strong, but today my money's on me. I'm a new animal, ready for wilderness.

"In the interest of atonement," says Grace, "we'll keep the truck, but ditch the Planets. We'll give them away. Agreed?"

She's perching her eyebrows, waiting on a yes.

I glance at the diamonds. "On one condition."

"What?"

I clear my throat. Grace's flavors are still on my tongue.

"Well, the guy who made these, he was trying to give someone a stupendous gift. . . ."

"And?"

"And if we give them away, we should do it like he did." I frown. I'm lousy at talking. "We should give each one away . . . stupendously."

She kisses me. "Stupendously it is."

I close the silver case. Grace and I are holding hands.

"Oh, one more thing," she says. "In the interest of bliss, we'll get married."

I stare at this red, radical woman. So far this morning there's been a hawk, sheep, and spilled blood. But Grace is the best crash yet in this bright, booming day.

I squeeze her hand. If she's bewitching, I'm bewitched.

"Deal," I say.

* * *

It turns out, though, that no one will marry us. Well, maybe a justice of the peace would, but Grace says we need a Christian wedding. After seven churches, though—Baptist, Methodist, Lutheran—we're still just Henry and Grace, lovers in a truck, crossing the Minnesota border. All the preachers we've seen—some women, some men, one guy with breath like a mutt—want addresses, waiting periods, birth certificates. But Grace and I truck on into Minnesota, and Grace says God will give us a sign.

"Like lightning?" I joke. "Like a river of frogs?"

Grace says just wait, I'll see. "It'll be cool. It'll be right."

She's in her Navajo dress, and I'm driving. It's still today, the day we met, but it's five in the afternoon. The sun's got some batteries left. There's an early peek of moon in the sky, and we've got the windows open. We breeze across the south of the state, still bearing west on the 90, and the sweetgrass smell of the wind is just right. Grace is just right too. She sits beside me with her legs drawn to her chest, her cheek on her knees, her eyes out her window. Her hair blusters, but she looks content, as if we're an adventure instead of a madness, and maybe we are.

Grace whoops. "Here! Get off here. The next exit, I mean."

"Why? How do you know there's—"

"Look." She points to a billboard that says BLUE EARTH, 1 MILE. "I've never heard a better name for a place. Blue Earth. It sounds like a poem."

"A poem?"

"A sign."

So I get off the highway, onto a rural road. We pass gas stations, a Burger King, farmhouses, a carnival. The carnival's set up on a sprawling, fallow field. It's one of those traveling-show midways, the sort that plunks down in a new town each week. There's a Ferris wheel, a Tilt-A-Whirl, and livestock shows and gaming booths. It's Friday, and even though the midway lights aren't glowing yet, they will be soon. I can almost smell those lights, just like I can smell the hundreds of Blue Earth children aching to arrive here tonight, aching to hurl darts at balloons and devour taffy. I recall Bella Cavasti, and our Foster Ave. magic, until Grace leans over and tongues at my neck.

I nod at the fairgrounds. "Should we stop?"

She shakes her head. We pass farms and fields, then homes

with sweeping lawns and gabled roofs. Along the road before one such estate are shiny Cadillacs, sports cars, limousines. The limo closest to the house has a JUST MARRIED sign.

"Pull over," says Grace.

I don't know what she's thinking, but I park. We walk up the driveway, which is full of James Bond–type cars. I've got my Planets case in one hand and Grace's hand in my other, and I'm loving the evening air. Like me, Grace doesn't know a soul here, but there's shiny music from the backyard, so we round some white-brick corners and there's the party.

"Damn," says Grace.

Spread out on a lawn that looks blue in the tapering sun are three busy dance floors, and a brass band, and fountains of arcing waters. There's an inground pool with no one in it, and there are hundreds of guests. All the men wear smooth black tuxes, while the women are in red. I check the men out first, looking for marks, for danger, but there's not a gun-toting temper in sight, just martinis and big, easy bellies. The women are a trip. They're chatting in squadrons of three or four, and their dresses and suits are as varied as valentines. Some are ruby, some pink, some are spitfire bright, and near a dance floor stands the lily-white bride, one hand on her veil.

Three waiters in gray blouses pass by, bearing bowls of caviar.

"Let's find whoever married them," says Grace. "Let's find the preacher."

We split up and wander different sides of the gig. I watch for holy folks, keep a bead on Grace. A small man with a pocket watch on his tux takes me aside.

"I'm the father of the bride. I don't think we've met."

"I'm Roger," I tell him. "Roger Pobrinkis."

Mr. Pocket Watch smiles, does the math. His breath smells like sour mix, like a woman's drink. "I don't recall your name from the guest list, Roger."

"I'm with the band. I do keyboards. And anthropology."

"Ah. The band." He nods at my denim jacket. "Hence the attire."

"Henry! Over here!"

I turn, and beyond the pool is Grace. She's standing by a white wooden fence. I walk over.

"In here." Grace leads me through a door. The fence, it turns out, is an enclosure with four tall walls and no roof. It's been built around a black metal monolith, a humming power box. It's a filter, probably, a gizmo that keeps the pool clean and upper-class and warm. Sitting in deck chairs around the machine are three men. Two are waiters, sharing a joint, their blouses untucked, and the other's a priest in a Roman collar. The priest looks my side of forty. He holds a tumbler of whiskey.

"Found him," says Grace.

The priest wears a black shirt and black pants and has his bare feet against the monolith. "I'm Arthur Kelly," he declares. "This is my third drink."

"Dude." The waiter holding the joint shakes my hand. "I'm Joe Kelly. I'm his cousin."

The other waiter looks Cuban. His sideburns are as long as thumbs, and his eyes are delighted with Grace.

"Joseph and Alphonse are smoking weed," says Arthur. "I am not, though I did in my past."

"I work for the Timbersons." Joe Kelly drags, holds his smoke. "Ron and Sheila. This is their house, man. You look like party crashers."

"I forsook cannabis and took the cloth."

Joe asks if we want a hit, but we don't. Beneath us all is thick green grass.

"Alphonse speaks no English," says the priest.

"Please join our hiatus," says Joe.

"We're happy to meet you," says Arthur.

Joe's eyes are bloodshot. "What's in the suitcase?"

Grace clears her throat. "I'm Grace McGlone. This is Henry Dante. We're trying for heaven."

The priest swishes his tumbler, making the whiskey seesaw. "Again, please?"

"We need to get married," explains Grace, "but I have questions for you first, please, Father Kelly."

Alphonse frowns. The conversation is clouding his fine Caribbean high.

"Um . . . Listen here, call me Arthur. But I'm not sure I—"

"I have to make sure you're legit, Arthur. Just a couple questions."

Beyond the fence are party sounds, but we're in the eye of the storm. The black machine hums on.

"My cousin's ordained, man." Joe passes Alphonse the roach. "He's blessed and shit. I was there."

Grace faces Arthur Kelly. "Can you tell me, please, Father Arthur, which book of the Bible contains the four songs of the suffering servant of Yahweh?"

The priest sets his whiskey in the grass. He sits up straight and looks at Grace, intrigued. "Isaiah."

Grace nods. "And . . . hmm. It says in the Old Testament, and I quote, 'Whoever gets up early to seek her will have no trouble but will find her sitting at the door. For she searches everywhere for those who are worthy of her.' " Grace adjusts her bra strap. "Well, Father? Who's the 'she' in that quote?"

Joe pokes his cousin's shoulder. "Guess Mary. I'll bet it's Mary."

Alphonse drags on the roach, crosses himself.

"Wisdom." Arthur shoos Joseph's poking fingers. "The answer is Wisdom herself, Wisdom personified as a woman."

Grace looks at me. "This guy's pretty good."

"All right," I say.

"I'll ask him one more."

"All right."

Joe crosses his arms. "Fifty bucks he gets it, man."

Grace thinks. The band outside plays "Silhouettes." Despite the warm black box, Grace has goose bumps on her arms. I take my coat off, give it to her.

"Is this all really necessary?" says the priest.

Grace arranges my coat on her shoulders. "All right, Father. In the Gospels, Jesus cures a possessed man. The Lord makes the demons leave the man, but lets them enter a nearby herd. Then the possessed animals charge down a hill and drown in a lake. What kind of animals were they?"

"Goats, Art," whispers Joe. "In Bible times the world was chock-full of goats."

Arthur says, "Pigs. I'm not a fundamentalist, and we could debate the literal veracity of the incident, but the animals are pigs."

"Dude, hold up. Are you sure? It's pigs?"

"It's pigs," confirms Grace.

Joe throws his arms up, Rocky style. "It's pigs! It's pigs, man! Arthur wins!"

"Well done, Father. We'd like you to marry us now." Grace fixes her hair.

"Marry you?"

"Yes. Right here, right now, please. Sorry about the questions, but I had to check your credentials."

Joseph lights up a fresh joint, drags. "You know who it sucks to be in that story? The pig farmer. His porkers go ballistic and drown themselves? Guy's wife must've been ripshit."

"*Cerdos muertos,*" says Alphonse.

"You want me to marry you?" The priest is standing, facing Grace and me.

"Yes, please," says Grace.

Arthur looks us over. He's probably sizing us up in some sneaky way they taught him at seminary, but I'm unafraid, curious. My hand is in Grace's, and the power box is churning, and it's spring.

"Is either of you Catholic?"

"We're Christians," says Grace.

I tell him I was baptized Catholic.

Arthur rubs his chin. "Are you going to quiz me too?"

I don't remember much about church. There were smells, stories, boredom. I study the fence around us, the way it hides us from the real guests.

"Nope," I say.

Joe Kelly throws his head back, peers at the sky. "Henry and Grace have got a suitcase. What's in the suitcase, Henry and Grace?"

"Marry us," Grace tells the priest, "we're ready."

And the thing is, we are. I know I shouldn't have the truck, or the two guns. I know there's supposed to be years of fights and picnics, and she hates cats, and I learn to listen. But sometimes it's not that way. Sometimes it's fast, barely lawful. Sometimes it's two strangers with sex in their teeth and they just want a green light.

"And you really crashed this party?" The priest is close to us. "You just drove in from nowhere?"

"From the east," I say.

"And you stopped at this house because . . . ?"

Grace puts her palm to his cheek. Her bosom is rising and falling, and great things inside me are rising and falling too.

She pats his cheek softly. "We were looking for you, Father. We honestly were."

"Right here, you say." The priest gazes at the length of me, the stance of Grace. "Marry you, right here, right now."

"We'll devote ourselves to Christ," promises Grace.

Joe is still staring up. "Tell you what. Ron and Sheila have a bitchy daughter."

"And screwing," adds Grace. "We'll devote ourselves to Christ and screwing and bliss."

Arthur laughs. "Will you indeed."

"The bitchy bride beyond these walls," says Joe, "is Jane Timberson."

We can all smell the joint and the tiki torches being lit outside the fence.

Joe nods at his cousin. "Go ahead, Art. Marry them."

The priest draws a breath. As if amazed by the taste, he draws another.

I kneel, open my suitcase, turn it toward the men. There's a couple of spare tikis inside the fence, so I spike them in the ground, grab Joe's joint, fire up the torches. When the tikis spit flame, the Planets gleam.

"Holy shit," whispers Joe.

Alphonse leaps up. He crosses himself, points at the suitcase. *"Los Planetas!"*

"Are those diamonds?" says the priest. "They're enormous."

"Los Planetas de don Canto!"

Joe jumps up and seizes Alphonse by the shoulders. They spew Spanish to each other.

"These are the Planets," I announce. "They're worth forty million."

"They're beautiful," says Arthur.

"Alphonse has become way stimulated," says Joe. "He knows those diamonds. He's asking where you got them."

"None of his business. Or yours." From the suitcase I pluck out the Saturn stone. With the grooved band etched around it, I figure it has a nuptial theme.

"Here." I place the diamond in Arthur's hand. "A present. A stupendous gift. You know, for marrying us."

Grace studies the suitcase, the foam crater where Saturn lived. She nods at me, proud.

"I—" Art Kelly clears his throat. He pets what's in his palm. "I can't accept this."

I tell him he can. Alphonse squawks and blusters.

Joe says, "Alphonse claims you can't split up the Planets. He says they're mythical or something. They're supposed to be together."

"*We're* supposed to be together," says Grace. "Henry and me. That's what this is about."

Alphonse starts fussing, so I hug him. With one arm around his thin, bony shoulder, I guide him to the door and open it.

"We love you, Alphonse." I push him out. "Thanks for being here. Go away now."

Alphonse starts to protest, but I hold up a finger, shut the door in his face.

"You shouldn't piss off Alphonse," says Joe. "His brother's a cop."

I turn to the priest and tuck my shirt, which is a red flannel deal, into my jeans. "Look, Father, you can keep the diamond, or give it to Alphonse, or hock it and treat Minnesota to steak and potatoes."

"Marry us," says Grace. "We don't care about certificates. Just the vows."

The priest stares at Saturn. Outside, around the fountains, men and women are downing wine, clinking glasses. The band plays Benny Goodman.

Arthur glances up. Stars are out. "Well." The priest grins at the heavens. For a second, I imagine he's the pastor of some nineteenth-century town of gold miners, whores, hurdy-gurdy men. In my vision, he sits at a saloon table with gamblers, and when he wins, there's a diamond the size of a fist among the coins.

"All right." The priest's voice is quiet, and his fingers close around Saturn. He pockets the gem. "All right."

I close the suitcase and stand. Grace and I clasp hands, lock our gazes. I think of my dead mom and dad. I remember Honey, Roger, Floyd, men I'm stronger than.

Art places a hand on Grace's shoulder, one on mine. "Is Joseph your witness?"

"Sure," I say.

Joe has his back to the monolith, like a sentry. He watches us with wide eyes.

"Make your promises," the priest tells us.

"This is so fucking cool," whispers Joseph. The tikis flicker. They're like candles the size of men.

Grace kisses my lips. "Henry Dante. I promise to be your woman, always, and to take care of you, always."

I kiss her back. "Grace McGlone. I'll always be your man. And I'll always take care of you."

Grace sighs, happy. We hug, then stop hugging.

"And will you take care of other people?" asks the priest. "Especially children, if you have them?"

"Sure."

"Yes," says Grace.

With his thumb, Arthur Kelly makes the sign of the cross on our foreheads. "Oh, wait." He pulls a little bottle from his pocket. "Holy Water." He wets his thumb, marks our foreheads again. "Henry and Grace, in the name of the Father, and of the Son, and of the Holy Spirit, I pronounce you husband and wife."

Grace and I kiss.

"That's it." Art Kelly smiles. "That's all."

Joe lets out a whoop. He does some sort of rain dance. The brass band thumps out "Mack the Knife."

* * *

For our honeymoon, we drive to the Blue Earth carnival. As we walk to the midway, the sod beneath us smells like manure. I'm carrying the case, the six remaining Planets.

Grace wants candied apples, so we buy some. I want a Ferris wheel ride, so we pay for one. As we get on, I give the guy twenty bucks to stop the ride when we're up top.

"I love Ferris wheels," I tell Grace. We're forty feet in the air, and it's cool out, and Grace is in my coat. We swing the car like it's our front porch swing, and we watch the night. Kids on the Tilt-A-Whirl scream, and some guy dressed in a wolf costume is taking tickets at the haunted house. Once, near Halloween a few years back, I had to clobber a mark dressed in a similar outfit. The mark was leaving a costume party, and he owed Honey four grand, and he was dressed as a wolf—a really good wolf, with a lolling red tongue and convincing hairiness about the arms and legs. I knew it was him because I'd been staking out his Miata and I watched him key open the door, then I appeared and pounded him. I tell Grace about this Miata-driving wolf.

"The thing is," I say, "some other guy tried to intervene, but he was dressed as a Rubik's Cube. You know, he was wearing a big cardboard box, and it was painted little blocks of colors, and he tried to be a hero. But the paint job on his box was quite shitty."

Our car is stopped in midair. Grace is trying not to laugh at my story, but she's my wife now, and laugh she does, for a moment.

"What I mean is, I was already fighting a Wolf-man, and clearly winning. But I was trying not to ruin Wolf-man's costume too much. I was throwing mid-body punches, you know, soft-tissue punches. Wolf-man had supercool, homemade fangs, and I wanted to give them a sporting chance. But then this other guy, not a mark at all, he intervened, and I had to pulverize him a little too."

Grace isn't laughing anymore. Her face goes serious.

"All I'm saying is, I'm a pretty big guy."

Grace takes my face in her hands, and I feel lousy. I mean, there's moonlight, and I'm telling this violent tale.

"Henry, baby. We're responsible for the harm we do."

For some reason, I'm crying a little.

"I know." My teeth are clenched. "I know I'm responsible. But I'm big. That's how I turned out."

"All right," says Grace. There's some wind, but not much. There's a smell of fried dough.

I rest my head on her shoulder. "I'm just big."

"All right." Grace strokes my hair.

We sit there. It's Friday night, and in the tide of fairgoers I make out Alphonse the waiter. He's standing by a booth where a well-tossed Ping-Pong ball wins you goldfish, and beside him is a cop who looks like him. They have matching sideburns, anyway, though the cop is roly-poly, and Alphonse stabs a finger in our direction, leading the cop's gaze.

I wipe my eyes. "There's Alphonse," I say, but the Ferris wheel jerks, curves us back to earth.

We walk to the fried-dough booth. It's a white shack, and it smells like a diner at breakfast. Off to one side is a stage. The band setting up is a bunch of punks, three boys with guitars and drums, and a lead singer chick with green hair. The crowd gathered before the stage contains dubious farmers and parents, but mostly other punks. One woman has a stroller and a squalling baby.

"Two fried doughs," I tell the kid in the shack.

"They're beignets," he says. He looks fifteen. He has spastic red hair and pimples, and his shirt tag says *Rupert*.

"Well, they're *made* of fried dough, right?"

"I don't know." Rupert shrugs. "They're beignets."

Grace pets my arm. "Two beignets, Rupert."

"Gotcha."

Grace keeps petting me. The baby in the stroller is shrieking, squealing her heart out. I remember I'm married. I remember the ladybug on Grace's panties.

"Hurry up," I tell Rupert.

Rupert grumbles, brings our beignets. He powders them with sugar, I pay. We walk off, biting our beignets, which are hot and greasy. I grab Grace, pull her behind the shack.

"Uh-oh," she giggles.

It's dark behind the shack. There are good shadows. The band and crowd are forty feet off, but they're living their lives, and I back Grace against the shack.

"Henry. We haven't said I love you yet."

"I love you."

Grace spreads her work boots in the dirt. "I love you too."

"Keep eating."

Grace chews and chews, watching me.

"Here we go," says the green-haired chick. Her words echo in the microphone.

I finish my beignet, drop the suitcase, hike Grace's dress. The pink ladybug's right where I dreamed she'd be. I coax my hand into the panties, and the ladybug comes alive, shucking and jiving on the black cotton over my working fingers.

"Oh." Grace scootches back and forth on my hand. "Oh."

"Keep eating."

Grace nods, swallows. I drop my pants then, tug the ladybug aside. Guitars begin jamming, and I'm inside my wife.

"Oh my God. Oh my God."

We're humping hard, pounding the shack. Grace's fried dough is gone, and we're smiling, screwing.

"Did—" Grace grooves her hips with mine. "D-did I tell you I'm a runner?"

"No." I'm snarling. I'm grinning.

"I am. I'm—God, yes. I'm really fast."

We thump the shack. The baby's still crying, but the punk song is louder. The green-haired girl wails, and the shack's back door opens.

Rupert sticks his head out. "What's going on out— Holy blue balls."

Grace says, "Hey, Rupert."

Rupert stares. In the light from the shack, his pimples are blatant. I keep screwing Grace.

"Rupert. My wife needs one more beignet. Go get it."

Rupert disappears.

Grace leers into my eyes. Her hair is crazy on her shoulders. She bites at my ear. "You're a tough one."

I nod and ram her, slam her, to the rock and roll.

Grace growls into my neck. "You're a tough motherfucker."

Rupert comes back. He hands me the beignet, which I feed to Grace's mouth.

"Um, that's two dollars, sir."

Grace's hips get faster. The beignet's still in her mouth, but her hands are on my ass, drawing me in. She makes new noises, like something special's coming, like we're staking holy ground.

Rupert's watching, and I'm thrusting, and there's powdered sugar on Grace's chin, and that's when I decide that this *is* holy ground, this whole freaking carnival. I'll give back, I decide. I kick open the suitcase.

"Goddamn." Rupert stares at the Planets.

"Take the one on the right," I pant. "The farthest-out one, Uranus. It's yours."

"I . . . I can't take a diamond."

If Grace and I weren't climbing toward the yelps, I'd talk. I'd tell Rupert the stone's not only for him, it's a far-out gift for this far-out night, and he's just an ambassador. But Grace twists and moans, and I'm way past explaining.

"Take it," I grunt. "Take it and leave."

Rupert obeys. He takes the diamond, stumbles inside, shuts the door. I kiss Grace's jaw, love her hard.

"Have some," she sputters. "Have some, have some."

The beignet hangs, half-chewed, from her lip. Her ankles rise to my ass, lock around me.

"Oh my God," she whimpers.

"Wife," I whisper. "Wife, wife."

I'm up on my toes. I grind into Grace. There's manure smell on the wind, and screaming baby, and dough in my teeth, and the singer hits a high note. I'm married, and proving it, but I turn my head, see the diva.

"Henry," whimpers Grace. "Henry."

There's some rough, bright magic in the diva's lungs, her green hair, her waving arms. She swans her body forward, touches her fingertips to the microphone like she might lick it—then, incredibly, just for a second, just for Grace and me, she does.

CHAPTER FIVE

Grunts

ROGER LIT A CHESTERFIELD. HE WAS DRIVING WEST on Route 90, crossing into southern Minnesota. Floyd rode beside him, reading aloud the signs they passed, pronouncing the towns.

"Witoka," said Floyd. "Eyota."

"Shut up." Roger was irritated to be steering a two-door, faded-lime Chevy Nova—the lowest-ranking rig in Honey's fleet—rather than the four-door, badass Buick that a hawk had crunched two days ago. Roger had always felt the Buick was a car of his own steel-blue temperament. Heavyset but sleek, it blew past its lesser peers like a charging, armored knight. The Nova, to Roger's thinking, was more like Floyd, a shifty, deadbeat thing, born in the 1970s, devoid of class.

"High Forest," read Floyd. "Grand Meadow."

"Annoying car-mate," said Roger.

"Dexter," read Floyd. He snapped his fingers. "Hey. I knew a Dexter once."

Roger sighed. Each time he blinked, his swollen, blackened right eye tingled. Also, itching his right jawline were the two raw sockets of skin where Henry's knuckles had plugged into his face.

"Dexter Weepcheek," said Floyd. "Year ahead of me at Belzer High. Oh, man. Dexter Weepcheek. What a specimen that guy was."

Roger knew what was coming. He tried to stave it off. "Keep an eye out for Blue Earth, Floyd. It's somewhere in the next little while."

"Dexter Weepcheek." Floyd shook his head with portent, as if his high school days—which had ended just eight years back—were relics about to be unearthed. "Dexter was a specimen." Floyd drew a solemn breath. "He wrote a play."

Roger groaned.

"We performed it the winter of my junior year. The play was called—"

"*Anti-Matter,*" finished Roger. "You've told me a million times. The play was called *Anti-Matter,* and it was brilliant and tragic, and when the main character got sucked into the vernal equinox, you tolled the fucking bell. I *remember,* Floyd."

Floyd gazed at his partner. Floyd's left eye was exactly as black as Roger's right, as if they were fraternal twins, each punched once at birth.

"It wasn't an equinox, Roger. It was a vortex. A black hole of sorts."

Roger stared grimly at the road. "We are not having this conversation today."

"It was called the Vortex Sans Pity," explained Floyd. "*Sans* is French for 'without.' "

"I'm turning on the radio," said Roger. But he didn't, because the Nova had no radio. Nor did it have air-conditioning, cruise control, or remotely comfortable seats.

"The main character in *Anti-Matter* was called Hospice Lumm." Floyd stared out his window, lost in reverie, entranced by his own voice. "Hospice was a plucky astronaut, but he sacrificed his life for the shuttle's navigator, Magda Babevitch."

"Okay." Roger feigned a smile. He patted Floyd's shoulder, offered him the pack of Chesterfields. "Well done, Floyd. Good story. Now have a smoke."

Floyd glanced at the cigarettes, met Roger's gaze. "Magda was Russian."

Roger fixed his eyes through the windshield again, tuning Floyd out. He willed himself to think of the university, of the eight months of the year he devoted to mental calisthenics and the bedding of women. Roger loved his master's program in anthropology, loved sitting around oaken tables, pondering the history and habits of mankind. Around those tables with him were always a half dozen male charisma-free losers, who'd never learned from their mothers to wear T-shirts under their button-downs and thus avoid disgusting armpit sweat stains.

The female U of C students, though, were the prize of Roger's life. He was taking only one course each semester—most students took four—in order to stretch his master's over eight years (most students finished in two) and expose himself to as many potential lovers as possible. The women pursuing postgraduate degrees at Chicago usually ranged in age from twenty-five to thirty-five, and most were from out of town. To

Roger, such were an ideal quarry's qualifications. He believed that by twenty-five, a woman was bold enough in body and character to be seduced by a high-minded thug like himself, and if she wasn't a Chicagoan and wary of the Pobrinkis name, so much the better.

During the previous year, his fifth season of master's classes, Roger had hit his stride. He'd conducted affairs with seven women, nearly half the roster of female first-years. Like many women graduate students in obscure fields of study, Roger's conquests were obscurely attractive. During the past nine months, he'd had Amy Bainbridge, who wore owl-eyed glasses but never brassieres, and also Pauline Grock, a Communist in thongs. Young Jennifer Schoolcraft, the ticklish vegan, had thrilled Roger's November, but for the holidays he'd kept company with the Solzhenitsyn-mad Kira Woo, who lowed like a Tibetan monk during intercourse, then denied it afterward. February brought Carla Chopping, who followed opera, then Queeny Reese, who squeezed, every day, the juice of eight fruits into her hair.

Roger drank in these women—their habits, their smells and talking—one at a time but in fast, greedy gulps. Over late-night coffee in Queeny's apartment, he'd held forth on the swirling theories of Teilhard de Chardin, then groped Queeny's breasts. It intoxicated Roger that with university women, if he flashed the badge of his intellect, then showed some muscle, he almost never slept alone.

This approach had worked particularly well with Roger's seventh woman that year, Hilda Reisch. Hilda was a towering, pale-skinned adjunct professor visiting from Denmark, maybe thirty-five, a woman who rarely showed smiles but always showed leg. She shod herself daily in skirts and low boots. She wore her black permed-out hair like an explosion on her head, and her eyes, also black, dismissed almost everything they saw. It was she who'd taught Roger the Fierce Leaders course, the study of dictators and demagogues. Roger had determined, at the class's first session in January, that he'd land Hilda by the first day of spring. When he got her, on March 15, to consent to dinner out that night, he took her to Ferryman's and talked straight.

"I'm a study in male paradox," Roger declared, during their second carafe of Syrah. "I'll fascinate, then ravage you."

Hilda snorted, ate her steak.

Roger leaned in close. "I've killed five men."

Hilda showed him her teeth. "Bullshit," she whispered.

They were in a corner booth, sharing a cushioned half-circle seat. Roger slid himself closer, so his thigh was touching his teacher's. He set down his wineglass and put his arm around her waist.

"I made one of those men eat spoonfuls of wet cement." Roger bored his eyes into Hilda's. "He swallowed fifteen bites before he died."

Hilda waited for a punch line. "Hold on. You're kidding . . . right?"

In a practiced move, Roger slid his hand down the back of Hilda's skirt, gripped her right ass cheek in his fist. Professor Hilda Reisch made a quick, meeping sound, and sat bolt upright. Her eyes darted around the restaurant, at the faces of strangers.

"Am I kidding?" whispered Roger. He squeezed firmly, held the woman in place. "Am I kidding, Hilda Reisch?"

An hour later, Roger and Hilda were tearing into each other

in bed at Hilda's town house. Roger worked her body savagely as she clawed his neck and shoulders. Later, when they'd finished, Hilda asked quietly whether he'd really ever murdered someone, and Roger had said nothing. He'd merely closed his eyes, a mute force in history, a monarch who would never negotiate.

"Roger?" said Floyd. "Are you hearing me? Are you hearing what I'm saying?"

Roger adjusted his grip on the steering wheel. "No."

"I'm saying that, in the end, Hospice Lumm throws himself *willingly* into the Vortex Sans Pity. You see? I'm saying he *becomes* antimatter."

"I don't see, and I don't care."

"I'm saying his is an act of sacrifice."

"Here I sit," said Roger, "not caring."

Floyd crossed his arms. "Oh, man. You don't care, huh? Well, I'll tell you who did care. Rhea Cicconetti, that's who."

"Blue Earth." Roger pointed at a sign. "Here's our exit." He steered off the highway. From his coat pocket he pulled a piece of paper that read *Juan Ortiz, Blue Earth Police,* with a phone number. This policeman, Ortiz—who'd lost to Honey in a Reno poker match and owed him heavy—had spotted Henry at a carnival and, having received Honey's all-points bulletin, had phoned Chicago. Honey sent his hounds north, and Juan, in the meantime, had been shadowing Henry's truck.

"I gotta call this cop." Roger pulled onto the shoulder, whipped out a cell phone, and dialed.

Floyd was polishing his switchblade. "See, Rhea Cicconetti played Magda Babevitch. Rhea was just a sophomore, but—"

"Yeah, Blue Earth Police? Juan Ortiz, please. Yes, ma'am, I'll hold. . . ."

"She had some sexy little earlobes, that Rhea did."

Roger tried to sit patiently as he held the line, but he couldn't resist. "Listen, Floyd. It was immature for the playwright to name the Russian girl Babevitch, okay? Unless *Anti-Matter* was satirical, and you've never said it was, then fusing the slang word *babe* into the leading lady's name was jingoistic and reductive."

Floyd pointed his knife at Roger. "You wouldn't criticize Rhea if you'd seen her in her space helmet. It had glowing Christmas bulbs inside."

"Fuck Rhea. I'm talking about the text. I'm dispassionately deconstructing the text."

"The bulbs and foil in the helmet lit up her earlobes."

"What kind of guy fixates on earlobes?"

Floyd clucked his tongue like a father. "I see. So, even in our civilized times, a young man still has to, like, obsess over a girl's mammaries, or he's a fag?"

"They're not mammaries, they're tits." Roger's face fell. "Oh, no, ma'am, I wasn't talking to you. . . ." He listened to his phone and frowned. "Hasn't reported back from lunch?" He glanced at his watch. "It's four-thirty. . . . Yes, it seems strange to me too. Listen, I'm Juan's cousin, Hector, from Chicago and I'm here in Blue Earth . . ."

"Truth is, Rhea recognized Dexter's talent just as I did. She had insight, see."

"Well, if you know where Juan takes lunch, maybe I'll . . . what's that? The Garbage Plate Pub. All right, great."

"Rhea had earlobes and insight."

Roger covered the phone, punched Floyd's shoulder. "Hey. Alistair Cooke. Could you pause the fucking sound track while I get some directions?"

Five minutes later, the partners were driving back roads in silence. Roger steered and kept his eyes peeled for the Garbage Plate. He thought again of women he'd conquered, and, annoyed with Floyd, he let his mind drift toward one particular conquest. Two summers back, Floyd's sister, Gretl, had come through Chicago and stopped to visit her brother. She was twenty-three at the time, a year Floyd's junior, and she was backpacking solo around the country. She'd dropped by Ferryman's one afternoon during an August that was dry for Roger, womenwise.

He'd been alone at Ferryman's that day, standing behind the bar, bored, reading racing forms. It was his malicious good fortune that Honey had business in Toronto that afternoon, with Henry and Floyd along as bodyguards. So when the lean, flaxen-haired Gretl loped into the empty restaurant, dumped her backpack, and asked after her brother, Roger, just to see if he could, got to work. He chatted up the vagabond, fed her bratwurst and plenty of whiskey. An hour later, he scuttled a woozy, hiccuping Gretl down to his uncle's walk-in vault. The vault's control pad featured the alphabet, and Honey had a password he believed no one could crack. But Roger knew his uncle's mind, his yen for things mythical, his love of his dead father. So, after experimenting for months, Roger had struck upon the lock's trigger: the word CHARON, the name of the ferryman who steered the dead across the River Styx into the Underworld.

Stabbing out those six letters on this August afternoon, Roger opened the vault and shoved Gretl inside. Relishing her protests, he pinned the girl on the plush carpet, got her naked, worked her into a gasping fervor. Gretl had an ectomorph's bone structure, a patchouli smell, and unshaven legs. As he urged cries from her, Roger memorized these details. Later, when Gretl hurried dizzy and shamefaced out of Ferryman's, Roger watched with a pleased nonchalance, knowing she wouldn't come back and wouldn't tell Floyd what had happened.

It thrilled Roger that he'd done this, that he'd connived his way into two supposedly sacred spaces, violating both Floyd's and Honey's trust in ways they'd never know. To act boldly, on demand, and breathe easy afterward was the essence of power, Roger thought. Floyd believed the two of them were blood brothers, boon companions who argued but whose mutual loyalty was unshakable. Roger knew otherwise. While he looked for the Garbage Plate Pub, he thought of Gretl's spread thighs and smirked.

Meanwhile, Floyd slouched in his seat, oblivious. He watched for the pub, too, but his mind was daydreaming, rebuilding the backstage nooks of the *Anti-Matter* set. Back in high school, skinny and sixteen, Floyd had been the props manager of Dexter Weepcheek's play. He'd gotten kicked off the wrestling team the previous fall for habitually biting his opponents when losing a match. So he was almost tearful with gratitude when Mr. Fulikkis, the drama teacher, gave him a fresh extracurricular chance that winter. As Floyd hid backstage, close to the curtains, it was his duty to hand props to actors. There was no competition in this and so, ostensibly, no reason for Floyd to bite anybody. He performed his duties well, now making sure that Hospice Lumm had his flavor pellets, now handing Ensign Celia her Holy Sword of Collateral Damage.

Floyd enjoyed huddling backstage because Dexter Weepcheek often huddled next to him, listening to the actors beyond the scrim. Dexter was a weakling, a tall, sticklike boy who avoided beer and eye contact, and who was too shy to watch his own creation from the audience. Floyd had a soft spot for the playwright. The two never spoke, even when kneeling side by side, but Floyd suspected that, deep down, Dexter was a grunt like he was, a clumsy boy made for behind-the-scenes labors, a guy with few friends, no dates, no limelight abilities. That's what made Floyd so proud to work on *Anti-Matter*: he believed someone of his own graceless nature had reached down against the adolescent odds and produced a great work.

Thinking they shared this camaraderie, Floyd was happy to crouch beside Dexter, to wince when Dexter winced as an actor flubbed a line. Then, on *Anti-Matter*'s closing night, Floyd got a slap in the face. It happened toward the end of Act Two, just as, onstage, Hospice Lumm was preparing to leap into the black papier-mâché pit that was the Vortex Sans Pity. Crouching between Dexter and the bell rigged at backstage right—and gripping the mallet he used for tolling the bell—Floyd listened to Hospice Lumm's farewell monologue. Alone onstage, Hospice delivered his swan song words to a cold, empty universe. When Magda Babevitch, in her astrosuit, floated onstage just in time to see Hospice Lumm's oxygen tube get sucked like spaghetti into the Vortex, Floyd always choked back a sob.

On this night, though, as Hospice gave his own pre-Vortex eulogy, Floyd glanced across to the stage-left wings where Rhea Cicconetti, in astrosuit and space helmet, was staring into a mirror, applying last-minute lipstick. Suddenly Rhea turned, caught Floyd's eye, gave him a sultry come-hither smile. Thunderstruck, Floyd dropped his mallet. Rhea's gaze burned into him. She licked her lips suggestively, and Floyd's heart swelled. Then Rhea lifted the top of her astrosuit, revealing her pale white belly. Making crude red letters with her lipstick, Rhea wrote the words DEX = SEX on her stomach, and grinned in Floyd's direction. Horrified, Floyd glanced beside him at Dexter Weepcheek, who was leering a smug, proprietary leer at the exhibitionist astronaut. Rhea blew Dexter a kiss, adjusted her suit, and disappeared onstage, wailing for Hospice.

"Toll," whispered Dexter.

Floyd was angry, confused. "What?"

"Toll, goddammit." Dexter nudged him hard. "Toll the fucking bell. Where's the mallet?"

Floyd had lost the mallet in the dark. He rapped his knuckles on the bell, which produced a flat, feeble dung-dung-dung.

"You fuckhead, Webber!" Dexter scowled in Floyd's face. Floyd, flushed and furious, still picturing the characters on Rhea's belly (and knowing he'd never inspire such an equation), did the first thing that came to mind. He grabbed Dexter's forearm and chomped his teeth into it.

Dexter howled. In the lobby afterward, several parents complimented the playwright on the offstage primal scream that had sounded just as the curtain fell on the bereft Magda.

Floyd never told anyone the closing-night story, especially not his onetime failure with the bell. He did admit to Roger, though, as they parked at the Garbage Plate Pub, that Dexter and Rhea had danced indecently close at the cast party.

"I'll tell you what." Floyd sheathed his knife. "Seeing Dexter lick her earlobe under a mirrored ball? That broke the cake."

Roger killed the engine. "Took the cake. Takes the cake. Never mind."

The Garbage Plate Pub was all but deserted. It wasn't quite five, so the evening patrons hadn't arrived yet, and only two Blue Earth drunks sat at the bar, one nursing whiskey, the other vodka. These men hunched over their glasses like stooped, thirsty trees, and their hair was gray and greasy. Behind the bar was an enormous woman chewing a toothpick, watching a television talk show. Her face was all jowls, her rear end was held miraculously aloft by three adjacent bar stools, and as Floyd and Roger approached, she never took her eyes off the TV.

Floyd whistled, impressed. "Jesus, God. You must weigh four hundred pounds."

"Quiet, Floyd," said Roger.

"Four-fifty," said the barkeep.

On the television, a young boy tearfully confessed that his mother once made him swallow a bottle cap.

"You," said Floyd, "are hands down the plumpest woman that I've ever met."

"Thank you," said the barkeep.

Roger asked, "Have you seen Juan Ortiz?"

In an unseen kitchen area, something sizzled.

The fat woman chewed her toothpick. "Juan's in for lunch, most days."

"Oh, man." Floyd admired the woman from all angles. "You're like a battleship. What do you eat to stay so humongous?"

"Was Juan in for lunch today?" asked Roger.

The whiskey-drunk glanced at Roger's black eye, then Floyd's. "You fellows from out of state?"

"Chicago," said Floyd.

"Quiet, Floyd."

"The bottle cap lodged in my anus."

The whiskey-drunk grunted. "Looks like Chicago took a pounding."

"I'm partial to veal chops," the barkeep told Floyd.

The vodka-drunk sighed.

"So, did he?" Roger faced the fat woman. "Juan. Did he come in today?"

"Came in a while back, during the lunch rush."

"Never left," said the vodka-drunk.

"Doctors got involved." The talk-show boy sniffled. *"They saved me."*

"Veal chops." Floyd nodded sagely.

"Wait," said Roger. "What do you mean, 'never left'?"

"Juan never left." The vodka-drunk yawned and pointed. "He's in the shitter. Been there an hour."

"News to me," said the barkeep.

The whiskey-drunk frowned. "No one's business but Juan's."

In the men's room, Roger and Floyd pushed open a stall door and found Officer Juan Ortiz slumped unconscious, wearing his uniform. The cop had been propped in a seated position on the toilet bowl, but the only things in the toilet water were a police-issue Glock handgun and nine bullets snapped from the gun's clip. Also, blood was drying around a gash on his chin, while on the skin of his right jaw shone two red, round welts.

"Oh, man." Floyd's fingers flew to his own cheek. "Devil's horns."

Roger stared at the cop. The fourth man Roger had killed had been a pimp who'd attacked him in a Hyde Park restroom. Roger had crushed the guy's face with a metal paper-towel dispenser, then left the body sitting on a stall in the same position as the out-cold Juan Ortiz.

"Yeah," said Roger quietly. "Devil's horns."

Floyd poked the cop's stomach but couldn't rouse him. "Shitbox. This guy was supposed to be on Henry's ass. Now who's tailing him?"

Roger clenched and unclenched his fists. "We are."

CHAPTER SIX

Monsters

JUST OFF THE HIGHWAY NEAR CACTUS FLAT, SOUTH Dakota, Grace is running wind sprints on the shoulder. It's our fifth morning together, sunny again and warmer than it's been. I'm sitting on the tailgate, not moving, not anxious, just watching my wife and a world of creamy stone. I've got my suitcase beside me, but there's no need to open it and behold the Planets, because the Badlands around me are trippy enough. The terrain looks like a cave with the ceiling ripped off. There are crags and bumps and hills of rock, all the color of dirty salt, and they stretch to the horizon. It's barren and still, and even with Grace a quarter mile off, I can hear her panting. It's a steady, living sound, like a pulse, and the sky's giant blue, and this could be the surface of the moon, except then we'd be floating, Grace and I.

I dipped the truck off the 90 last night and we slept here on the roadside, on Route 240. Grace has never seen South Dakota and I wanted her to wake to something dazzling. Watching her now—she's rubbernecking, kicking up dust—I figure I'm falling in love, not just with her but with wherever we're going, which is who knows where. The San Juan Islands, maybe, or Banff. Or to that palace in Sri Lanka, the place we can buy if we keep just one diamond.

"Hey." Grace walks up to the tailgate, spent and heaving. Back in Blue Earth, she used the ATM card that's been funding our danger to buy the sweats and running shoes she's wearing.

"Hey," I say.

She kisses my chin, and I hug her close, smelling her hair, blinking up at the sun. We hold each other, look at the day.

"Let's tell the truth," says Grace.

"Say again?"

"It's such an amazing morning, we should each tell the other the truth about something."

"All right," I say. "You first."

Grace mops her temples with her sleeve. "Well, the truth is, I miss my mother. I wish she could've been at our wedding."

"If I remember right, we eloped."

"I'm just *saying*, if I'd called her, I wonder if she'd've come. Driven to us."

My arms are locked around her waist. She leans back, pets my jaws, which have a stubborn, five-day beard.

"My daddy..." says Grace. "He was a trucker, and he did that once, before I was born. Called my mother out onto the road, I mean. He phoned her from Topeka. Said he had a migraine so bad he was blind in one eye and could she come tend him."

"Did she?"

"Yep. But when she got to Kansas, no migraine. It was a ploy. My father was at the Tip-Top Truck Stop, where some good old boys were throwing a summer clambake in the meadow out back, and Daddy wanted to treat Regina to a shindig. When she pulled up in the station wagon, he was drunk as a monk. He'd been dancing for hours, there was some garage band playing, and Regina slapped his rascal face." Grace grins, looks off at the Badlands. "She claims she sat and stewed in the station wagon all night, refusing Daddy's dance card, but from the way she talks about it, remembers it so sharp and angry, I think she kicked up her heels and danced with him. You know, embraced the rhythm."

I kiss Grace's neck. "When in Topeka . . ."

"Your turn now. Tell the truth about something."

I move my hands over her back, feel her bones underneath it all. I want us to stay like this, easygoing, but gripping each other.

"Come on, Dante," she teases. "Out with it."

I should take the easy route, maybe, chat about my father's love for Maker's Mark, my mother's crush on Gorbachev. But Grace needs to know some things.

"All right," I say. "I have a confession to make."

"What's that?"

"I pounded a cop."

She leans her forehead into mine. "I know, baby. You hurt a lot of people before you met me. But now we're together."

"Not before I met you. Yesterday. I pounded a cop yesterday."

"What?" She breaks our embrace, stands back. "What cop? When?"

"In that restaurant where we had lunch. The Garbage House or whatever. Before we left Minnesota."

Grace puts her hands on her hips. She's peeved, perspiring, wearing a ponytail. We made love three times last night in the truck. Between the second and third times, she read aloud from one of Charles's smutty paperbacks, *Little Julia Among the Elves*.

"I didn't see any cop."

"I pounded him in the bathroom. I had to. He was following us."

"Following us? Since when?"

"Since that carnival."

Grace stares at me, waiting for more.

"Honey Pobrinkis knows some cops, all right? Not the National Guard or anything, but a couple guys owe him favors. So he's probably got the word out to boys like Ortiz."

"Who's Ortiz?"

"The cop I pounded. The Garbage waitress called him by name."

Grace shakes her head. "Perfect. I marry a guy and start screwing him, and he goes and pounds a cop named Ortiz."

I breathe in the morning. The breeze smells like smoke, and I grind my devil knuckles into my thigh. They're a fact I can't change, my knuckles are. They're spooky and lumpy, like the land around us.

"Look," I say. "That's how it's going to be. That's what you married."

Grace chews her lip. "Tell me again why we can't ditch this truck?"

I gaze at her cheeks, flushed from running, and think of how

Honey saved my life. It happened on a Wednesday three years back. I'd driven Honey to Burma's, a whorehouse he owns on a Chicago mansion property. The mansion's famous because the original owner, a rich, insane Soviet-hater named Connor Gout, built interlocking underground bomb shelters in his backyard. The mansion's empty now, but Honey converted the shelters into a plush whores' nest. As a gimmick, he pays the whores to live there, underground, 24/7, and never come out in the sun. They're ultrapale vixen vampires, and Chicagoans love them, including the police chief, a regular customer. Anyway, the grande dame of the place, Burma herself, fucks only Honey, and I drove him there one night for his midweek medicine.

I was waiting on terra firma, by the car. I dislike whores, and the walls down in Burma's are claustrophobic steel. So I was pacing around the Buick, when noise exploded, and my right shoulder and hip went electric with pain. I collapsed, aware I'd just been shot twice. I lay sucking wind, while Larry Nickel loped out of the shadows and came grinning toward me, holding a pistol. Larry worked for the Staff brothers, Duke and Victor, two meatheads who dealt low-level blow. The night before, I'd donated a cleft palate and a concussion to Victor Staff, who was into Honey for fifty grand.

"Vic sends kisses." Larry aimed at my head, but just before he fired, Honey's giant arm clubbed the gun from his grip. I was bleary-eyed, losing blood and focus, but I remember Honey was in his boxer shorts as he pounded Larry's skull on the Buick fender. I don't know how my boss came up out of the earth so fast to save my ass. All I can say is, three minutes after shooting me, Larry was folded dead in the Buick's trunk, and Honey carried me underground. He called an ambulance, while women with faces like ghosts whispered for me to stay, stay, stay.

"Honey deserves a sporting chance," I tell Grace. "If he has what it takes to find me, then he finds me."

"That's nuts."

"Yeah? So is tossing away forty million in gems, but I'm going along with that."

"We should lay low, though, right? Take back roads . . ."

"No." I arch my back, flex my shoulders. "No hiding, no pussy politics. We move free, where we want, out in the open. That's the secret. You get jumpy and careful, you get dead."

"You have a warped sense of chivalry."

"And you have a great rack."

Grace blinks at me, not laughing. She doesn't want jokes right now. She wants to know why I've done all I've done, wants to hear about all the bones I've ever cracked, probably so she can forgive me for cracking them.

"Don't look at me like that," I warn her.

Grace gives me the finger. I grab her arm, reel her in. My knees are spread, and her torso goes against my groin. She puts her hands on my neck like she'll choke me, but instead we kiss, heavy and hard. Our tongues battle till I'm dizzy, till I'm half sure that Grace will earn me, one day, a drop from some gallows, a trip to the coroner.

"Mmmph." She breaks free. "Okay. Enough. Jesus."

I'm on the tailgate. She's standing away from the truck. We trade stares, like we don't know each other, which maybe we don't.

Just south of the city of Wall we find a rest stop. It's an

adobe-looking building where a woman charges us two bucks each to use the shower stalls. The place is deserted, so Grace and I could shower together, but we clean up separately, her in the women's, me in the men's. We're fighting, I guess.

Back in the parking lot, we break out the Coleman stove. It's nearly seventy degrees out. Grace turns on the radio, I fry up the eggs and bread we bought last night at a Texaco. We eat sitting on the tailgate, and I burn my tongue on too-hot yolk. Grace and I still aren't talking. While Jim Croce finishes singing, I study the Badlands, wondering if they're as dead as they look. It's possible, I suppose, that underground mole persons live among these arid white hills, like the Burma whores in their bomb shelters. For a minute I contemplate getting the Planets and pitching them into the sky. The diamonds would land and glitter against the chalky earth, and the mole persons, sniffing along, would discover them. First they'd try to eat them, then they'd debate their meaning, and then, burrowing underground with their new, mystical artifacts, they would weep and hug and pursue joy.

"Hey." Grace leaps up, drops her egg sandwich to the asphalt. Her head is cocked, startled, listening.

"What?"

"The radio . . ."

I stay quiet. A folksy AM deejay is talking.

"Once again," speaks the deejay, "this'll be the kickoff of this summer's God's Will revival tour. It's this Friday night, eight o'clock, at the Hammerspread in Great Falls. Consider a road trip, believers, 'cause Bertram Block promises a barn burner."

"Bertram Block," whispers Grace. Her voice is worlds away. "Bertram goddamn Block . . ."

She shoves me aside, grabs the atlas. She grabs a pen, too, and a Little Julia paperback. On the book's inside back cover, she writes *The Hammerspread, Great Falls, Friday night*. She opens the atlas. "Where's Great Falls?"

I've confronted men in alleys, restrooms, sometimes in their homes. Their expressions always go grim and heavy, like Charles Chalk's did at the farm. Grace's face is like that now.

"Who's Bertram Block?" I ask.

"Where's Great Falls?"

"In Montana. Who's Bertram Block?"

"Montana." Grace paws through the atlas. "And what's today, Tuesday?" She finds a page of western states, traces her finger across Wyoming, then north. She stabs the map. "Great Falls. Bingo."

I stare at Grace's asphalt sandwich, remembering Bella Cavasti. Back when Bella and I fell in love, we spent our first months with just each other. This was before I'd found Honey or he'd found me. I was twenty-four and working in Palos Heights at Klayber's Furniture. I spent all day loading couches and sideboards into trucks, then at night, Bella would cook us linguine at my apartment. I can't remember why—it had to do with my job—but Bella gave me the pet name Hope Chest. She and I would dance around my kitchen, then fuck, then play Axis and Allies, an old board game I loved, and Bella would call me Hope Chest. Anyway, for eight weeks, we were an airtight twosome, like Adam and Eve. Then one night, we went out to dinner at Wong Yu's with another couple, Mary Bopp and Louis Dwyer. We were eating and laughing, then I left the other three and went to the can. When I came back a few minutes later, Mary wasn't there. She was probably just in the bathroom, too, but it didn't matter. Bella and Louis were at the table alone, talking low, grinning, their heads close together. I was five tables away, standing next to the lobster tank, watching how the ends of Bella's hair just missed brushing the tabletop as she leaned toward Louis.

In an instant, there was a bubbling green disease in my blood, a jealous nausea that felt as rank as the water in the lobster tank looked. In the middle of whatever story she was telling Louis, Bella said "Hope Chest"—the secret name she'd given me, a name I thought she'd never pronounce outside my apartment, and here she was speaking of it with another guy. My green disease exploded. I strode over, shoved Louis back, slammed my fist on the table. The shock sent soy-covered noodles flying. I hauled Bella outside, where she slapped my face and shouted what the fuck and stormed off down the sidewalk.

"Who's Bertram Block?" I ask Grace.

She stares at Wyoming, then snaps the atlas shut. "Henry, we have to be in Great Falls, Montana, this Friday night."

Grace is on the tailgate with her knees drawn beneath her. I can smell the almond shampoo she used, and she's in her fetching Navajo dress, but I want an answer.

"Who is he?"

She shakes her head. "I'll tell you when I'm ready. Right now, promise we'll be in Great Falls, Montana, this Friday. Swear that we will."

I crunch my top teeth on my bottom teeth. The husband is supposed to trust the wife.

"We'll be there," I mutter.

"Say that you swear it."

Grace probably swears things to herself every day, and the

swears probably have to do with her God. It occurs to me that—ladybug panties or not—I might have made a serious freaking mistake here.

"I swear it."

* * *

We rejoin the 90 in Wall, start west, drive in silence for an hour. On the outskirts of Sturgis, I see a hitchhiker. Normally I wouldn't stop, but there's tension between me and Grace. I'm used to loaded silences, but only between me and doomed men. Grace won't spill her Bertram Block story, and I don't know why. So I pull over, and Grace rolls down her window.

"Thanks for stopping." It's a short guy, maybe forty, in jeans and a burlap poncho. His face is windburned like a cowboy's, but he doesn't look mean.

"I'm Phil Weal," says the guy. "W-E-A-L. That's how my family spells it."

Phil has a deep, scratchy voice, like a blues singer. He carries no bags, and has hair the color of sand dunes. His poncho features swirling red and purple and yellow marks painted on the burlap.

"I'm Henry."

"I'm heading to Idaho," says Phil, "my native soil. You can drop me anywhere in the whole state and I'll be happy as a heifer."

Grace lets him in, introduces herself. Phil plunks into the makeshift jump seat. I get driving, and Grace gives the guy an orange. He nods his thanks, tucks into the orange, and looks around.

"I see a rifle on a gun rack," announces our guest.

"Does that freak you out?" I ask.

Phil eats his fruit. He makes snarfling noises, shoves his nose in the rind like a hound. "Idahoans do not freak out."

Grace braids her hair silently, avoiding my eyes. She was doing this before we discovered Phil Weal, and she's doing it now. For his part, Phil piles orange rinds in his fist. He scouts around, finds our trash pail, dumps the rinds. Then he looks back and forth between me and Grace. His skin, like hers, is dusted with freckles.

"There is unrest in this truck," says Phil.

The sun's winking off the hood. I'm doing eighty.

"Where you two from?"

"Henry's from Chicago. I'm from Janesville, Wisconsin."

"Never been to Janesville. What's excellent there?"

Two Corvettes that are friends clock past our truck, each going maybe a hundred.

"Provide an excellent detail is what I mean."

Grace stops braiding, thinks. "Well, there's this place I like, Pyle's Thrift Emporium. In the front window, there's a statue on sale for one dollar and forty-five cents. It's a Taj Mahal statue, a clay replica, maybe a foot high, covered in dust. It's been there since I was little, it never budges, and it's always been a dollar forty-five."

Phil slaps his knee, laughs a great, rasping laugh. "Yes. Fucking *yes*." He claps my shoulder.

"What?" I demand.

"A dollar forty-five, that's what!"

Phil seems overjoyed. He laughs again, and Grace laughs with him, like it's a slumber party. I consider introducing my fist to Phil's face. He was supposed to be a buffer, not a liability. I'd kick him out, but if I did, my Good Samaritan bride would piss and moan.

"Now," says Phil, "*I'll* provide a detail."

Grace faces him.

He leans forward. "It's hard to prove, and feel free to doubt, but I can tell after one bite, be it baked, boiled, whatever, whether any potato comes from Idaho."

"Come on," I say.

"I kid you not. That's how in touch I am with the land that sired me."

I glare out the windshield. The sky's a flawless, crushing blue, like it got orders this morning from God or the government. I should roll down my window and suck in that blueness, take it into my lungs as we enter Wyoming. I'm saying that crossing a border under a clean, pounding sky should taste as good as sex, but right now I'm lonely.

* * *

We stop at a Dairy Queen in Xander, Wyoming. It's late afternoon, and we sit on grass behind the restaurant. Phil and I have burgers, fries, Blizzard shakes, while Grace dozes. I've got my Planets case with me.

Nearby are picnic tables. They're empty except one, which has five high-school kids around it, three girls and two guys. The kids stuff down food, laugh, argue. One of them, a beanpole, flat-chested redhead, is writing down what the others say, so they're obviously the yearbook or debate club, banging out a manifesto.

"Nope," whispers Phil. He's eating fries one at a time, considering each one. "Nope. Nope."

"Cut it out," I tell him.

Across the lawn, the two boys break out a Frisbee. Grace twitches on the lawn, dealing with some dream. I look at her hand. We've got matching silver rings on our wedding fingers. We bought them in Blue Earth, fifty bucks each.

"Come on, Stewart," mumbles Grace, stirring. "Come on, Stewart. Come on, boy."

I shake her till her eyes open. "Who's Stewart?"

Grace yawns, sits up. She takes in the sky, the teenagers, me. "What?"

The green disease roars in my blood. "Who the hell is Stewart? You called for him in your sleep."

Grace's face gets defensive. "I did not."

"You definitely called for Stewart. Twice."

Grace stares at me, her expression tightening. I wish we didn't both have to be from somewhere. I wish we'd come alive the second we met.

"So, who is he? The first guy you slept with? The love of your life?"

Phil clears his throat. "Let's avoid unrest."

I tell Phil to shut his freeloading mouth.

Grace's hem is caught around her thighs from her sleeping. She tugs it down past her knees. "Stewart's the guy who always wanted me, but never got me. All right?"

"And did you want him?"

"Oh, gee, no, Henry. I never wanted any boys growing up. I knew exactly when I'd meet you, so I never looked at a boy or masturbated or anything. I was a lily-white virgin till you nailed me to a funnel-cake booth."

If my wife were a man, I could punch her.

She grabs my chin, tries to pull my eyes toward hers. "Who'd I marry?"

I don't answer. She sighs.

A gust of laughter blows up from the kids. We look over. The redhead court stenographer is blushing, hanging her head. The joke's on her for sure, because she's put down her pen and she's not laughing. Two tall, curvy brunettes—the future power-wives of Xander, maybe—whisper and point at the redhead. A Frisbee boy makes some crack, and the guffaws deepen. The girl's head ducks lower.

Watching all this, Grace sets her jaw. She gets up and climbs onto the picnic table nearest us. She stands tall, hands on her hips. "Hey! Hey, you kids!"

Their heads snap up. They check us out, their faces gone sullen. The two Frisbee boys stop playing.

"Grace," I say.

"What's she doing?" Phil asks.

Grace looks at me, sly and womanly. "Listen here a minute," she calls.

A brunette flounces her hair. "How come?"

"I have something to give you."

"Grace," I say. But I don't say anything else.

A Frisbee boy grins. "Is it pot?" The teenage posse laughs.

The brunette sits up straighter, fearless. "Well?" she says. Her tank top features the words LET THE WILD RUMPUS START. From her expectant, raised eyebrows, I bet she's headed for Stanford.

"Hey, Red." Grace eyes the stenographer. "What's your name?"

"Her name's Ginny," says a Frisbee boy.

"I wasn't speaking to you, young sir. I was speaking to Red."

I stand, move close to Grace's table.

"My name's Ginny," says the stenographer.

"Pleased to meet you, Ginny. I'm Grace McGlone." She peers at the others. "Seems like you were all having quite the cackle at Ginny's expense."

Phil gets up, too, stands by me.

"So, Ginny. Why were they laughing at you?"

Wild Rumpus bugs her eyes out like she's stunned. "Oh my God, Ginny. You totally don't have to tell her."

"It's all right." Ginny looks at Grace. "They were laughing about how I dance. I don't have a date for prom, and . . . these guys were saying it's because of how I dance."

"How do you dance?"

The sidekick brunette tsks her tongue. "Like it matters to you? Like, who the hell are you, anyway?"

"We're Henry, Grace, and Phil. Who the hell are you?"

No one speaks.

"I don't know," says Ginny. "I just dance how I dance."

"You dance weird," says the sidekick.

"Yeah," agrees a Frisbee boy. "It's like . . . monster dancing."

The teenagers laugh. They don't hate the IRS yet. They've never pounded a grown man's cranium.

"Show me," Grace tells Ginny. "Show me your monster dancing."

The sidekick brunette snorts. "Yeah, right."

Grace points her foot at the case in my hand. "Show me, and I'll show you something inside there."

The teenagers become serious. They stare at my suitcase, as if something sexual's been proposed, as if Pandora herself is nearby.

The bigger Frisbee boy steps forward. "What's going on here?"

"That's up to Ginny."

Ginny doesn't speak. Her eyes are locked with Grace's. I can't say for sure, but for an instant it seems as if millions of tiny female particles are streaming back and forth between Grace's heart and Ginny's. It looks like an invisible talking, where freedom and dignity and the smell of men get discussed through glances, and it ends with a smile on Grace's lips, a challenge in her gaze. Then, to everyone's shock, Ginny stands up, closes her eyes, starts swaying her hips.

"Wait." Wild Rumpus bites her lip. "Hey. Ginny?"

Ginny lifts her arms above her head, works her hands and fingers, massaging the air. She wears jeans, a black sweater, black Adidas. There's no music, but Ginny's knees jerk up like an Irishman's. Her feet tramp the grass.

"Ginny," says the sidekick brunette. "Stop."

But Ginny keeps it up. She's really flailing now, clawing and hooking out with her arms, like she's whomping unseen foes.

"Tallyho." Grace laughs.

Suddenly, Phil Weal makes a move. He dashes forward, gets close to Ginny, starts flitting his body around, matching her moves but never touching her. He wheezes and whirls. Ginny opens her eyes, grins at Phil, keeps churning.

"This is weird," says a Frisbee boy.

"What is this?" says the other.

Phil pounds and huffs. "Idahoans know how to groove!"

Grace leaps off the picnic table. She lands beside Ginny, starts twisting and kicking. "Come on, Henry! When in Topeka . . ."

I watch them gyrate. Just last month, I sent Jersey Ringo, a

Stickney loan shark, to the ER with a busted femur. But now I'm Grace's man, and she's looking at me, and I can see that in her own somewhat fucked-up way, she's trying to make things right. I take a breath. My blood clears. I clench my case, boogie onto the grass.

"Oh, for the love . . ." says the Wild Rumpus girl. She rolls her eyes, like she's saving her body for better things than this. But the Frisbee boys watch Grace, liking her moves. One of them shrugs, and they both start stomping.

"Gary," wails the sidekick brunette. "Andrew. Cut it out."

"Aw," says Andrew or Gary, "screw that."

There's a heat among us movers and shakers. Beanpole Ginny grinds in the center. My arm's heavy from the Planets, and my lungs haven't pumped like this in years, but I drive blindly on.

"Hey." The back door of the restaurant is open. A man with a name tag steps out. "Hey," he calls. "No, ah, no dancing at Dairy Queen."

"Screw that!" hollers Grace, whirling on. "Embrace the fucking rhythm!"

The restaurant guy looks startled. Grace claps her hands in time. Andrew and Gary join her. "Embrace-the-fucking-rhythm," they chant. "Embrace-the-fucking-rhythm."

The restaurant guy folds his arms. "I'll call the cops."

He goes back inside. There's bedlam on the lawn. We're thrashing like champs. The sidekick brunette capitulates, moves behind a Frisbee boy. She grinds her hips against his butt, her chest against his back. Just when it seems like an orgy's brewing, like the earth might open and swallow us, Grace shouts for us to stop.

"Stand still!" she hollers. "Everybody, stop! Just stand still, wherever you are."

We do. We're panting.

"Now," says Grace. "Who's the stupendous one?"

"What?" says Wild Rumpus. She's the only one still sitting.

"Who's the brave one?" asks Grace. "Who danced first?"

"I did?" says Ginny.

Grace grabs the case from me. She kneels and opens the suitcase. The teens gather around like ducklings. Staring at the gems, they coo and swear and whistle.

"They're diamonds," whispers the sidekick brunette.

"They're awesome," says Gary or Andrew.

Phil looks at the Planets. He glances at me, his face asking questions. I nod yes to him: yes, they're real, yes, they're stolen, yes, we're on the run. Phil inclines his head once, simply. This makes me like him. I punch his arm like we're soldiers.

"Here." Grace hands Ginny a diamond. "That's Mercury. It's the little one among bigger friends. Just like you."

Ginny says, "Damn."

"It's worth a couple million dollars."

Wild Rumpus snorts. "Yeah, right."

Grace shrugs, closes the suitcase, stands.

Ginny stares at the gift in her palm. It's catching the setting sun.

"My dad studies rocks," says Gary or Andrew. "That thing looks real."

"It is real," says Grace. "And Ginny's stupendous, and it's all hers, and she doesn't need any date for the prom."

Nobody talks. Someone in Nepal just became a corpse, I'm

sure, but here in Wyoming, there's five teens at a burger joint, and there's my wife, with a sheen of sweat on her forearms, and she's crazy and right.

"Grace," I say. "Let's hit it. That guy might really call a cop."

Phil, Grace, and I head for the truck.

Phil pats Grace on the back. "That was quite a gesture."

"Wait a minute! Hey! Grace, wait."

We turn. Ginny has run forward from her friends. She's maybe ten feet from us, but she's not an adult yet. She's a beanpole, and she's crying a little, holding Mercury out toward us.

"Wh-what do I do?" she stammers. She sounds grateful, desperate. "How can you just give this to me?"

Grace doesn't answer.

"I mean . . ." Ginny clenches Mercury. She scowls, like it's dawning on her she'll have to vomit and watch TV and lie with other human beings like the rest of us. "Grace, I just . . . what do I *do* with this?"

Phil stays quiet. So do I. Sometimes, after a fight or what have you, my old bullet wounds itch. They're itching now.

"You keep it," says Grace.

CHAPTER SEVEN

Glimmers

HONEY POBRINKIS HAD BEEN BORN HUNTER POBRINKIS, in Chicago, in 1938. At that time, the boy's father, Rudolph Pobrinkis, was the captain of the now-defunct *Racine Ferry*, a triple-decker pleasure boat that taxied tourists daily from Chicago to Milwaukee and back, stopping once each way in Racine, Wisconsin. Hunter loved his father and his father's ferry job, which Rudolph held annually between May and October. In the winter months, Rudolph painted houses with a cunning, alcoholic thug named Willis Enright.

Hunter lived for the summer days when he could accompany Rudolph on the ferry. By the time he was six, Hunter considered it vital that he stand beside Rudolph on the captain's deck—the small cabin on the ferry's uppermost level, with room for only two men—where he could scout Lake Michigan for German U-boats while his father manned the helm. Hunter was smart and into books early, and he favored grim fantasy tales in which ogres and dragons were vanquished. If the lake looked clear of enemy subs, Hunter would curl at Rudolph's feet with a book of such tales and read and doze in the sun and dream of his father kicking Hirohito in the balls.

When not on the ferry, Hunter was home with his younger sister, Christina, whose favorite possessions were her Raggedy Ann doll and her rosary beads. At noon on each summer weekday, Mrs. Meghan Pobrinkis made her children set a tray of two cheese sandwiches and two glasses of sherry outside her ground-floor bedroom door. The door remained shut while Meghan enjoyed her lunch inside, but Hunter noticed that Willis Enright's painting van was always parked in the neighborhood between noon and one, and from behind the bedroom door came strange, frequent moans and occasional scratchings that sounded like a window opening and closing. Hunter was too young to comprehend these noises, but they troubled his peace and filled his head with a weird, unwelcome heat. He yearned to report this heat to his father, but he never did, because each time Rudolph took Hunter in his arms and hugged him, the boy's mind cooled and gladdened and forgot all distress.

Then one summer afternoon when Hunter was eight his parents took him and Christina to Wrigley Field. It was blindingly hot out, with the sun tricking the eyes of ballplayers and fans alike. During the seventh-inning stretch, Hunter thought he saw Willis Enright about fifty yards off in the stands, staring at Rudolph, who had his arm around Meghan's waist. The mood of Willis's face was so malevolent that Hunter thought he was seeing a villain's mug from a comic book. The strange, troubling heat rushed over the boy's mind, and, feeling faint, he closed his eyes.

In that instant, Hunter Pobrinkis had a vision. For one sunspot second he saw his father being shoved by unseen hands over the captain's-deck railing on the ferry and plummeting, headfirst, onto the dock at Racine Harbor. Hunter shouted with fright and opened his eyes, but when he scoured the Wrigley Field stands, Willis Enright was gone. A grand slam had just happened, and fans were roaring. So, given the glare and the home run and the way his mind always bloomed toward the fantastic, Hunter bit his hot dog and stamped the morbid vision from his brain.

Twenty-four hours later, Rudolph Pobrinkis was found dead on the Racine Harbor docks. He had a broken neck, apparently from a great fall, but there were no witnesses, because the fatality had happened (the coroner later deduced) during the ferry's daily hour off, the time when Rudolph took his lunch break in Racine. Police found spilled motor oil on the captain's deck, and slippery footprints there that matched Rudolph's shoes, and it was determined that the poor boatman had lost his footing and gone over the railing by accident.

Hunter Pobrinkis did not cry, not once. He was shocked into an emotional freeze, but he didn't cry. A boy of only eight, he knew all through the funeral and the days that followed what had been done to his father and by whom, but he didn't tell anyone what he knew. And when his mother, Meghan, announced six months later that she was going to marry Willis Enright and take his name, Hunter didn't cry then either. Instead, he shook Willis's hand. Hunter was a well-built boy, but still a boy, so before the handshake, he went to the library and read. Gone forever was Hunter's interest in fairy tales. Instead, he read now about precognition, ESP, second sight. He read about puberty, and the selective service, and learned at what age an adolescent American male could expect to possess adult physical strength if he pursued good nutrition and used barbells. Then, having soaked up these facts, Hunter approached Willis Enright coolly in the kitchen of what was now the Enright home and shook Willis's hand and spoke.

"Sixteen," he said.

Willis, a man of reactionary politics and constant suspicions, frowned at his soon-to-be stepson. "What's that supposed to mean?" he grunted.

"Sixteen," repeated Hunter, and he ended the handshake.

For the next eight years, Hunter studied Willis Enright voraciously. He shadowed his stepfather, watched him slink in and out of bars, listened to the cruel snarls or spiffy apologies that Willis lobbed at Meghan, depending on his blood alcohol content. Hunter held his tongue, but tallied grievances every time Willis spoke sharply to Christina or mocked her rosary beads, which Christina prayed over each night. And on weekends and in summers, when he wasn't making crap wages on his paper route, Hunter found the city's underbelly. He skulked in South Side hovels and pool halls, being admitted both for his bulk (which by fourteen was considerable) and for his cold, peremptory gaze. He made the careful acquaintance of gamblers, debtors, prostitutes, bodyguards. He listened to drug fiends whining in back alleys, and absorbed the movements of club owners, restaurant owners, pimps, loan sharks. In this manner, Hunter came to know the weak, wheedling behaviors of men, their patterns and needs, their perennial vices. He saw the hangdog passion that men had for women, a passion Hunter vowed would never master him.

Hunter also endured the nickname that Willis Enright saddled him with the summer he was fifteen. Willis, whose hands and arms were always flecked with paint, was sitting by a corner of the kitchen table after dinner one night, listening to a ball game on the radio. Willis liked to slouch there at the table all evening long, drinking cheap red wine from a jug and eating blueberries, his favorite snack. Sometimes he poured the wine over the berries in a bowl and spooned up the treat until his lips were stained blue with juice. He was doing this one night, drinking himself blue, telling Meghan that her ass was sagging like the porch roof, when Hunter strolled in, back from a weight workout at the Y. Willis glared at his stepson while Hunter opened the fridge, pulled out a milk bottle, and chugged.

"How's little Hunter?" Willis wore a wine-enriched grin. "Little Hunter pumping iron? Getting tough?"

Hunter finished his milk and put the bottle away. "Yes, sir."

"Aw, sugar shit." Willis popped a berry in his mouth. "Tough's got nothing to do with Nautilus."

"It doesn't, sir?" Hunter stood with his hands behind his back, facing Willis like a pupil.

"Hunter," warned Meghan, who sat at the far end of the table from her husband. "Don't provoke your father."

"He's not my father."

Meghan looked up from her crossword and glanced anxiously at Willis. "Well, don't provoke him."

"He ain't provoking me," cackled Willis. "You ain't provoking me, little Hunter. You know why?"

"No, sir."

"Because you're a little cream puff." Willis was on his third bowl of Chianti.

Hunter peeked into the living room, to make sure Christina was safely watching television, which she was. If Willis and Meghan were arguing badly, Hunter sometimes escorted Christina down to the all-night corner grocery, where the owner, a kind Polish man named Levski, always made her laugh.

"You're a little cream puff," declared Willis, "and I'm going to call you Honey. Honey Enright." Willis slapped the table with his palm, hooting laughter.

"Willis," said Meghan, "don't tease him."

"Shut up, Meghan. I'm talking to little Honey Enright. That's his new name."

Hunter stood his ground. He was nearly six feet tall already. Willis cracked his knuckles, took in his stepson.

"Nautilus is bullshit," said Willis. "You know what tough is, little Honey?"

"Tell me," said Hunter.

Willis stared at him. "Tough is a nugget in your gut, boy. You're born with it, or you aren't. And you weren't."

"Oh," said Hunter.

Willis sighed. "Get the fuck out of my face."

Another subject of keen interest to Hunter was diamonds. He'd noticed that after his father's death, his mother had removed her diamond wedding ring and either hidden or sold it. Also, when Willis married Meghan at City Hall, he gave her a ring with no gem on it. It was just a cheap, plain gold band that matched one he wore.

The absence of a diamond on his mother's wedding finger

spoke volumes to Hunter. While his father had been alive, Hunter had adored touching the brilliant stone on Meghan's hand, turning her palm this way and that to see how the diamond flashed at him differently each time, as if, like Lake Michigan, it held deep, shining, adult secrets. Now his mother had no secrets from him. She drank sherry each night, while Willis consumed wine and berries. She did crosswords, withstood her husband's carping, and pursued screechy, wall-thumping sex with him in their bedroom, to the point that Hunter often sent Christina to Levski's for some Dots and some peace and quiet.

All of this came to a head on Hunter's sixteenth birthday. He skipped school that day, and walked to the house Willis was painting. He asked his stepfather for one birthday favor: that Willis remain sober for the day, and arrive home sober for dinner. He said he had something important to tell Willis that night. Willis scowled, but he remembered his own sixteenth birthday, the first day he'd driven a car, so he nodded curtly and agreed.

That night, after dinner, Hunter gave Christina some money for Levski's.

"I don't like her going down there alone," said Meghan. The entire family was in the kitchen.

"Neither do I," Hunter told his mother. "Please go with her. I have to talk to Dad in private, if that's all right."

A small hush happened, as Hunter had hoped it would. He'd never before referred to Willis as Dad.

"Well, I'll be." Meghan tousled her son's hair. "Someone's a gentleman after all."

Meghan and Christina left.

"So." Willis leaned back. He had a stomachful of rare roast

beef, Hunter's favorite food, and he was rooting between his molars with a toothpick. "Little Honey Enright is sixteen. He's a birthday boy."

"Please stand up."

"Excuse me?"

"Please stop picking your teeth and stand up."

Willis set down his toothpick. He creased his eyes warily, then stood.

"You're not drunk, right? You promised you wouldn't be."

"No, I'm not drunk, you little snot. Now, what's so private and important?"

Hunter wore blue jeans, work boots, and a white T-shirt. He stood six foot one, an even two hundred pounds. His hands were loose at his sides.

"I've been patient," said Hunter, "but now I have things to tell you."

"Is that right?" Willis weighed slightly less than his stepson. "Well, get to it, I'm *not* patient."

Hunter exhaled. "My name is Pobrinkis. Not Enright. Pobrinkis."

Willis scratched his head. His hair shone with thinner, which he used every night to lube paint splotches from his scalp. He grinned. "That ain't exactly a revelation."

"I know you killed him," said Hunter. "I saw it."

"What?"

"I saw it before it happened, in a dream. At the ball game." Hunter shook his head, dissatisfied. "Not a dream. I don't know. A glimmer."

The refrigerator hummed. It was August, and muggy in the kitchen.

"What the fuck are you talking about?"

"You killed my father. You drove to Racine and pushed him off the ferry and made it look like an accident." Hunter's eyes were the gray of granite. "You killed my father, Rudolph Pobrinkis, so you could keep screwing my mother, like you already had been all those years anyway."

Blood drained from Willis's face. "Honey. Take back every goddamn word you just said."

"You can have the first punch," offered Hunter. He spoke almost elegantly, for the words had been inside him for years, trimming themselves, getting leaner. "But by the end of tonight, if you aren't dead, you're leaving this house forever."

"That's it." Willis strode forward and shoved Hunter against the refrigerator. It was the only shove he got in.

Hunter's uppercut started down around his toes. It split Willis's chin, drove north into his nose. A crunching happened, blood shot from Willis's face, and the painter pronounced the name of God. He tried to cover his head, but Hunter's blows came quick and righteous, buffeting the older man's neck and skull and jaws. Willis sank to his knees, a dizzy white pain in his sinuses. He flailed with his hands.

"Hunter," he implored. "Jesus."

Hunter kicked his stepfather's ribs, cracked a couple. Willis wailed. He'd scrapped in bar fights, but he'd never faced a meanness stronger than his own.

"You killed Rudolph Pobrinkis." Hunter's fists were shaking, blood-covered. They pounded his stepfather's cheekbones. "You killed him."

Willis writhed on the floor, his head a softening pulp. He screamed, but Honey didn't relent. He felt as if he were striking out not with his fists but with his stomach, with the nugget of hate there that was harder than any knuckle. At some point, using his long, sharp thumbnail, Honey sliced off a third of Willis's ear. Willis shrieked, spat bubbled cries for mercy. Blood gushed from his ear onto Hunter's shoes, and then onto the foyer floor, as Hunter dragged his stepfather to the front door and kicked him out.

"Crawl away now." Hunter leaned close. He still felt composed, but he was surprised to see one tear drip from his face onto Willis's. "Crawl away down the street, and never come back. Ever."

Willis grunted, his mouth open against the ground. Three of his teeth were back in the kitchen, on the linoleum.

Hunter stood, stretched his shoulders, felt the twinge of a strained muscle. He looked down at the heap before him. "I'm going inside to clean up, Willis. If you're still here when my mom and sister get back, I'll put a chef's knife through your heart. Good-bye."

Ten minutes later, when Hunter finished mopping blood and teeth and earlobe off the kitchen floor, he looked out the front window. Willis Enright was gone.

* * *

The next morning, sixteen-year-old Hunter stared into his bathroom mirror. Overnight, as he'd slept, a bold streak of white had appeared in his otherwise black hair. It was the length of a knife blade and it slashed upward and back from his left temple. Hunter had heard of men who, after having faced down some mortal terror (the teeth of a lion, the barrel of a cocked Luger), found their hair turned entirely shock white. Peering at his own preternatural scar, Hunter guessed that the execution of terror could have a similar effect. He knew one thing for sure: Willis Enright would never return. But Hunter also knew that his own proclivities—his acquired ease with low people, his hatred of cowards like Enright, his anger at men who, like his own father, died foolishly and too easily—would not dissolve just because Willis was gone. He'd lived so long now with cloaked, acrid yearnings in his guts that the yearnings had become not means but ends in themselves, or at least their own excuses for being.

Thus, as the young man gazed, unafraid, at the new white emblem on his head, he got his second glimmer, this time a picture of his future. It was a future that involved him abandoning high school and rising to power on the streets of Chicago. It was a vision of muscle and cruel luxury, a glimpse of a life where he would eat meat and have women and kill men that crossed him, and he would effect such pursuits with sly, judicious nerve, learning, before any act, how certain funds could be vouchsafed, how each ingénue took her whiskey, where every corpse could be stowed.

Over fifty years, this vision came to be. The young Pobrinkis apprenticed himself to garden-variety hoods, then took over their rackets. He dealt always in cash, and introduced himself as Honey rather than Hunter, sensing that a casual, breezy moniker stuck better in people's heads. He also took the name Honey as a reminder of his triumph over Willis Enright, and, in perverse tribute to the man who'd murdered his youth, Honey started, in his thirties, to snack on red wine and blueberries each night. He did so, he felt, with greater panache and brio than Enright ever had. Whereas Willis had been a bitter, uncultured lush, Honey chose only the finest merlots, the choicest fruits. He sweetened the dish with sugar, and ate it proudly, in full view of patrons, in the foyer of the restaurant that he built and named in honor of his father. Over time, Honey's fondness for merlot and berries became a signature detail that, like his blue incisors and his infamous strength, etched his name ever deeper in Chicagoans' minds.

Honey's glimmers remained part of his nature too. They came irregularly, but sharply and intensely, like migraines. One such vision led Honey to have Ryan Vicario (his original copartner in founding Ferryman's) crushed to death in a trash truck's compactor. Another prompted him to catch his first wife, Babs, in bed with his lawyer, Terrence "Bifocals" Trilling. Honey had Babs and Bifocals frozen to death in a subzero meat locker. He then had his men stand these human ice sculptures in the lobby of the Trilling, Smith, and Cabou law offices at six-thirty on a Monday morning, so that when Mr. Washington Cabou (the new manager of Pobrinkis's accounts) got to work at seven, he would see the wisdom of keeping his dick in his pants.

As for diamonds, Honey collected them like baseball cards. He bought diamond necklaces and brooches and navel rings for his wives: first Babs, then Tasha, then Margarita. He wore a grape-size diamond pin in the lapel of his suit each day, and in 1985 he paid a dentist ten thousand in cash to pull his purple, infected molar and cement a five-carat gem into the socket. Meanwhile, in Ferryman's basement vault, he kept certain small but famous diamond collections that Charles Chalk had procured, including the three Norwegian stones known as the Fjords, and the original wedding ring and matching ankle bracelet of the famous 1920s Mexican film actress Villa Vente.

In the spring of Honey's sixty-fifth year, his fits of clairvoyance and his yen for diamonds dovetailed in two successive glimmers. In the case of the first, Honey was sitting at his table in Ferryman's foyer when into his mind crashed a picture of Charles Chalk and Helena Pressman on a flying red magic carpet. They were laughing and hell-bent for the Mexican border, and between them on the carpet was a silver suitcase that Honey knew contained the Planets, the diamond collection he'd sought his whole adult life. He dispatched Henry, Roger, and Floyd to the Chalk farm. When Roger and Floyd came back battered and empty-handed, Honey was stunned. He'd never once had a bringback or hit go awry, and it floored him that Henry Dante, his strongest and previously most reliable man, had run off with the Planets.

What floored Honey even more was his next glimmer. It came just days after the first, at four in the morning, while Honey was in bed with the twenty-nine-year-old Margarita. She had just finished performing on Honey her trademark sexual move, a technique she called the Old Salt, when Honey sat bolt upright in bed.

"No," he whispered. His eyes stared, vacant and terrified.

Margarita frowned. Men privileged enough to receive the Old Salt didn't complain afterward.

"Honey?" she said.

"He wouldn't." Thick, naked, and pale, Honey bunched the bedspread in his hands. "Henry's a gentleman. He wouldn't do that with them. . . ."

"Do what?"

Honey blinked, tried to erase the vision. His mind had been hazy with sex, filled with the blur and scent of Margarita. Then he'd seen outer space, the Milky Way. Floating in this cosmos had been the sun and seven planets and two enormous naked people. One was Henry Dante and one was a woman with a red celestial aura swirling around her head like hair. Henry and the woman had been making love, kicking stars around in their passion, but then they'd reached their hands toward the planets as if to scoop them up and—

"No." Honey slapped the mattress. "It doesn't make sense. It's not sporting. Why would he give them away? Unless . . ."

"Honey, you're scaring me." Margarita was dark-haired and tan and she knew what lay in Ferryman's basement. But she'd never witnessed a glimmer firsthand.

The mobster closed his eyes and concentrated. For a moment, he saw Henry again, Henry and the universe-size woman. Honey tried to focus on her. It was just a dream, a quick flicker, but there was something in this woman's aspect that reminded him of Christina, his rosary-obsessed sister. For decades, Honey had sent money to Christina, but, disapproving of his life, she'd always returned it. Not only that, she'd barred him from paying for their mother's golden years, nursing home, and funeral.

Honey opened his eyes. He glared at Margarita.

"What?" she said nervously. "What'd I do?"

"A woman." Honey stood up, paced. "A woman is making him do it."

Margarita put on her robe. She felt exposed, in peril. "Making *who* do *what*?"

"Just give me the goddamn phone."

"Give it to yourself." Margarita hurried from the bedroom, afraid.

Honey found his phone among the sheets. He dialed the cell

number of his only nephew, the son Christina had disowned once he'd started working for her brother. Honey stood flexing his muscles, waiting. Then Roger Pobrinkis, lost in South Dakota, answered, and Honey related with fury the sin he knew to be taking place.

* * *

On a roadside in Greybull, Wyoming, Grace McGlone was having, if not glimmers, at least some portentous, ranging thoughts of her own. It was two in the morning, and Phil Weal was stretched across the truck's front seat, asleep, while Henry and Grace lay in their air-mattress nook, a curtain drawn between them and the cab. Henry was as deeply asleep as Phil, but Grace lay awake, listening for coyotes and other Big Horn sounds. At Phil's urging, Henry had steered the truck off the 90 onto 14 West, which would bear them straight through Yellowstone into Idaho. It was Wednesday morning, just twelve hours after they'd met Phil, so Grace had no problem with the route. She and Henry had time to get Phil home, then backtrack northeast and reach Great Falls, Montana, by Friday night. All Grace knew was, she was a married woman, and she was going to face Bertram Block.

She glanced at her husband's back, at the stallions emblazoned there. The horses bore black armor, and their Jolly Roger jockeys, with swords raised in bony fists, wore purple shrouds and wicked grins. As Grace beheld this dark prophecy, two mythical creatures loomed in her mind. One was Gehenna, the devil bird that had ruled Hell in her girlhood imagination. The other was a man made of stones, a hero Grace had once looked upon in a tree house. This man had seemed forged from earth itself, not from a woman's rib or womb but from the bulging stuff of mountains.

Grace shook her head to clear it. She looked down at the slight guttering in her stomach skin that came with each breath out. She was a woman now, a wife, not some one-night screw for an arrogant cleric. She hadn't yet told Henry that she'd lost her innocence to the preacher they were driving to meet, because she wasn't sure how to play the meeting. She wanted to give Bertram Block a bullet where his mystical third eye should have been, because he'd pressed into her something no man had any right to press into a fifteen-year-old girl. On the other hand, Grace thought, the reverend—or the P&V that preceded him—had wakened in her some profound carnality, some desire to clutch and drink down all the truths under heaven.

This carnality, Grace knew, had led her to Henry, but she didn't know what it would prod her to do once she saw Bertram Block again. She figured facing the preacher would be dangerous, but somehow correct, or gallant, or, as her husband said, stupendous. She sensed Henry felt the same way about having commandeered the Planets, about having married her. She'd chosen in a flash to wed this stranger because she believed he was no stranger, but the answer to an ache in her heart. Everything in life that had first felt dire to Grace—her father's death, her faith—had whispered to her that peaceful, calm living couldn't make her happy, that bright, irrational lurches of the body and soul were the worthwhile paths. Grace couldn't decide now whether this was true.

I should want peace, she thought. *I should. I should.*

As she listened for wolf song, though, Grace felt tugged

toward something besides peace. She guessed that whatever this tug was, it was what told Henry not to cower from pursuers. It was some call for reckoning, and it hounded her and her man, and, like a hunted animal, Grace feared and hoped and knew that soon she would have to whirl, bare her teeth, and fight.

* * *

Roger clicked his phone shut, thinking about the news his uncle had just roared at him. It was past two in the morning, and Roger was tired. He was behind the wheel of the Nova, which was parked outside an all-night bowling alley named the Snapdragon. The bowling alley was in Rapid City, South Dakota, and Floyd was using the place's men's room. The car windows were open, and a cool, tart breeze flowed in from the east.

Roger blinked wearily, removed his porkpie, scratched his head. He needed a shave, and the muffler had started coughing a few towns back and Roger didn't want to be chasing Henry anymore. He wanted what most men want when they're lonely and tired at night. He wanted a woman's warm thigh under his hand. He wanted a shower and a pint of ale and a hamburger cooked hot but rare, with bacon and three melting slices of cheese.

Floyd came out of the Snapdragon, stuck his head through the shotgun window. "Hey, Roger. They've got a nice two-holer in there, in case you need to dump."

Roger winced.

"Plus, we should bowl a few frames. The lanes look smooth."

Roger said nothing. The fifth mark he'd killed for his uncle Honey had been a guy named Tobias Ploughman. Tobias had owned a video arcade called Ploughman's Playhouse, a building whose cruddy façade was similar to the Snapdragon's. One night, after hours, Roger had come to collect the twenty thousand that Tobias owed Honey, and when Tobias drew a gun, Roger was obliged to shoot him three times in the face. He then hid the corpse in the vat of sponge balls that normally contained frolicking children and Ploughman Pogo, the arcade's bouncy mascot, who was played by a college kid wearing, for reasons unclear to Roger, a Dalmatian suit.

"How about it, Roger? Want to take some R & R? Bowl a few frames?" Floyd was still peeking his head in the window, eyebrows raised.

"Honey just called. He's had a glimmer."

"Oh, man."

"Henry's with some redhead, Honey thinks. The two of them, Henry and this chick, they're unloading the Planets."

Floyd's ponytail hung over his shoulder. He swept the tuft of it along the door. "No problem. Your uncle knows every diamond man and pawn hocker in the States. As soon as the stones turn up—"

"They're not selling them." Roger rubbed his neck. "They're giving them away. Honey saw it."

"Giving them away?" Floyd frowned like a scientist. "Why would Henry do that? I mean, who's he giving them to?"

Roger wanted sustenance, a barmaid, a good book. "I don't know. People. Civilians."

Floyd looked at the sky, exhaled long and loud. "Oh, man. This chaps my ass. Here we are, at the Snapdragon bowling alley, and Henry's making time with babes, giving away Planets, living the life of Smiley."

Roger kneaded his temples. "Riley."

"Riley?"

"The life of Riley. Henry's living the life of Riley. That's what you mean."

"I'm saying Henry's probably giving the diamonds to, like, random soccer moms, in exchange for boning them. He's probably all smiles right now. You know, the life of Smiley. It's a phrase."

"There's no such person as Smiley, Floyd. You're saying it wrong."

"Yeah? Who the fuck is Riley, then?"

Roger closed his eyes, felt the breeze on his cheek. He tried to think, then laughed. He had no idea who Riley was.

"I am so goddamn sick," he said, "of being in this piece-of-shit car."

Floyd nodded sadly. He felt bad when Roger got down.

"I hear you, buddy," said Floyd.

Roger smacked the steering wheel. "We're driving blind here. Henry could be in Oklahoma. Honey says, keep heading west, don't worry, we'll pick up their trail, but how the fuck . . ."

Floyd watched Roger with motherly concern. "If Honey says we'll pick up their trail, we will. How often is Honey wrong?"

Roger shrugged.

"So we'll keep heading west. In the meantime, we're both beat. We should take it easy, you know? Get some R & R."

"What do you mean?"

Floyd rubbed his hands together. "Oh, man. I wasn't going to say anything till Wyoming, but my sister Gretl works at this spa out here. In a town called Cody."

Roger looked at his partner. Floyd had never before spoken

of his sister's whereabouts. Roger smiled a secret, wicked smile, remembering the blond, downy hairs above Gretl's knees, the pleading gasp of her voice.

"A spa, huh?"

Floyd nodded vigorously. "I haven't been there, but it's always in magazines. They swaddle you in mud or somesuch goo and you become supremely at ease. And Gretl will hook us up for free, I bet."

Roger sat up straight. He was a Pobrinkis and a killer, so he would not get swaddled in goo. But an encore of sexual roughhouse with Gretl Webber—whether she wanted it or not—sounded first-rate.

"We could pop inside here," said Floyd. "Have a few beers, bowl a few frames. Then, you know, head to Cody."

As far as Roger could tell, the darkness and the breeze weren't whispering any secrets about where to find Henry Dante.

"All right, Floyd."

"Honestly?" Floyd's grin quivered like a puppy's ears.

Roger redonned his porkpie. Recalling Gretl's patchouli scent, he got out of the Nova. "Sure."

"All right!" Floyd pumped the air with his fist. "Fucking A, baby!"

Roger stretched. Then, before heading to Cody, he and his partner entered the Snapdragon and had a few beers and bowled a few frames, because, manhunters or not, they sometimes had fun together.

CHAPTER EIGHT

Peace

FOR ONCE, GRACE IS DRIVING. AFTERNOON RAIN slams on the hood in long silver nails that look like prison bars. Dips in the road are two-foot-deep puddles. Thunder shakes the sky.

"Maybe we should pull over." Grace squints her face forward.

We're inching west on Route 14, moving through Cody, Wyoming. Phil Weal's quiet in the jump seat, disliking the thunder. As for me, I'm holding our silver suitcase, the four remaining Planets. A mile ahead, lightning jolts the road.

"We're pulling over," says Grace.

She edges the truck onto the shoulder. We stare out the windshield, rain drumming the roof. More lightning spikes before us.

"This is bad," says Phil. "We should be indoors."

I almost say how a car's the safest place, but I don't. For one, it might be bullshit, and for two, rain's dripping in through the doorjambs.

"Hey." Grace points toward my window. "Look."

Phil and I look. Beyond a blowing field of rain and a few giant oak trees looms an enormous five-story mansion. It has gables and cupolas. Over the porch hangs a hip neon green sign that reads, if I'm seeing it right, 'QUILLITY.

"Quillity?" I say. "What's that?"

"It's indoors," says Phil.

Grace peers past me. "You know what? I've read about this place. It's a spa." She turns into the long, splashy driveway.

I frown at the massive estate.

"It's like a famous retreat," says Grace. "For celebrities and stuff. *Powergirl* magazine did their spring shoot here once."

"We aren't celebrities," I say.

"It's indoors," says Phil.

Grace parks in a lot beside a Maserati. We behold the mansion. Extending off one side is a mammoth greenhouse whose windowpanes are translucent and the same color green as the 'Quillity sign. The whole place looks straight out of a sci-fi story, the kind where your soul gets sucked out your ear by a ficus plant while you nap by the pool.

"It looks expensive," I tell Grace. "And I thought by Friday you wanted to reach—"

"We'll just stay one night." Grace crawls into the truck bed, shoves clothes in her satchel. "Come on, we can't keep driving, the road's flooded. Plus, it looks romantic. You know, honeymoonish."

"I'm broke," says Phil.

"I'm paying," says Grace.

"I'm in," says Phil.

I drum my fingers on the Planets' case. There's something about the mansion telling me to stay away. It's an indistinct feeling, like I've been here in a dream or my ancestors are buried under the greenhouse. I can't place it, but I don't have time to reflect because a young man in a black robe hurries out of the mansion and splashes toward my door. He has curly black hair and sandals, and he's holding an umbrella with a Stealth bomber's wingspan. Embroidered in bright green on his robe, over his left breast, are the letters *T-i-n-e*.

I roll down my window. Rain clatters on the pavement.

"Welcome," says the guy.

Grace jumps into the front seat and leans over me. "We'd like rooms, please."

"What's Tiney?" I ask.

"Tine is my name. Not Tiny. Tine. Tine, like fine."

Phil and I look at each other.

"Tine." Phil tries it out loud.

"We have three overnight slumber cells left."

"We'll take two," decides Grace. "One for us, one for Phil Weal."

We all enter the mansion lobby, which is done in black chrome. Behind a reception desk is a wall with a giant inset fish tank rimmed by green fluorescent lights. Swimming in the tank, of course, is a freaking baby sand shark.

"Tallyho," says Grace.

The lobby's carpet is green. A few guests pass, all wearing sandals and robes like Tine's, but with no names. The guests have wealthy haircuts. Tine leads us to the desk, which holds a brochure rack. One brochure is called "The Shamelessness of Guilt."

Grace pays. Tine gives us keys and directions.

"For the next twenty minutes, the restaurant is still serving the midday meal." Tine waves toward the greenhouse. "Treatments are offered in the solarium, toward which I'm pointing. Our most celebrated treatment is the Fetal Herbal Hammock Wrap. I urge you all to succumb to it both physically and psychically."

Grace herds us down a hall. We find our adjacent slumber cells, Phil goes into his, me and Grace into ours. The carpet's black and the bed's incandescent green, like the walls. A nightstand card says the robes and sandals in our closet must be worn in public areas. Grace hands me a robe, which is black and silky.

I hold it with pinched fingers. "This is absurd."

"When in Topeka . . ." says Grace.

I pick lint off the stupid thing. Grace was right, though, the storm's no joke. Plus, at least for the night, we'll be laying low like she wants, because Honey's boys would never seek a scruff like me in a castle like this. So I suit up.

We meet Phil, and find the restaurant, where each table has a green lantern. A skinny blond maître d' seats us. Her robe says *Gretl* and she looks vaguely familiar. She moves off quickly, though, and while we read the menus, our waitress appears. She's tall, with Mediterranean skin, frazzled black hair, exhausted eyes, great cheekbones. Her robe says *Lucia*.

"No luggage allowed in here, sir. I'll put this in the coatroom." Lucia reaches toward the case that I've stashed below my chair. I catch her hand.

"That doesn't leave my side."

Lucia pulls her hand from mine. "Very well."

"How are the littleneck clams?" asks Grace.

Lucia inspects her thumbnail, looking tired. "They're heaven on a half shell."

It's clearly the end of Lucia's shift. The other tables are empty, except for dirty plates.

"Excuse me?" says Grace.

"I'm sorry." Lucia speaks to her cuticles. "What I meant was, our clams are a gustatory wonder. Golly, they're something."

"What a bitch," says Grace, when Lucia's gone.

Phil spreads his napkin on his lap. "She's just having a bad day."

"Who's Bertram Block?" I ask Grace. I'm not sure why I'm asking this now. It has something to do with the black weather outside.

Grace watches me deeply, decides something. "He's a guy from my youth."

"Stewart. Bertram Block." I prod my utensils around the tabletop. "Stewart and Bertram, my wife's mystery men."

"Henry." Her voice is a warning.

"It just sounds like you had a busy youth, that's all."

Her face goes scarlet. She looks at her lap.

Lucia brings our plates. Grace has clams, Phil has hummus, I have balsamic chicken. We eat in silence, and my stomach roils with vinegar. When Grace goes to the restroom, Phil taps my shoulder.

"Brother," he says, "let it go."

"Let what go?"

"The past, man. *Her* past. And yours." Phil ignores his hummus. His eyes are worn and brown like leather. He's looking at me plain, unafraid, a way men rarely look. "Listen, Henry. I'm older than you'd guess, and I'm no idiot. You haven't said much about yourself, but one look at you, I know you've seen combat. You've mucked with the heavy shit."

I glance around. We're alone.

"And?"

"And I'm saying, if you want it to stay good between you and your girl, leave the heavy shit behind. Hers and yours."

I study his shoulders. They're sturdier than I first thought. They've done work, maybe.

"So, what, you're a hitchhiking marriage expert?"

Phil rubs his jaws. "I'm just a guy. But I've mucked with the heavy shit, too, and I'll tell you this. A woman's past is a giant thing, brother. It's a story in her heart. You'll never really get her story, and she'll never get yours. So let it go. Look forward." He starts eating.

I stare at our lantern. I've never gone in for gypsy counsel, and if we were in a bar, I'd have decked Phil by now. But as Grace walks back from the bathroom, I think, *Try*. I stand up.

"I'm sorry," I tell her. "I'm sorry."

Grace studies me, waits for more. Her shoulders look tense.

"I won't ask about them again. I mean it."

Grace unclenches her shoulders, leans into me. I can feel her breath on my chest. She bites my robe between her teeth, lets it go. She boxes two punches at my stomach.

"Thank you," she whispers.

We finish eating. On Grace's plate lie empty clamshells, open on their hinges like mouths. Lucia materializes and says no dessert, the kitchen's closed.

"Well, Lucia," says Grace. "You've been a lousy server."

"I beg your pardon?"

"You heard me." Grace reaches below my chair, grabs the Planets' case.

Lucia folds her arms. "You can't talk to me like that just because—"

"Be quiet, please." Grace opens the suitcase, grabs Venus, holds it up.

"This is Venus." She plops the gem into a shell on her plate. "It's priceless. I know tips are included, but this is for you anyway."

Phil makes an impressed noise.

I gaze at Grace. Maybe she feels generous because we just made up. Maybe she figures we're a tag-team charity, and since I gave out the first two Planets, the next two are her turf. Either way, she's being stupendous.

"Is that a . . . diamond?" Lucia bends toward the plate. She looks thunderstruck.

"You're beautiful, Lucia." Grace inhales, her nose near our server's hair. "You're wearing beautiful perfume, and I'll bet you look beautiful naked, like the Venus on the shell in that famous painting."

"I—" Lucia doesn't continue.

Grace shuts the case, stands, pats Lucia's shoulder. "Technically, I should try to get you fired, but lucky for you, Henry and I have a different M.O. Enjoy your diamond."

Lucia stares between Venus and Grace. She looks like she wants to rally, to react, but she doesn't get a chance, because my bride struts out of the restaurant, with me and Phil in her wake.

* * *

In the late afternoon, we head for the solarium in our robes. We wind through hallways, follow signs, and come to an area that resembles the inside of a hut. The walls are wooden, like in a sauna, and the floor is dirt. The wall farthest from us has a green door, above which hangs a sign reading SOLARIUM. Between us and the door is a low wooden table that holds a teapot and teacups. Kneeling at the table is my main man, Tine.

He pours tea in three cups. "Before entering the solarium, all guests must partake of our kava tea."

"Why?" asks Phil.

"It cleanses your body and your aura."

I roll my eyes, but we all three kneel. Tine urges the cups toward us.

"Hey, Tine," I say, "I thought you worked the front desk."

Tine smiles cryptically. "We are a collective."

None of us has an answer for that. We lift our teacups.

"Sip slowly," advises Tine. "Let the kava fill your molecules with calm."

We sample the brew. It's piping hot and disgusting. I put my cup down.

"Is the kava filling your molecules with calm?"

Grace frowns. "Is there *dirt* in this?"

Tine smiles patiently. "The kava contains the natural elements of the earth."

"Meaning dirt?"

Phil says, "I notice you're not drinking any, Tine."

Grace takes another sip. She's trying to enjoy the sludge, trying to make this a honeymoon day, a good space. I suck her earlobe a moment, then stand and head to the solarium door. Tine looks miffed, but Grace and Phil join me.

"Whoa," says Grace, once we're inside.

Phil says, "Holy crap."

The solarium, which is gigantic, is what I thought was a greenhouse. The walls are plates of cloudy green light, and the ceiling is high. There's a kidney-shaped swimming pool cut in the black stone floor. Tall green plants sprout up everywhere, and floating in wisps is a steam that smells like wintergreen.

"What are those . . . things?" asks Phil.

I wave away steam and see what Phil's seeing. Around the pool, sticking up from the floor, are bamboo poles. Strung between these poles are fluorescent green hammocks. They're set in clusters of two or four, and they're holding guests, but that's not the half of it. The hammocks are solid cloth instead of mesh, and they cocoon the guests' bodies, except for their heads, which poke out from the ends.

"Oh." Phil exhales. "They're people."

I gaze around, speechless, my case is in my hand. Each hammock sags slightly, because the guests are in sideways, fetal positions. The heads of each pair slant toward each other, and the members of each couple or foursome talk to one another. They look like mutant, chatting pea pods.

"Behold the Fetal Herbal Hammock Wraps." Tine has come up behind us. He sweeps his arm forward. "As you lie in your prenatal coils, you will breathe eucalyptus and feel utter peace."

We stare. Black robes hang from the bamboo poles, so the hammock-folk are evidently naked in their cocoons.

I nudge Grace. "I am not getting in one of those things."

Tine vanishes. Grace and Phil and I meander through the pod people. We come to the pool, in which nude men and women are floating. One man with gray hair hums a Beatles song. A gorgeous young woman doing the backstroke has an hourglass figure and a Caesarean scar. She looks like the box-office dream girl Katie Nullify. In fact, she *is* the box-office dream girl Katie Nullify.

"Now what?" says Phil.

"Let's sit a minute," says Grace. We sit at the pool's edge and soak our calves and feet in the water.

"So anyway"—we hear a woman's voice—"Jasper and I spent an hour Monday at the Painted Pots, near Old Faithful."

Phil turns his head. Grace and I do too. There's a cluster of three women and one man—Jasper, apparently—slung in hammocks nearby. Resting below them are green frozen drinks. Skinny Gretl, our onetime maître d', hustles among the hammocks, lifting the drinks to the mouths of the larvae.

"The Painted Pots are exquisite," continues the woman. She has sharp, plucked eyebrows. "Jasper and I stood in awe before them."

"Actually," says the slung-up man, "I dropped my sunglasses in one."

The woman nearest Jasper titters. Her beehive hairdo is parallel to the ground. The third woman, in an orange swimming cap, sucks from her straw, which Gretl holds to her mouth.

"Jasper," says the eyebrows lady, "don't mock the Painted Pots."

"I'm not mocking them, Suzanne. I just dropped my sunglasses in one. You should've seen it, Carol. My shades melted into this yellow gunk."

Carol scrunches her nose.

"Hi, folks." Phil waves. "Phil Weal, here."

Suzanne and posse glance over.

"You know," says Phil, "the Painted Pots are just ten miles from my home state."

"Is that right?" says Jasper. "They're only a couple hours from here, too."

Phil gives Jasper the thumbs-up.

"What are the Painted Pots?" asks Grace.

Gretl is staring at my devil's-horn knuckles.

"They're these bubbling pits of mud and springwater," says Phil, "with goopy colors coming out of the earth."

"Let's go." Grace elbows me. "Let's go tomorrow."

I know what my wife wants, at least right now. She wants us to have fun, to belong here. So I sigh, clowning for her. "Yes, dear."

Katie Nullify swims past my knees.

"Hey." Gretl's still looking at my knuckles. "Hey, are you famous? You look familiar."

"Another drink," calls the swimming-cap woman. Gretl fades into the mist.

Grace stands and walks among the strangers. "Pleased to meet you all. I'm Grace and this is my husband, Henry. We're trying for heaven."

Phil and I walk over.

"What's in the suitcase?" asks Jasper.

I hold one finger in front of my mouth. Jasper gives me a wink, copacetic style. "That's my lady friend, Suzanne. That's Mimi, this is Carol. I'm Jasper."

"Trying for heaven?" asks Beehive Carol. "How's that work?"

Rain beats the solarium windows.

"It works because we're Christians, Henry and me. We follow Jesus."

Suzanne snorts. "We are all facets of the Tao. The Tao contains Jesus."

Grace looks quietly at the floor. "Nothing can contain Jesus."

Phil crouches next to Mimi. He whispers to her, and her orange-capped head nods okay. Phil starts rocking her hammock, like pushing a child on a swing.

"Deep down," says Jasper, "I guess I'm a Quaker. That's how I was raised."

"You're not a Quaker," says Suzanne. "You're a facet of the Tao."

"Wheeee!" says Mimi. Her hammock creaks as Phil rocks it.

"I don't *feel* like a facet of the Tao."

"Well, you are."

Carol says, "I came up Methodist."

Suzanne wriggles in her hammock, looking perturbed. She sneezes.

"God bless you," says Carol.

"I sort of liked those Quaker meetings," says Jasper.

Suzanne makes a frustrated grunt.

* * *

Later that night, Grace and I have sex in our bathroom. Grace hangs by both hands from the shower rod, and I balance like a puma on the tub, thrusting upward, my arms clutching her ribs. Afterward, as we lie in bed, Grace weeps.

"We could stay here," she sniffles. "I mean, we could live somewhere like this, you and I. Right?"

I don't answer. Grace sighs, frets, falls asleep in my arms. I pet her, smell her smells. After a while, I get up. I put on my robe, grab the Planets, slip out of our room.

Somehow I wander down to the solarium. It's midnight, and the green door's locked, but I know doors and I want in, so I monkey the lock and enter. Inside, there's no steam, no people, but the air's warm. The hammocks hang empty, like skins that've squeezed out snakes. The pool is still, and an eerie green light glows from the bottom. I set down the Planets, chuck my robe, and dive in. In the middle of the deep end there's a tall column of black rock with a hollowed-out top where a person can recline and pretend he's Poseidon. I nestle in this chair.

First I try to do what Phil said, try to look forward. I think loose, good things, like maybe Grace and I really will settle somewhere. We'll bypass Banff and fly to Africa, dig wells, make zebra soufflés. My hips are still happy from screwing, and I kick at the water, glad to be naked. Then I remember Honey and my thoughts toughen up. I let my arms and legs fall slack. Leaning back, with my hair in the water but my face in the air, I think how, despite my strength and luck, things might not go my way. I think of Grace dying. I picture myself alone in the truck, or in prison, with Grace buried far from her home.

"No," I say. My voice fills the solarium. "No," I say again.

Up in the ceiling, there's a round, clear skylight, like a telescope eye in the swampy green glass. Through this skylight, stars are visible. The clouds and rain have quit, and if God ever wanted to talk to me, Henry Dante, now might work.

"Go for it," I tell the skylight. I've tried this before, mostly on the shore of Lake Michigan, but also one night in bed with Bella Cavasti, when she was asleep and breathing so sweetly that I begged the darkness for eternity to come right then, for nothing ever to change. The darkness didn't oblige me, though, and the skylight won't tonight.

I make myself still, one foot raised above the water. I keep my body frozen in the chair, and stir what's around me with one big toe. The thing about my wife is, she thinks God's a guy who walked the earth. She thinks he's a man who swam like I'm swimming, and I won't argue with her. I'll get back to my robe and my Planets in a minute, but right now, I'm stirring this pool, and I'm thinking maybe God's not a man, and maybe he's not up in the skylight, either. Maybe he's subterranean, impossible but there, worrying the ground beneath us like those Badlands mole persons or the Burma girls. That's what I'm thinking.

CHAPTER NINE

War

IT WAS A THURSDAY, TWO HOURS BEFORE NOON. THE spa employees' schedule of rotating duties had Gretl Webber working reception that morning. The young woman squealed when her only brother, Floyd, walked into the lobby. There were hugs and tearful hellos, for the siblings hadn't seen each other since before the millennium turned.

"How's Chicago? What happened to your face? How long can you stay?" Gretl's arms were a loose lasso around his shoulders.

"I'm not sure. Hey!" Floyd pointed at the fish tank. "That's kick-ass."

Gretl caught her breath. Walking through the front door was a brute in a porkpie hat, a man she'd banked on never seeing again.

"Roger," she said softly.

The nephew of Honey Pobrinkis sneered. He'd been parking the car, but now he strode across the lobby, looking the woman up and down. "The robe suits you."

Floyd looked at his sister brightly. "How'd you know his name, Gretl?"

Gretl kept her eyes on the floor. She still had her arms around Floyd's neck, but her face had lost its joy.

Roger continued to take in her body, which was fuller than he remembered. "Yes, Gretl, how'd you know my name?"

A silence happened. The oblivious Floyd looked back and forth between them.

"Anyway, sis ... we were hoping to score some back rubs."

Roger chuckled. "Or whatever else you're offering."

Gretl avoided Roger's gaze. She cleared her throat, searched for words. Lately she was dating a small, bookish man from Cody. His name was Eliot and he was, at that moment, visiting his dentist.

"I ... um. You know what's weird, Floyd, is I got your vibe yesterday."

"What pretty blond hair you have, Gretl," said Roger. "It's so pure-looking."

"I can't believe you've got a shark," said Floyd. "What does it eat?"

To collect herself, Gretl laid her cheek on her brother's shoulder. She'd done this sometimes when they were little and they watched scary films late at night. "Wait ... I know what gave me your vibe. It was a guest here."

"What was a guest?" asked Floyd.

"Don't you know a guy with two raised-up, freaky knuckles? You told me once that you worked with—"

"What about this guy?" Roger was inches from Gretl's face.

"Hey. What's the— Back off."

Roger took her arms off Floyd. He held her shoulders, made her face him. "What about this guy?"

Gretl glanced at Floyd, nervous.

"Don't look at your brother, look at me. What about this guy? Have you seen him?"

"He . . . Ow . . . He checked out half an hour ago."

"Holy hell," whispered Floyd.

Roger still held the woman. "This man's name was Henry, yes? He was with a girl?"

"And one other guy. Please let me go."

"One other guy," repeated Roger.

"Shitbox, Roger. If we hadn't stopped for waffles—"

"Shut up, Floyd."

Gretl was wriggling. "Floyd, make him let go."

Floyd swallowed. Outside of argument, he was not in the business of confronting Roger Pobrinkis. "Yeah . . . um . . . Roger. You don't have to—"

"This Henry." Roger bored his eyes into Gretl's. "Did he say where he was heading?"

"If you don't let me loose, I won't tell you. "

Roger pulled Gretl closer, then lifted her off the ground till his chin was practically down her robe. He stared at her cleavage, held the stare. "I remember these two little beauties," he whispered.

Gretl blanched.

"Roger?" Floyd tapped his partner's arm. "What'd you say?"

Roger smirked, let go. The young woman stumbled, cinched her robe tighter, rubbed her shoulders.

"Gretl." Floyd's voice was quiet, sorry. "Please. Just tell him where—"

"Fine. This guy and the other two, they're heading to Painted Pots. It's in Yellowstone, just west of here."

Roger steered her to the reception desk. He grabbed a pad of paper and a pen and put them in front of her. "Directions," he said.

Gretl looked anxiously over her shoulder at Floyd. Then she picked up the pen.

* * *

"They're beautiful," said Phil.

"They are," said Grace.

The two of them and Henry stood on a wooden observation deck in Yellowstone National Park. Bubbling below the deck and spread out before them in a field of white rocks were the famous Painted Pots. Other tourists were on the deck, too, including a whiny boy with a zinc-covered, red-skinned nose. It was a sweltering day, and the boiling pools of colored mud and springwater seemed to draw power not just from the earth but from the sun, which reigned in the sky unrivaled by clouds.

"I left my camera in the truck." Grace wore her Timberland boots, cutoff jean shorts, and a luminous green T-shirt she'd purchased in the spa gift shop. It read 'QUILLITY in black letters across the chest.

"They're like my poncho." Phil pointed at the Pots. "Same colors."

Henry and Grace glanced at the swirls on Phil's stomach, and they both nodded. From a wristwatch worn by the zinc-covered boy's father, twelve digital bells rang out the noon hour. Henry clutched his silver suitcase. Grace gazed into a purple-red puddle below her, thinking of Perry Danning and the days of their gesso dresses. Then she recalled a second dress of hers, the white item she'd worn once at Lake Loomis, then hung like a prize ribbon in the treetop lair of Stewart McFigg.

"I'm going to grab my camera," said Grace. "Be right back." She tramped off to the parking lot.

Henry and Phil leaned against the wooden fence that kept visitors from tripping into the steamy natural cauldrons. For a time, the two men said nothing. They basked in the glory of the day and kept their own counsels, while below them, the hues of creation stirred and mixed and popped. The air smelled of sulfur.

"Hey." Phil nudged his friend. "Can I hold one of those Planets a minute?"

Henry opened his case, plucked out a diamond, and handed it to Phil. "Just be careful with it."

"This place sucks," said the zinc-covered boy. He was bickering with his father.

"Which one is this, Henry?"

"That's Mars."

Phil gripped the Planet in his left fist. He looked at the diamond and the hot, swirling Pots.

"Just think," he said. "This diamond is made of the same stuff as that gunk down there."

"Not exactly the same stuff."

"Well, like, the same *elements,* but in different combinations. Different recipes."

Henry smiled. He liked Phil Weal.

"Zachary." The wristwatch man sounded stern. "You are getting on my last nerve, boy."

"Not only that." Phil held the diamond up in the sunlight. "The real planet Mars, even though it's way the hell away, it's also made of the same shit as this gem. Right?"

"Maybe."

"Think about it, Henry. No matter where you go in the universe, everything, all of us—I bet we're all made of the same shit."

Henry laughed. Both men were still leaning against the fence.

* * *

"What'd you whisper to my sister?"

"It doesn't matter."

"Just tell me what—"

"Shut the fuck up, Floyd. We have a job to do. Focus."

Floyd sat in the shotgun seat, fiddling with his switchblade. Roger had been driving through Yellowstone for over an hour. They'd passed grazing buffalo, and the Grand Tetons were sharp on the horizon, but Floyd noticed none of it. He opened and closed the butterfly handles of his knife, thinking sadly of Gretl, with whom he'd shared just five minutes.

"Stop dicking around with that knife. . . . Wait. That sign says Painted Pots. Yeah, here it is."

Roger had a Chesterfield lit. He sucked from it deeply, turned the Nova into a parking lot, and wheeled into a space away from other cars. He and Floyd got out.

"Oh, man," breathed Floyd.

"Calm down." Roger tossed his smoke, unbuttoning the holster under his coat. "You see the truck?"

Floyd looked around, but a Bluebird bus was loading tourists, blocking half the lot from view. Floyd was still fidgeting his knife, open and shut, open and shut.

"Never mind. Let's go."

"What's that smell?" Floyd's face was screwed up, alert. "It smells rotten."

"Just come on." Following trail signs, Roger strode down a thin dirt path through trees and shrubs. Floyd stayed two paces back. The flicking of his knife made scissor sounds.

Roger turned, grabbed the knife. "You sound like a gardener."

"A gardener? Fuck you, that's a vintage blade. Its handles are whalebone."

Roger got walking again. As he moved, he set the safety catch on the switchblade, locking it open so it might be of use if trouble broke.

"Give it back," snapped Floyd. "It's an antique. It's whalebo— Whoa."

The path ended, opening abruptly onto a wooden deck. Maybe thirty feet away stood Henry Dante, holding a squat silver suitcase. Beside Henry, a man with sandy hair and a poncho that looked like a tie-dye experiment had his left fist in the air. Farther off, another man stood scolding a boy with a smeary white nose. Beyond the deck were wide, puttering hot springs, but all Roger saw was the glittering rock in the poncho wearer's fist. He reared back his right hand, which held the open switchblade.

"Wait," began Floyd.

But Roger didn't wait. He was a Pobrinkis, a man with a cold soul and a knowledge of weapons, and he'd driven a thousand miles and it was time to make a point. He brought down his cocked arm like a pitcher.

"Hyike," grunted Phil Weal. He'd been holding up Mars in the sun, when a flying knife buried itself between his heart and left shoulder.

Phil fell on his ass. His fist tightened on the diamond. His face was bewildered. "Henry?" he asked.

"Oh, fuck." Henry whirled. Roger Pobrinkis was stalking toward him, a gun in his hand. Floyd was right behind him.

"H-Henry," gasped Phil. "A knife. In me."

Henry moved quickly. He knelt, pulled the knife from Phil's chest, and dropped it. Blood pulsed down Phil's poncho. Henry ripped the diamond from Phil's fist and jumped up. He pressed his boot on the wound, making Phil howl. Leaning out over the fence, Henry held Mars and the suitcase over a bubbling, muddy pit.

"Lie still, Phil," ordered Henry. "I'm keeping pressure. If you can, pull my boot down harder on the wound."

"Hey, a gun," said the zinc-covered boy. The boy's father snapped his head around, saw Roger's piece, heard Phil's anguish. The man scooped his son up under one arm and made a Johnny Weissmuller leap into the shrubs.

"I want to see," wailed the boy, but his father bore him toward the cars.

Roger trained the gun on his former partner's face. "Greetings and salutations."

Phil whimpered. His teeth were clenched, and his right hand pushed on Henry's boot as best it could.

"I'll drop them, Roger." Henry waved the stone, rattled the

suitcase. "You take one more step, twenty million dollars is going in that fucking quicksand down there."

"Cold," pleaded Phil.

"Hey, Henry, that's my knife by your foot. Could you kick it over to me?"

Henry stared at Floyd, and a tumbler—a tumbler named Gretl—clicked in his brain. "That's how I knew her. Shit." Henry put his free boot on Floyd's blade and swept it into the hot-spring mud. It splashed, hissed, and sank.

"You dick!" cried Floyd. "You asshole! That was whalebone!"

"Blood," moaned Phil, whose poncho was soaked with red. Sweat poured down his face.

"Your move, Roger." Henry kept his body contorted, trying to help Phil and balance the Planets. "Back off, or the stones go bye-bye. I've ditched four, I got no problem tossing these."

Roger said, "I'm not going anywhere."

"Hey."

All four men looked down the deck at Grace McGlone. She held a handgun, the one Henry had lifted from Roger at the Chalk farm. She was pointing the gun at Roger's head.

"I heard Phil screaming," she told Henry.

"He'll stop in a minute, once he's dead." Roger started to turn toward Grace.

She cocked her gun. "Don't move, mister."

Roger froze. He smiled over his shoulder.

"Throw your gun over that fence," she said.

"Grace," began Henry.

"Idaho," begged Phil.

Floyd shook his head. "Fucking whalebone, man. What a waste."

Roger's eyes danced. "Any woman who walks around Yellowstone packing a piece and tits like yours can suck my cock dry any day."

"Toss your gun," said Grace.

Henry was stuck between Phil and the fence. The sun glittered on Mars. The sulfur stench from the Pots was thick.

"Hmm," said Roger. "Your bitch is ballsy, Henry. Can she aim, though? Could she hit, for example, that humongous tree that's only ten feet away?"

Grace looked at the tree.

"Grace, wait," said Henry.

She frowned with concentration, aimed toward the tree, fired. The gun kicked hard, and Grace lost her footing and fell. She jumped up, expecting Roger to be upon her, but he hadn't moved. He was laughing.

"Well, you missed, but someone in Alberta might drop dead in a second."

"Fuck you." Grace blushed. She recocked her gun and thrust it toward Roger. "You . . . you put your hands up."

Phil's poncho was no longer multicolored.

"Oh, yes, ma'am." Roger hooted so much that Floyd joined in. "Come on, Floyd, let's put our hands up." Roger spread his arms, grinning at Grace. "Let's put our hands up on the outside chance that this cunt can—"

Grace fired at the slur. In a moment of honed anger or dumb luck, her bullet tore through Roger's outstretched right hand, ripping his pinky, ring finger, and gun from his possession, spraying them into the Painted Pots.

"Fuuuuuuuuck!" Roger sank to his knees, his hand sprouting blood.

"You bitch," shouted Floyd. "Fucking bitch, you shot my *partner*!" He moved at Grace, but Henry was fast. He flew off the fence, pocketed Mars, and tackled Floyd's legs.

"Henry," wailed Phil.

Henry and Floyd tussled. Grace fumbled with her gun, trying to cock it and scamper free of Floyd's arms. Roger lay curled up, cursing, pressing his hat to his hand like a bandage.

"Fucking woman. Fucking bitch." Floyd seethed, rolled, clawed for Grace. Henry hammered his chest, kept him down.

"Elements," whispered Phil. "Idaho."

Grace was sobbing. Henry drove his knee into Floyd's collarbone, causing it to pop. Floyd howled and went down. Henry coughed. The gun quaked in Grace's hand, and she was about to lower it, when the lithe, wiry animal sprang up, teeth flashing, biting hard into Henry's neck. Henry cried out, but Floyd's teeth held tight. A whine of rage curdled in Grace's throat: she shoved her gun at Floyd's temple and pulled the trigger. A cannon went off. Grace was jolted back and down. Her eyes closed, she smelled the wood of the deck. Her ears rang. It got quiet.

"Okay."

Someone stood. Grace winced.

"Okay, baby." It was Henry.

"What'd I do?"

Another man was cursing softly. Roger, guessed Grace.

"It's okay, baby." Henry touched her cheek. "It's me."

"What'd I do?" Her chest heaved panic. She opened her eyes.

Around her was a tableau. Floyd lay dead, half his head open, a blur of blood and bone. Phil had quit this world too. He was flat on his back, his right hand flat over the slice in his chest, like he'd died pledging some allegiance. The other pieces of the scene were the cheerful blue sky and Roger, curled between the corpses, muttering to his hand. The teakettle sounds of the Painted Pots hissed on.

"Come on, baby. Get up."

Henry dragged her to her feet. Grace looked around with a hollow, terrible calm. She tossed the gun blankly into the Painted Pots, as if she'd discarded weapons this way all her life.

Henry stumbled to Roger, frisked his pockets. Roger flailed with his good fist, and Henry rabbit-punched his neck.

"Fucking kill you," spat Roger.

"Yeah, yeah. What're you driving?" Henry pulled a key chain from Roger's coat. "The Nova."

Henry threw the keys into the Pots, punched Roger again, and grabbed his suitcase. Grace was gaping at Phil.

"Honey, we have to go. Grace, make your feet move. We have to go."

Henry tugged her to the lot, propped her against the truck. He opened the back hatch, and got in. Blood ran down his neck. He rummaged, pawing oranges and Little Julia books out into the lot, out of his way. He pulled down the shotgun and filled his shirt pocket with shells.

"Grace." He was at her side. "Grace?"

She stared straight ahead, weeping.

Henry ran to his boss's car, fired one barrel at a front tire, the other at a rear. "In case he hot-wires it. All right, let's go."

"Phil," whimpered Grace.

"There's nothing we can do. Get in the truck."

"Dante, you prick." Roger was three cars away, lurching toward the truck, cradling his blasted hand in his porkpie.

Henry grabbed shells, shoved them home. "That's close enough, Roger."

"Pussy-whipped prick."

"Get in the truck, Grace."

Roger glared at the woman. Grace clutched her stomach. Her abdomen bucked.

"Go on, sweetheart," said Roger. "Spew."

The Bluebird bus was gone, the lot otherwise empty.

"Grace, that man whose brains you just made a tourist attraction, his name was Floyd Webber. He was a close friend of Henry's."

Grace swayed on her feet. Vomit dribbled, then shot from her lips.

"Yeah," snarled Roger. "Yeah, Henry and Floyd worked together a good five years."

"Grace, get in the goddamn truck right now."

She wiped her mouth, clattered through the passenger door.

"Give me a reason." Henry trained the barrels on Roger's chest. "Take a step."

"Nah." Roger grinned. It hurt to, but lots of things hurt at the moment. "I'd rather admire your moral code from afar. Hey, sorry about your buddy. The poncho guy."

Henry had been heading for the truck door. He paused.

"Kept saying 'Idaho.' I hope when I go, I say something pithy like that." Roger laughed, winced, kept laughing. "We should toast your pithy little pal."

"Should we?" Henry fished in his pocket and brought out Mars.

Roger's expression dimmed. "Henry—"

“No, I like your idea.” Henry faced the Pots. He gave Roger the finger and cocked his arm. “To honor the fallen.”

“Wait—”

Henry released. He sent Mars over the shrubs, into a pit of steam and mud.

“You fucking idiot!”

Henry stalked over, got Roger’s right palm in his own, and squeezed. Roger cried out.

“You really should get this hand looked at.” Henry got in the truck, peeled off.

Roger was left on the gravel. He cursed himself hoarse, tugged off his coat, wrapped it around the hand, which was bleeding again full force. For ten minutes Roger sat sweating, applying pressure, staring at a white wall of pain behind his eyes. Then his vision cleared and he gazed at a Yellowstone National Park Services van, which was, at the cell phone behest of the zinc-covered boy’s father, rolling belatedly to the scene. Making a brief note that the van read Sanitation rather than Security, Roger looked away, spent. Oranges and paperbacks were strewn around him. He peered at one novel. It had a flapped-open cover that bore the handwritten words *The Hammerspread, Great Falls, Friday night*.

CHAPTER TEN

Keening

AT CORK RIVER, NEAR RINGLING, MONTANA, GRACE starts screaming. She's been comatose-quiet for ninety miles, ever since I burned us north out of Yellowstone. We're on Route 89, making for Great Falls, and suddenly she's bawling and gasping.

"Grace. Grace, Jesus. Breathe. Try to breathe."

Grace wails, stamps her boots. She tears off her 'Quillity shirt, which has puke and blood on it. Livid, she starts punching me.

"Stop it. Dammit, stop!" I keep Grace at arm's length, screech off the highway. I park under a willow, by the bank of the river.

"Grace, calm down."

But she isn't calm. She slaps my face hard, bursts out her door, surges into the river. I watch from the truck as Grace boils and rages. She punches the water, which comes to her hips. She hollers and keens. A sleek, alarmed doe stands on the far shore. Grace dunks herself under, brings up a rock, hurls it at the doe. The deer flicks off through the woods.

"Grace." I get out of the truck and stand on the bank.

She's stock-still in the river, staring daggers at me, water churning around her. Her face and fists let me know that this is crucial, that she'll cling to my words or else swim off alone.

"Get away," she shouts. "You're just like him. Like Roger."

"No, I'm not."

Grace sobs to the sky. "I killed him. I killed Floyd Webber." She slumps like she's fainting.

I charge into the water. She lies back against my arms. The water's like ice.

"Come on out."

Grace shivers. "No. I killed Floyd. I blew his head open."

"He would've killed you if he could've. Look at my neck. He did this."

Water splits around my back.

Grace puts a hand to my raw, punctured throat. "It's still bleeding."

"Just a little. Come on out now."

She splashes some water on my neck, wipes off dirt and dried blood. I haul her to the bank. As she sits in the sun, I get dry shirts from the truck and wrap them around her.

"You're a dick," she says. "I love you."

"I love you too."

Grace takes off her boots, pours them out. "I scared off a deer."

"I saw."

She toes at a stone in the riverbank. It's midafternoon. I

brought Charles Chalk's first-aid kit from the truck so she can clean up my neck.

"I'm afraid, Henry."

"That's okay. That's normal." I squeeze water from her hair. The sun warms us. I comb my fingers through wet, red magic.

"Floyd would've killed me?"

"He was a loyal guy. He could be nice, but he was tougher than he looked." Something comes to me. "We were on a roof once, Floyd and me, where we'd cornered this mark. It was two stories high, the back porch of the mark's apartment. Anyway, the guy's wife shows with a gun and shoots me in the neck. Her other five shots miss, and she really only winged me with the first, but there's lots of blood. Now, this woman's out of bullets, see, and her husband has no weapon, but that doesn't stop Floyd. She'd shot me, and I was his partner, so Floyd pushed that woman off that roof."

"Jesus," whispers Grace. "Did she die?"

"No. But she broke like ten bones, and if I hadn't stopped him, Floyd would've run down and bashed her head till she stopped breathing."

Grace looks at her hands. "We're all so awful."

"Who?"

"People," she says.

I imagine that I'm sunlight. I imagine I'm getting under my wife's skin, charging her arteries, replenishing her.

She gazes at me. "Phil died because of us. Because of being with us."

"He knew we were ducking someone. He could've split."

Grace's tears are regrouping. Behind her, on the far shore, is a pine tree so enormous, I could build a bridge from it, a bridge across this river, maybe most rivers.

"Grace." I take her hand. "Listen. I've never killed a man. I crewed for Honey for seven years and never personally killed a man. But I would've killed Floyd today to keep him from hurting you, and if I had, it would've been all right."

Grace nods. Her tears stand down, but Floyd's on her mind. He will be all her life.

"Henry . . ."

"Yeah?"

The sun's good on our faces. She leans back on her arms. Living things tick in the grass.

"I want to tell you something."

"Okay."

"I want to tell you who Bertram Block is. But you have to do something for me."

I stare at the giant pine. "Okay."

"You have to get new license plates for the truck. You have to get them right now, today." Grace looks away. "I know you can do it, so go do it. No more sporting-chance bullshit."

"Okay."

"You're my husband. You have to keep us safe. After tomorrow, after the Hammerspread, we'll ditch the truck altogether, make some new start. But for now, go get plates. Don't hurt anybody, but get them. A few different ones. I know you know how."

"Okay," I say.

Grace swipes a gnat off her knee. Then she tells me a story. I sit, listening. The riverbank turf is strong, the Cork gurgles. My jeans are soaked through, like Grace's were the morning we met. The story she tells is hard and clear, like real stories are. I listen. There's a rape scene, and strange moonshine, and a dress that got buried and a man I want to kill.

"So I want to face him," finishes Grace. "I don't know what I'll say, but I . . . I have to face Bertram Block again."

"Maybe I'll face him. Maybe I'll put his fucking head through the wall."

"No, baby." Grace touches my cheek. "I'm a grown woman. This is for me."

I make a fist, unmake it. "What am I supposed to do?"

"Go get us new plates, is what."

Phil Weal comes to mind. I remember him outside the Dairy Queen, whirling, galumphing.

"I'm sorry, Grace." My voice is low. "I'm sorry Phil died. It's my fault. And I'm sorry you went through what you did."

Grace's face is quiet.

"I'm sorry. I'm sorry that I'm not a better—"

She covers my mouth, leaves her hand there till I kiss it. I keep kissing it. Then she springs the kit open and dresses my wound.

* * *

Around four, she urges me into the truck. She says she'll stay here, near the willow, gather wood for a fire. She says she wants to sleep outdoors in my arms. She says don't hurt anyone, leave the Coleman stove and cooler, hurry back.

I drive south twenty miles to Wilsall, where I saw a used-car dealership on our way north. I park down the street, sneak into the lot. At least ten cars out back belong to salesmen—I can tell by the doughnut bags and legal pads cluttering the dashboards.

Dealers are forever switching plates for test-drives, so Grace and I should have the weekend before these chumps miss their tags. I swipe three sets of plates—two Montanas and one Wyoming—and I'm back beneath the willow by seven. I set the truck up with Wyoming plates and look around for Grace.

She's down at the riverside. She's built a tee-pee of logs and branches for a bonfire, and there's a stash of kindling nearby. I kiss her hair, and we don't speak. On the Coleman, Grace has brewed up coffee. In a pan, she's frying the garlic and sausage we've been saving on ice. She slides these piping hot onto bread, and we eat, drink our coffee, as the sun closes up shop.

After dinner, I light the tee-pee. The flames grow as tall as a person.

"Get the Planets," says Grace. I fetch the suitcase. There's just Jupiter and Earth now, the largest and the most familiar. We hold them up in the firelight.

"No matter what happens to me," she says, "it was good what we did. Sharing these diamonds."

"What do you mean, no matter what happens to you?"

I have Jupiter. Grace has Earth.

She leans against me. "I just feel like something might."

I shake my head. "No way. No goddamn way. I won't let it."

She picks up the empty suitcase, tosses it into the flames. "Let's each carry one now." She slips Earth in her pocket. "I'll hold Earth, you hold Jupiter."

"All right." I stash the diamond in my pocket beside shotgun shells. I'm in my red flannel, and the pocket has a button.

Grace has a bottle of brandy. She must've found it in the cooler, and she pours a long shot in my coffee, then hers. She clinks her cup with mine.

"To Phil Weal," she says.

"To Phil Weal." I'm about to drink, when Grace stops my hand.

"Not yet." She clinks our cups again. "To Arthur Kelly."

"To Arthur." Then, because I know my Grace, know what she wants, I say, "To Rupert Beignet. To the chick with green hair."

She nods. "To Tine and Lucia. To Dairy Queen Ginny."

"To Ortiz the cop and that Garbage Plate fatso."

"To Alphonse."

"To Gretl."

"To the sunrise bench of Carlson's Car Wash."

"To the lovely Katie Nullify."

Grace laughs. I laugh too. When our faces sober up, we clink glasses one last time, drink.

We take our clothes off slowly. We're both sore from the Pots, from all that's happened. But we're naked, too, and married, and we pull each other down in the dirt. We make love soft, then not soft. We bite, thrust, and moan like we're saying good-bye, like a war's on, a ship's leaving, and one of us, me or Grace, is embarking. Firelight plays in her eyes, and mine, too, and I flash back through time, and we're rutting cave people. I lick her breasts, she sucks on my tongue, and our hips are one action, refusing to part. We're grunting, surviving, we're saving our species.

Grace tenses, orgasms, calls out my name. "Again," she wails, gripping me. "Do it again."

I keep up my rhythm. I don't let us rest. She claws me and clings, and we kick over kindling. Inside my mind wash the faces I've pounded, the men I've punished, the lives I've made bleed. All the cold things in me, all the hard, jealous sorrows, they catch fire and burn, turn to smoke, join the sky. There's tears in my eyes, and there's mud on my arms, and I know I must finish, must surge, for my wife. But Grace is giving with her hips, sending sounds from her mouth, and I'm sending some, too, and our sounds join the river. Just before I come, I pray for these sounds, for our moans, pray that they mix with the black, secret water. I pray that they rollick off east to the Mississippi, that they spirit themselves down to New Orleans, where some blues-guitar boy and some dark bayou lass wait for music or love to deliver their bones.

CHAPTER ELEVEN

Hell

HONEY POBRINKIS SAT IN HIS VAULT IN FERRYMAN'S basement, reading and drinking wine. It was late on a Thursday afternoon, and for once Honey was trying to ignore the diamonds on his walls, the prizes he'd reaped and preserved like a big-game hunter who keeps the heads of his kills. Instead he was deep into *Tender Is the Night* and a bottle of Châteauneuf-du-Pape.

The one item in the vault that allowed intrusion by the outside world was a small red telephone resting by the reading lamp's base. It was an emergency line, and only three people had the number, and if one of them called it, he or she had to impart news of drastic import to warrant having disturbed the gangster in repose.

On this Thursday, when the red phone rang and Honey answered, the doomsayer's voice belonged to Roger Pobrinkis. As he listened, Honey gripped more and more tightly the bulb of the wineglass in his hand. The glass finally exploded, spraying shards and Châteauneuf onto Honey's linen pants and the chair leather.

"He threw it away?" barked Honey. "Threw it where?"

Roger's voice, coming from his cell phone, was a crackling presence. "Into this muck. Into a geyser. Anyway, it's gone, and I don't know how many are left, and the Nova's toast, and Floyd's dead."

"Floyd is immaterial. You understand? Floyd is completely fucking immaterial to the crisis at hand. Fuck Floyd."

"Yes, sir."

Honey glared at the Fjords, the Norwegian diamonds on his wall. "Where'd you say you were?"

"A hospital in Bozeman. They just treated my hand."

"And what're you driving?"

"A Yellowstone sanitation van. I had to kick some old custodial coot in the balls to steal it."

"Fuck the coot, Roger."

"Yes, sir. Fuck the coot."

Honey glared at the phone. "You cracking wise?"

"I just had two fingers shot off, Uncle Honey. Cut me some slack."

A glass shard stuck out of Honey's palm like a toothpick. He removed it, sucked blood from the wound, spat.

"All right. All right, Roger. Here's what's going to happen. There's an airport on the west side of Great Falls. You'll pick me up there tomorrow at three P.M., mountain time."

"Yes, sir."

"By the time you get there, you'll already have cased this

Hammerspread place. Find out what's going on there tomorrow night. It's probably some sappy fucking bobbing-for-apples square dance that this piece of tail, Grace, wants to see."

"I'd guess otherwise, sir."

Honey sucked more blood, spat more blood. "Why's that?"

"I've met the piece of tail. She's not the sappy type."

"How do you know?"

"Because she blew my goddamn hand apart."

Honey stood from his chair. He threw his shoulders back and shook his legs out, like an animal quitting hibernation.

"I'm just saying she's trouble, Uncle Honey."

"Yeah?" snarled Hunter Pobrinkis. "And what the fuck am I?" He slammed down the phone.

* * *

Henry drove with Grace beside him. It was an hour before sundown, and the couple watched the ribbon of the road unspool before them. Around the truck lay Montana, its trees holding the sky like rafters. Henry and Grace thought what lovers and travelers always think in the bold quiet of dusk: that they belonged to the landscape, that they were privileged, strong, radically free.

Grace especially felt inspired. She believed she and Henry had turned some corner the night before, with their talk, their riverbank passion. They were more together now, somehow, more alive, and the green, thriving land seemed to confirm this as the truck rolled north, passing silos, pastures, the odd home or tavern.

If it had been raining, perhaps Grace's mood would have tempered. If they'd come upon some roadkill, perhaps she would've recalled the gristle of Floyd's brains, the fragility of her skin. Instead, as she watched crows strutting on a barn roof, a mischief rose in Grace's heart. She felt like doing something large, like screwing Henry atop the Eiffel Tower. She felt, she decided, like making Bertram Block suffer.

"You follow my lead tonight," she said. "When I find this preacher, you back me up, no matter what."

Henry raised his eyebrows. "Feeling frisky?"

"Damn straight."

Grace stared out the window, remembered Bertram Block's water bed. She'd been weak on that water bed, susceptible. Now she was a woman who made love in the dirt. She felt strength, a wild, winging force, lift off in her stomach.

"And if I back you up," said Henry, "what do I get for my trouble?"

"Blow jobs. A Corvette. Eternal blessings."

"Deal."

With a growing, plotting pride, she squeezed his hand.

* * *

Ten miles north of Great Falls, Montana, near Benton Lake, stood the Hammerspread, an open-air amphitheater that could host five thousand people. The stage and seats had been carved from spruce, and, given the cloud-piercing pines that surrounded the place and the view from any row not just of the act onstage but of the rambling stars and moon, the Hammerspread was steeped in big-sky charm. From Scout troops to office executives, UFO enthusiasts to backwoods militias, virtually every club or cabal of American humankind sought to book the Hammerspread. Since its 1963 founding, the theater had been a touchstone, tour-launching venue for each generation's edgiest musical acts, from the Tribals in their Nixon-era heyday, to Smithy Grit, the pouty, hermaphroditic lord of the eighties, to Friend of Pig, at the millennium's close. In fact, it was during a sweltering, all-day Friend of Pig concert that lead guitarist Pig Wilson and bassist Pig Ritter threw down their instruments and raced to help their fans and local firefighters snuff a blaze that had reared up in the dry-as-a-bone forest around the Hammerspread. After a drug-induced loss of bearings led Pig Ritter into a smoking stand of bramble, where he doddered and collapsed and coughed his last breath, the Hammerspread became more legendary than ever as a zone of adrenaline-driven public action and, possibly, self-sacrifice.

The latest performer seeking to tap the Hammerspread's galvanizing vibe was celebrity preacher Bertram Block. The reverend was fifty-seven now and feared that his annual God's Will tours were straining for vigor, for relevance. Over twenty-nine summers, Bertram had unleashed, in every contiguous state in the Union, night upon night of fervid oratory. He'd cast out devils, championed the Gospels, laid hands on townsfolk. Under this latter category, he'd also furtively enjoyed relations over the years with no less than two hundred farm girls, pastors' daughters, and moony-eyed female event coordinators. The Reverend Block had long ago convinced himself that these one-night sexual booster shots were not only the wages of the road but God-given chances for him to learn new coital maneuvers, which he then parsed out to his Memphis wife, Annabeth, between each September and April.

Yet the reverend had begun to feel unsettled in recent years. For one thing, he could've sworn of late that when he phoned

Annabeth at night from out of state, there was another body breathing beside her. Also, polls indicated a declining population of those listening to the God's Will Tennessee Power Hour, Bertram's nightly radio talk show. In the final, deepest insult, the reverend found fewer and fewer Christian coeds milling around his RV when he finished each summer revival gig. It just showed, thought Bertram, how young believers were straying ever further away from proper moral role models and losing themselves to the Internet, to mammon, to pink-martini bars.

It was to stem this tide of strays that Bertram had secured the Hammerspread and its launchpad reputation for the first stop on his thirtieth annual God's Will caravan. Needing promotional dollars, the reverend had also signed a contract with Quick Fix Chicken, a national fast-food behemoth. Jeremiah Kendall Quick, the president of Quick Fix, was a lifelong believer in the Tennessee Power Hour. During the preceding months Jeremiah had funded publicity for Bertram's looming summer road trip, plugging the reverend's tour dates on radio and TV, and convincing some private high-school lunch programs to offer Quick Fix Chicken and Power Hour cafeteria signage. In exchange—this pricked Bertram's pride slightly—the reverend had to allow a loud-lunged actor to don the eight-foot-tall feathered mascot suit of Fixxy the Chicken at each tour stop.

It's worth it, thought Bertram, in his RV behind the Hammerspread stage. It was a Friday night in May. The reverend listened to the crowds in the theater outside the trailer. Thousands were congregating, just to hear him. True, as these ticket-holders arrived, they were being waylaid or hugged by a strutting, clucking Fixxy. *But it's worth it,* the reverend told himself.

He stared into his mirror, combed his thick white hair, arranged his monogrammed handkerchief in the breast pocket of his suit. *It's worth it,* thought Bertram, *to be a corporation's lackey if I can keep sowing the Word over America's hills and dales.*

Yet, on this warm, seminal night, Bertram felt a prayer stir inside him. It was an honest, quiet, shame-faced prayer, one that rarely rang through anymore, but, as the reverend stared at his mirror, at his sad, aging eyes, he let the prayer speak.

Dear God, prayed the prayer. *Dear Lord, if I really am sinning, deep down, if I'm testing your patience by lying with young women, then send me a sign, make me stop it forever. I'm an old man, dear Lord, and my habits are hard, but if you want them broken, then break them. Send me your justice, and send me a sign. Send me a sign that I cannot ignore.*

A knock came on the trailer door.

Bertram turned. He shook his head. Absurd, he thought. Absurd coincidence. He checked his watch. It was nearly showtime. He opened the door.

Before him stood a ravishing red-haired woman, her fists on her hips. She wore a buckskin dress and work boots. Drinking her in, Bertram thought God had answered his prayer in the most generous way imaginable. Then the preacher saw the man with a bandaged neck and two hideously wrong knuckles, the man aiming a shotgun at him.

"Before whom will you shudder?" demanded the woman.

The preacher blinked, confused. Overhead was a dramatic twilight sky. Cities of gilded purple clouds were built above the setting sun. Near the God's Will RV stood the trailer of Fixxy the Chicken. There were no crewmen milling around, though.

They were all at sound and lighting boards, for the show was scheduled to start in five minutes.

"Whom will you serve, Reverend Block?" The redhead's voice was imperative. "Before whom will you shudder?"

"I . . . Um . . . I'm afraid I—"

"You don't remember me."

The preacher had been looking at the shotgun barrels, but when he switched his gaze to the woman, her eyes looked equally lethal.

"No, I don't, ma'am." He tried to bow. "Um . . . What's your name?"

"I don't expect you care. You didn't ask for it last time we met. You didn't call me *ma'am* either."

"But we *are* acquainted?" Bertram tried to ignore the ill-knuckled man.

"I'm Grace. This is my husband, Henry. If you do anything other than what I tell you, he'll pump you full of six-shot. Come down out of that trailer."

"I don't see why I—"

Henry cocked the shotgun. Bertram minced down the steps.

"Head toward the stage," ordered Grace. "We're right behind you."

The reverend opened and shut his mouth, then obeyed. He walked a corridor of dirt and grass that snaked through amps and sound equipment. The sky above him gleamed, portending darkness. Grace stalked along behind him, Henry in her wake.

"Braaapp!" A giant feathered creature jumped from behind a speaker, landed before the preacher. *"Braaapp!* What's up?"

"Jesus." Grace put her hand to her chest, staring. "Oh my God. Gehenna."

The reverend glanced sharply at Grace. "What did you say?"

"Hey, Rev." The beast clucked and chuckled. "It's me, Fixxy! *Braaapp!* What's up?"

Henry showed the chicken the business end of his shotgun. "Hit the bricks, bird."

"Fuck me. Yes, sir." Fixxy hurried away.

Bertram glared at Henry and Grace. "What do you want?"

"Keep moving," said Grace. The chicken guy had scared her, but in her heart she clung to her plan. Bertram Block was a public man, she thought, and when a public man sins, he does public atonement.

She prodded his ass with her boot. The three proceeded over the grass. They reached the stairs that led to the stage.

Bertram stopped. "They need to introduce me."

"I'll have that honor tonight." Ready to strike him again, Grace lifted her left boot. Wedged safely in this boot, against her ankle and hidden from view, was the Earth diamond.

Bertram took a final peek at the shotgun and mounted the stairs. Henry and Grace followed. A control-booth technician, seeing the reverend take his center-stage mark ahead of cue, hurried to flip switches. The stage flooded with light.

The crowd erupted. From the first row of seats, seven feet below the stage, Gladys Corinth, the Hammerspread's owner, and Jeremiah Kendall Quick waved at the night's main event. Their smiles, though, and the crowd's clamor faded once Grace and her weapon-toting husband joined Bertram.

A podium with a microphone stood beside the preacher. He reached toward it, but Grace nudged him aside. She loosed the microphone and strode to the edge of the stage.

Henry kept the shotgun trained on Bertram. He watched

Grace with some concern for her brazenness, but mostly with admiration. She was a slinky buckskin powerhouse, he thought, and he was used to helping settle scores.

"Good evening, Montana," said Grace. "I'm Grace. That's my husband, Henry."

Uncertain applause came and went. People whispered. The stage manager flipped furiously through her notes.

"Hey, believers," Grace's voice boomed from speakers. "Are you prepared to sink your teeth into the truth?"

Audience members looked at each other. Many grinned, thinking a gutsy testimony was unfolding, something swash-buckling, like the famed 1972 alighting atop the U.S. Capitol by antiwar spiritualist Lana Clovenstein. Lana had been deposited via hot-air balloon, and tonight's crowd wondered if a similar spectacle was under way.

"Yes," yelled some daring souls. "We're prepared."

"Are you ready to meet the real Bertram Block?"

A louder whoop went up.

"All right, then. Here we go." Grace moved to Bertram's side. "Reverend Block, strip down to your Jockey shorts."

The crowd gasped. The stage manager, hidden in the wings, waved frantically at Gladys Corinth.

Bertram flushed an incendiary red. "I most certainly will not."

Henry jabbed Bertram's shoulder with the shotgun. When the preacher shook his head, Henry laid the base of the barrels atop Bertram's head, angled the gun at the sky, and fired.

"Owww!"

Bertram rubbed his scalp and started peeling off clothes. Henry pulled Jupiter from his bulging shirt pocket. He wedged it between his chin and chest, rummaged out a new shell, replaced his spent cartridge, and repocketed the diamond. Meanwhile, the theater aisles surged with bodies. At the gun's report, half the audience had leapt for the exits. The remnant that held their ground stared rapt and appalled as the preacher disrobed.

"This is weird," said Jeremiah Quick. He was a no-nonsense Arkansan who'd flown in to watch his investment perform. That investment, however, was tugging off his pants, revealing pale, spindly legs.

Jeremiah nudged Gladys Corinth. "What is this?"

Gladys didn't reply. She had thirty years of rock-and-roll chaos under her belt, and she didn't spook easily. If her stage had endured, in 1983, the unchoreographed heart attack of Lester Runion, the blimp-size lead singer of Shoddy Rocket, then it could handle a striptease.

"Well, well," Grace said into her microphone. "The reverend unmasked."

Beside her, Bertram had shed every stitch but his sky-blue briefs. His face remained blushed, though his gut was as milky as his legs. Given his near nudity and its certain career-crippling ramifications, he might have been expected to cover his genitals. But Bertram Block stood defiantly, his chest swelled, his feet spread like a soldier's at attention, his hands clasped behind his back. His face spoke at once of his bewilderment and his refusal to let that bewilderment break him.

"He almost looks like a superhero." Grace paced around the reverend, inspecting him. "With his fine posture and blue briefs, he looks like he could really save the day."

"Whatever it is you think I've done—"

Grace got face-to-face with him. "Shut your mouth."

The audience gasped again. More headed for exits. Those

that stayed glanced toward the stage wings, expecting security guards to charge the man with the shotgun. But Bertram was an evangelical, and he employed only two security men, and both were unarmed and smaller than Henry. What's more, they were doing tequila shots with Fixxy the Chicken in Fixxy's trailer.

"Ladies and gentlemen," said Grace, "you're probably alarmed to see the reverend undress. I don't blame you."

Jeremiah Quick scowled. "Bertram, what is this, dammit?"

"I don't blame you," Grace told the microphone. "I was surprised, too, twelve years ago, when he stripped down and stripped *me* down on his cozy little RV water bed."

The audience was no longer shocked, merely waiting, like a crowd at an execution. Bertram stared at Grace, a catalog of female faces and bodies ripping through his mind. Then a memory crash-landed, a lakeside night, a girl in a painted dress.

"Wisconsin," he whispered.

"It wasn't an abduction," Grace promised the crowd. "I'm not pressing charges."

The stage manager had caught Gladys Corinth's eye. She drew a finger across her throat, ready to kill lights and sound. But Gladys shook her head.

"I mean, I went pretty willingly into that RV." Grace sighed. "It's just that I was fifteen and a virgin, and I'm not sure this minister of the Lord should have given me head and then fucked me."

Henry was proud of the way Grace was talking. It was raw and true, he thought. It was meant for people like him and her.

Meanwhile, Bertram eyed the floorboards. He knew now that he wouldn't be gunned down in a traditional manner. Jeremiah

Quick stormed from the amphitheater with no intention of returning.

"I'm all for sex, by the way." Grace threw her arm around Henry's shoulder. "My husband's a real battering ram."

Henry waved at the crowd. Several people laughed. A few clapped. To a person, though, they were listening.

"Like I said," continued Grace, "I intend no legal malice against the reverend. But, as your sister in the Spirit, I say that when Bertram Block proclaims, as he always does, that we are sinners all, he's speaking from experience." Her amplified voice was sober and plain. "He fucked me without honor, and he's probably fucked dozens of girls that way. That's what I came to say. The Reverend Bertram Block fucks girls without honor, and if you're trying for heaven, you should know that."

The Hammerspread was silent.

Grace exhaled into the mike, as if expelling something she'd held far too long. She extended the microphone toward Bertram. "Reverend? Anything to add?"

The audience waited. A retort, a showstopping rebuttal, was coming now or never. But Bertram hung his head, and ever so slightly shook it.

"Jesus," whispered Gladys.

"Dante, you prick."

Henry whirled. At stage right, atop the stairs from the backstage grass, stood Honey and Roger Pobrinkis. It was Roger who'd spoken. He was holding a black nine-millimeter Glock, training it on the head of Grace McGlone, who stood forty feet from him beside a pale, mostly naked stranger.

"That guy must be the reverend," Roger told his uncle.

"He's immaterial." Honey loomed in the lights. The glare galled him, but he relished the provocation. When they'd arrived and seen Henry onstage, Roger had suggested they pounce after the show, in the parking lot, in a motel room. But when Henry pulled out Jupiter for his shotgun reload, Honey—fearing a charity toss to the crowd—had rushed the stage.

"I've come for my diamonds."

Bertram cowered behind the podium, hid from Roger's line of sight.

Henry had his shotgun trained on Roger's chest. "Honey," he said. "Roger tried to rape Helena."

"Yeah, he does that. It's a grievance of mine."

"Well, I had to do something."

"Ah," said Honey. "You had to do something."

Neither man had a microphone, so the audience couldn't hear each word. They caught the gist, though. They watched the man with the bandaged neck and the giant with blue lips.

"You had to do something," repeated Honey, "so you stole my diamonds and ran off with some hussy and you're giving away Planets like Robin fucking Hood?"

"I'm not a hussy," declared Grace. "And you're a coward with more money than Wall Street, so what's a few precious gems to you?"

Honey and Roger stood still, the matching streaks in their hair lined up on their cocked heads. Neither had heard a woman speak to Honey this way.

Henry cleared his throat. "Grace, I'll handle this negotiation."

"We're not negotiating, Dante." Roger tapped his Glock.

"I've got fifteen rounds, you've got two. Hand over the Planets or your lady's going to spend some quality time with Floyd."

"You fire one shot at her, you'll be minus a rib cage."

Gladys stared, eyes glittering. Even more of the audience was slinking out, but Gladys knew this was front-page press.

"Jupiter's right here, Honey." Henry tapped his pocket. "But I've got a proposition for Roger."

"Henry . . ." began Grace.

"Unless Grace mangled your self-esteem along with your hand, let's drop the guns. See if you're as tough as you think."

"Oh, man." Roger shook his head. "Are you kidding? I've killed six men."

Two hawks circled over the Hammerspread. One cried out, then both wheeled into the night.

"You killed them with a taxi, a meat hook, a towel dispenser. When's the last time you went skin to skin and didn't get your ass handed to you?"

Roger's face fell.

Honey touched his nephew's shoulder. "Roger, this isn't—"

"Behind us, Dante." Roger sneered. "We toss our toys behind us on my mark, then we'll see what we'll see."

"Deal."

"No, baby," said Grace.

"Go," said Roger.

The Glock and shotgun clattered to the stage. Henry and Roger charged each other. They ran hard, tired of talk, their blood jumping from seven furious days. And if the atoms of the world had teamed up to make Henry choose Grace, they'd also teamed up to make him vicious and hard with his hands.

Roger led with his left, clocked Henry's temple. Henry danced in, gave a haymaker to Roger's jaw. The Hammerspread had fine acoustics, and knuckle on bone was audible.

"Henry," cried Grace. He and Roger had each other locked up like rugby players, grappling each other's necks.

Grace eyed Honey, figuring he'd go for the Glock a few yards beyond him. Honey thought she'd turn for the shotgun a body-length behind her. Seeing each other's guesses, though, they remained frozen, as Roger and Henry grunted.

"You forget something?" Roger ripped the bandage from Henry's neck, scratched open his wound. "I'm a Pobrinkis."

Henry brought up his knee, bashed the gauze pad of Roger's hand. Roger roared, tore free.

"You're a two-bit excuse for a master's student," panted Henry, "and you won't see graduation."

They traded kicks, uppercuts. Blood flowed from Henry's neck, Roger's eye leaked pus, and with every landing fist the crowd exclaimed fear or favor. Roger got Henry in a headlock.

"No," shouted Grace, but Roger choked down as Henry sputtered.

"Now we'll see," Roger hissed. "Now we'll see what we'll see."

He strained to twist his arms, to crush Henry's windpipe. But Henry's neck muscles were strong walls, and Henry, stooped forward and seething breath, met the stare of Honey Pobrinkis.

Honey was a betting man. He knew how to calibrate odds, on numbers, horses, anything. So he recognized the dark will in Henry's face.

For one instant, Honey's eyes spoke. *Don't,* they said. *Don't.*

And Henry's eyes spoke back. *I have to,* they said. *Like with Helena, I have to.*

"Hyarg." With one massive shrug, Henry stood, lifting Roger off the ground.

"Wait." Roger tried to tighten his forearms, but Henry locked his fists on Roger's wrists, stumbled to the stage edge. He crouched, balanced Roger on his back, wrenched Roger's wrists free of his neck, and heaved. The anthropologist Pobrinkis, who'd killed six men, got pitched like a shot from a catapult. He flipped out from the stage toward the audience and crashed headfirst to the ground.

Gladys Corinth screamed. Honey rushed to Henry's side. They stared down at Roger's body, which lay in the grass like a discarded doll. His head was twisted, eyes gaping, neck broken. The remaining audience, including Gladys, fled.

"I had to," said Henry. "It was me or him, Honey. That's how he played it."

Grace relaxed for a fateful moment. She couldn't see over the lip of the stage, but she figured, from Henry's words, that Roger was dead. She also figured, since Honey wasn't close to the Glock, that Henry was in control.

"Yes." Honey spoke quietly. "Yes, that's how he played it."

Henry pressed his neck wound. Honey seemed at ease, or resigned. On the plane from Chicago, the gangster had wondered what he'd do if Henry got the drop on Roger. He'd told himself that if it happened, there might be amends, there might still be a place for Henry in the Pobrinkis clan, if he coughed up the remaining Planets. What Honey hadn't counted on was the splay of Roger's corpse. He couldn't have predicted that his sister's only son would lie dead in the pose that Rudolph Pobrinkis had lain on the Racine ferry dock. Staring at Roger, Honey saw his father's snapped neck, the break that had ended one boy's happiness.

Behind his closed blue lips, Honey's teeth clenched. He didn't glance toward the Glock. He merely turned toward Henry, flexed his forearm, making his silver gun pop snug from his sleeve to his palm.

"And here's how I'm playing it." Honey fired twice into Henry Dante's heart.

Henry stumbled backward, fell.

"Nooooooooo!" Grace skidded on her knees, caught his head. Henry coughed. Blood welled from two neat punctures in his chest. He pressed two fingers into the gashes, choked what might have been a laugh. He waved his devil knuckles at Grace, mock-aimed them at his heart.

"Could've done it to myself." He grimaced.

Grace was sobbing. "Baby!" she shouted. "Baby!"

Honey bent, pulled Jupiter from Henry's pocket, and slipped it into his coat. He patted Grace's head like he might a puppy's, then put his gun to her temple. "You, too, I'm afraid."

Grace stared murder at him. When the blast came, it was louder than she'd expected, and she was surprised to be conscious. Someone screamed, but it wasn't her. Honey reeled back. A quarter of his face had been shorn off. His cheek was flayed open, pouring blood, and Grace could see blue teeth through the hole.

"What the—" Grace turned.

Bertram Block stood close to the podium. He held the shotgun on his shoulder like a man who knew how and aimed his unspent barrel at Honey's chest. "Drop that gun."

Honey was hopping, shrieking, his gun still in his right hand. From his blue mouth came howls and squawks. He touched his free hand to his bloody cheek. He swayed, reached in his coat, pulled out Jupiter, stared at the stone smeared with his life. Spitting, he aimed his gun toward Bertram.

The second shotgun blast bored a crater in Honey's solar plexus. He blew back, dropped flat, dead. A fat diamond was clutched in his palm. From the void in his cheek shone his five-carat molar.

"Henry," wailed Grace. "Henry."

Henry's hand was in hers. "Wife," he said softly. "Wife, wife."

Bertram knelt, looked hard at the man's heart. He put his hand on Henry's forehead.

"May... May the Lord Jesus welcome your soul," spoke the preacher. "May He—"

"Shut up!" Bawling, Grace shoved Bertram. "Don't touch him!"

The amphitheater was empty, the stage still lighted.

"Grace." Henry squeezed her hand. "I love you. Listen."

"No! Don't die, baby. I love you. Stay. Please stay."

"Listen."

Grace bent to him.

"Again, sweetheart." He coughed blood on his teeth. "Do it again."

Their hands were tangled. His shirt was soaked through.

"What?" she begged. "Do what again?"

Henry's gaze shared all it could with hers, then traveled to the preacher, to the concert hall, to the spruces beyond.

"This," offered Henry. "All this." Then he died.

CHAPTER TWELVE

. . . Earth

NINETY MILES NORTHWEST OF GREAT FALLS, MONtana, ranges the blue-green world of Glacier National Park. Wild bear roam the land, and the lake waters, from spring to fall, stay as potently cold as a high-proof vodka. Just within the park's eastern gates, clustered around Lake Saint Mary, below Mount Cleveland, stand a phalanx of campsites. They are spare, basic plots, frequented not by lovers of sunshine or Grand Canyon vistas but by those who crave the north, those whose hearts are drawn by ice, by thin atmosphere, by the planet's poles. If a man and woman stand barefoot in early summer beside Lake Saint Mary, and the man yaks about soccer, or affirmative action, or his bullish, ticker-tape dreams, the woman is within her rights to wander off in the bracing waters. Glacier is, like its name, a massive, appropriate silence, a place where nature, dense and drifting, crushes time and other trivia.

* * *

Grace had left her husband's body with the stripped-down preacher. Before she could be caught or questioned, she'd sprinted, sobbing, from the Hammerspread, and blundered north in the truck, alone. She'd driven without map or purpose, and when the truck ran out of fuel at Lake Saint Mary, Grace ran out of fuel too. She'd steered dizzily off Route 2 into a pine-needle clearing that happened to be a campsite. The truck's front grille banged smack into a thick ponderosa pine, and as it did, Grace passed out cold, her face on the steering wheel, her arms limp. She slept that way for twenty hours.

When she woke, day had come and gone. It was early night again, and when Grace lifted her head, her vertebrae cracked out loud. She glanced in the rearview mirror. Her face was a lattice of steering-wheel dents, her eyes two gothic craters.

I'm a widow, thought Grace.

She sat in place, weeping. A young girl in a red windbreaker from a nearby campsite rapped on the truck window and waved a steaming ear of corn at Grace, who ignored the child. Later, after midnight, Grace drank water from the cooler, then stumbled to the lake's edge, where she threw up, falling to her knees on round, flat rocks. She passed out again, facedown on the shore.

This time when she woke it was morning. Someone had covered her with a black, scratchy, wool blanket. Grace was hungry, but remained stubbornly where she was, the rocks aching her thighs. At noon, the red windbreaker girl appeared and tapped her boot on Grace's buttocks. Grace peeked out.

"Give it back." The girl pointed at the blanket.

Grace handed it over.

The girl stared at Grace's matted hair, at the curled-shrimp pose Grace made in the rocks. She shook her head. "You shouldn't sleep on stones. You're stupid."

On the third day, Grace ate sticks of jerky. She dug out Charles Chalk's license plates and screwed them back on the truck. After this, she took anything that had belonged to Henry, his shirts and pants and Sprite cans, and made a pile beyond the ponderosa pine. She dumped the remaining Little Julia books on the pile and threw in the stolen license plates, the air mattress, her vomit-stained 'Quillity shirt. Then, standing by her work, she lit matches, dropping them until the pile flared. The air mattress popped, writhed, smelled like poison. Grace peeled off her Navajo dress and added it to the carnage. Braless, in her black panties and Timberlands, she watched the flames, felt their heat on her belly. She kicked pine needles away, made sure the pyre didn't spread. She plucked two long hairs from her scalp and dropped them in the fire.

"You're stupid."

Grace turned. It was the red windbreaker girl.

"That pit." The girl tossed her chin toward a rock circle. "You should've built it there. You'll burn the whole park down. Plus, your fire smells."

"You smell," said Grace.

The girl frowned. She was twelve, and she stared at Grace's breasts. "We have a crazy naked neighbor back in Billings. She waters her petunias in the buff."

Grace gazed into the flames. *I'm a widow. I'm a widow like my mother before me.*

"Bye, stupid." The girl scampered off.

Grace started walking on her fourth day in Glacier. She woke first at dawn, and pulled on her jeans, her Carlson's Car Wash T-shirt, her boots. She stuffed her pockets with jerky and two oranges and tied two water bottles to a belt she made from rope.

Thus shod, she struck out toward Mount Cleveland, beat through six hours of bogs and thatch and stands of massive trees. She wandered trails, pressed her mouth to cold, purple-lichened mosses. At a river's waterfall, above iron-colored boulders, she shoved her face in the pounding gravity of the current, daring the pressure to snap her neck, to dash her down on the rocks. All this time, she kept the Earth, the final diamond, wedged tight in her left boot, where it chafed her ankle like a dungeon ball. She couldn't bring herself to hurl it into the forest, just as she couldn't bring herself to swan-dive from the cliff promontory she reached. So she ate an orange wearily, turned her back on the mountain, made for the truck. Seven hours later, with Henry's twice-pierced heart on the slab of her mind, she limped into her darkened campsite.

"Welcome back."

The red windbreaker girl sat on pine needles, her back to the ponderosa tree. The air smelled imminent with rain, and the girl held a stack of graham crackers. She was eating them carefully, dropping no crumbs. It was nine o'clock.

"I didn't hear you coming," said the girl. "You're supposed to make noise."

Grace collapsed in a heap. She pulled off a boot, keeping the gem inside hidden from view.

"When you're hiking around here, you're supposed to make noise as you go. That way, if there's a bear up the trail, he knows you're coming and you won't surprise him. If you surprise them, they freak."

Grace inspected her ankle, which was raw and blistered.

"Freak, as in attack you. Wow, that ankle looks horrible." The girl stood. "Have you got first aid?"

Grace stared at her blisters, recalled Henry's laughter. She nodded.

"Well, you damn well better use it. Bye."

In the truck that night, Grace slept in fits. Rain beat a staunch percussion on the roof, and Grace dreamed of Roger's neck, Floyd's pulpy brains.

In the morning, she repeated her routine. She stocked her jeans with jerky and oranges, lit out between the trees, swatting aside leaves that spit rain upon her. She'd sprayed her ankle with Bactine, wrapped it with tape, but she'd shoved the Earth right back in her sock, too, so her limp returned. It worsened with each step. Cursing, she doubled back, spent the afternoon in the truck bed. She tried praying, but panicked instead, bolted outside, hugged the giant pine, held it tight, smelled its century-old smells as she wept and wept.

* * *

On the fifth day, Grace came upon a baby black bear. She was limping along a trail, the diamond in her boot like a penance, when there the bear was, just off the trail, sniffing a berry bush, nuzzling fruit into its mouth.

Grace stopped, watched. She knew she was experiencing what should have been a tender thing, a moment of animal quietude. She waited dully, wondering if harmony or comfort would flood through her. Instead, nothing happened. The baby bear kept eating. Grace stared at it, resenting its appetite, its concentration and ignorance of her affairs.

A blood-frightening roar rattled the air.

"Jesus!" Grace whipped around, her heart in her throat.

Five feet from her towered a mother black bear. Its mouth was open, charging noise into Grace's face. Its eyes were malice, and its six hundred pounds of muscle and hairy height blotted out the forest.

"Jesus," whispered Grace. Urine ran down her legs. She stood motionless, petrified. She was between the bear and its child, but she wasn't conscious of this logistic. She was conscious only of her bowels, the mortal shaking within them.

Again, the mother bear roared. Her teeth, a rack of long white knives, showed themselves, gleamed. Spitting from the bear's mouth, along with the next roar, came saliva. It sprayed on Grace's chin, and one fat drop of it fell on her tongue.

Grace smashed her eyes shut, trembled. Her stomach spun. All in one instant, visions and voices clamored through her mind. She saw her father, Max McGlone, the sloppy-haired hero of her adolescence. She saw her campsite's giant pine, pictured herself scaling it, climbing higher than gangsters and beasts could reach. The bear's hateful breath blasted her scalp, smelling like hot, rotten cabbage, and Grace, eyes still clenched, recalled Bertram Block saving her life. Finally, she saw the Planets. They hurtled like comets, burned through the sky of her mind till just one was left.

Grace heard Henry's voice. *Again,* said her husband. *Do it all again.* Then another voice, a brassier one, came clobbering through, pointed itself at Grace like a finger.

You, commanded the voice. *You're supposed to make noise.*

Grace clenched her fists. She was shaking. She tasted on her tongue the ancient, forever-ago bite of P&V. Then, eyes still rammed closed, she opened her mouth and screamed. She howled and wailed, brought shrieking up from her guts. She leaned her face forward, roared her own roar at the one coming at her. She keened till her cheekbones ached, till her diaphragm gripped. She pealed and bawled out decibels till she felt herself no longer a daughter, wife, or widow, but merely a noise, a strong, insistent sound.

Then she stopped. She was done. She opened her eyes, panting, and looked around. She was alone on a forest trail. There were no bears, neither baby nor mother. She was the only thing there.

Unclenching her fists, she gazed at her hands, the dirt, the trees, the high blue above her. She wiped her eyes. Her heart took a minute to find its pace, then she sighed, threw back her shoulders. She was done crying, done screaming.

"Good-bye, Henry," she said softly.

* * *

Grace borrowed gasoline from the red windbreaker girl's father. In exchange—though the father asked for nothing—Grace removed her silver wedding band and passed it to the man, with a note telling him to give it to his daughter.

She left Glacier, steered her truck into southern Montana. There she found Lou Feeper's Bozeman Truck Stop, the roadhouse famous among tractor-trailer drivers for its two-inch-thick rib-eye steaks and its bordello of a bunkroom. It was here at Lou Feeper's, Grace knew, that her father had died at the hands of some shadowy foe, some gambler or harpy or creature of the night.

Grace didn't go inside. She gassed up the Charles Chalk–mobile, paid with her ATM card, then sat on the hood in the sunshine, staring at the roadhouse. She wore a clean pair of jeans, her Carlson's T-shirt, her Timberlands. Three men in Mack truck caps whistled at her, invited her for a rib eye, their treat, but Grace ignored them till they vanished inside.

She drove east. At Billings, at the split of interstates 94 and 90, she took 94, the more northern, less familiar route. She cruised east, nonstop, with the wind. She moved through Treasure County, Montana, and Stark County, North Dakota. She dropped down through South Dakota, past Fergus Falls, past St. Cloud. At midnight, she ate meat loaf in an Eau Claire diner named Selena's, in her home state. Then, in Selena's parking lot, feeling unable to move closer to Janesville, she slept for eight hours in the truck bed, her boots on, her diamond still crammed against her ankle.

The next morning, a knocking woke her. Grace yawned, blinked hard, stared out the windshield at a middle-aged Latin-skinned woman. Grace crawled into the driver's seat and opened the window.

The handsome, imperious stranger spoke. "I'm Selena. This my diner. My cook tell me, you here all night. Parked. No leaving."

Grace didn't reply. Her tongue and whole person were incapable of rapport.

"You police?"

Grace remained silent. Her eyes were a dark limbo that Selena, a widow herself, recognized.

The matron crooked her finger. "You come."

Limping, Grace followed the woman inside. Selena ushered her into the kitchen, fixed her eggs, left her alone. Grace sat on a chilled industrial refrigerator, ate her eggs, watched waiters and cooks work and bicker. She sat until it was clear to Selena that this girl hadn't the will to do much else. So, later that afternoon, Selena set a box of tomatoes on the counter. She gave Grace an apron and knife, pointed at the tomatoes.

"You cut," said Selena.

Grace cut up the tomatoes. When she finished, Selena gave her a box of onions and Grace sliced those up, too, all without speaking. That night, Grace ate the burrito that Selena prepared for her. Then she went out to her truck, crawled in the back, and slept.

The next morning, Selena woke Grace again. She fed her, gave her the knife, set her to labor, left her alone. Day after day, it became a ritual between the two women. Grace worked at Selena's diner, and wore an apron, and chopped things, and didn't speak. At night, she lay alone in her truck, the curtains drawn. She thought of Lou Feeper's Truck Stop, wondered if there was a Selena there, too, a woman who owned and served. She thought of Janesville, just thirty miles away, and felt perhaps she should stay in Eau Claire forever, always orbiting but never returning to her home. She knew that no one would come for the truck, that some Chicago justice that had lived in both Henry and Honey had died with them too. Mostly, though, she slept.

It went on for weeks. Gradually, Grace's limp disappeared, though she at all times carried the diamond stowed in her boot. Selena never asked the stranger about the lump in her foot. She gave the girl work and food, never advice. She waited for the day when the girl would realize that, no matter what had befallen her, she was herself. On that day, the older woman knew, the silent girl would vanish.

* * *

The predawn clouds were rosy fingers across the sky on the early June morning that Grace drove into Janesville. She got to Carlson's Car Wash at five-thirty. Chubb Gesthoffen wouldn't arrive till seven, but Grace fetched Paul Carlson's office key from under the sunrise bench and opened the place. It would be her last time performing these tasks, but she turned on the clack-track tunnel, filled the detergent vats. After pressing the Super Deluxe wash button on the wall, she ran back to the truck and drove it through the tentacles, through the clean-smelling lather. When she eased the steaming truck from the tunnel, she turned the engine off, left the keys in the ignition for whoever might want them, and walked away from the car wash for good.

Main Street Janesville was empty. Dawn hadn't reached the sidewalks, so streetlamps were still lit. Grace strolled, looked at the town, reorienting. Plastered on telephone poles were posters begging for the safe return of Tom Pfordresher's lost seeing-eye Doberman, Cassius. The dessert menu at Mackidew's, taped on the diner's front door, listed Our Famous and Astounding Homemade Pecan Pie, which Hollis offered only when the Cubs were winning.

A man and woman in matching sweat suits jogged past, but Grace didn't know them. She studied the vines that gripped the east wall of the Bryson Inn. They looked to her like the tributaries of some great river viewed from outer space. As a girl, she'd decided they were a map of the Nile, or the Yangtze, or some mighty, surging body that she herself would find, name, and navigate.

At the display window of Pyle's Thrift Emporium, Grace stopped. She gazed through the glass at a few new items—a hibachi grill, two kites—but mostly at totems she recognized. There was the marble chess set that Francis Pyle had been trying to sell since October, and the maritime telescope, and the toaster. Then Grace caught her breath. In the corner stood the clay Taj Mahal statue, the one that cost a dollar forty-five. As ever, it was covered in dust, its price tag dangling like a listless flag, but it had been shifted from its plot. It was a move of only inches, a move perhaps no other Janesviller would detect, but Grace marveled at it. She could see the old space, one band of white exposed wood in the window-casement soot.

"Good morning."

Grace turned with a start. Beside her, in blue jean overalls, each arm hugging a stuffed grocery bag from Todd's Supermarket, stood Color Danning-Tate. Grace shouldn't have been surprised, because Color and her husband lived one block down, beside the Bryson Inn. Also, once a week, Todd Wilcox opened his market at five so Color could shop undisturbed before other patrons came at seven. Children invariably shrieked with fear or wanted to follow and pet her when they saw Color in the aisles, and Todd and countless parents had had enough of both. Color herself became sapped or driven to distraction when thrown among so many souls whose secrets called to her.

"Hello," rasped Grace. She hadn't spoken since Glacier.

Gleaming above celery stalks were the famous gray eyes, the strong silver hair.

Grace coughed to jump-start her voice. "So . . . how are you, Color?"

"Pregnant."

"That's wonderful. Congratulations."

"Thank you." Color sniffed the air. "Hmm."

"What?"

"You've been out prowling, Grace McGlone. Roaming."

Grace's heart seized. She looked away. "And do you . . . do you know what happened to me?"

"I have some guesses."

Grace's eyes rimmed with wetness.

"Oh, honey." Color set down her groceries, hugged Grace. Grace let out one bark of a sob. She let herself be held.

"It's all right, honey. It's going to be."

"I don't know . . ."

"It is."

Grace wiped her eyes.

"You're Grace McGlone. Nobody nowhere has got nothing on you." Color stood back, but held Grace's hands. The streetlamps clicked off. Dawn was building.

"What will you do now?"

Grace sniffled. "I'm not sure. I've been thinking . . . I've half a mind to do something fairly wacked."

Color cocked her head, listened. "Dammit. It's Cassius Pfordresher."

Grace glanced around, saw no trace of the dog. "Where?"

"Loomis Forest, sounds like. His leg's caught in a woodchuck hole or something. I better go find him."

Color took Grace's chin, raised it. Her eyes glinting, she nodded toward Morgan Street, which was three blocks away.

"Seems like we've all got places to be this morning, don't we, Grace?"

Grace swallowed, looked away. "I . . . I don't know. Do we?"

"I don't know," said Color Danning-Tate. "Do we?"

* * *

On Morgan Street, Grace strode to the house of Stewart McFigg. The front door was unlocked, but when Grace peeked in, Stewart was asleep in his clothes on the couch, one bar of sun stealing through the window toward his head. Grace hesitated, thought. She jotted him a note, slipped out the front door.

The walk to the Oval Office took almost an hour. Grace went slowly to accommodate the stone she refused to loose from her boot. When she arrived at Uncle Treemus, she put her hand to the bark, peered up. It had been nine years since she'd touched this tree. She'd never beheld Uncle in honest morning light, and she wondered, gazing skyward, whether she could still climb the giant.

Halfway up, she slipped, caught a blunt branch in the gut. She rested on one of Stewart's ancient platforms, pulled up her T-shirt, checked her stomach. There was no blood, but she saw a grand bruise in the offing.

At seven-thirty, Grace reached the tree house with the chimney. She sat on the porch, took in the rising sun, wondered exactly what she was doing here. When she finally went inside, she was surprised that the bearskin rug and bookshelf remained, though the rug was tattered almost to crumbling. The room's startling additions were the arsenal of water bongs, hash pipes, and hookahs. They were everywhere, on the bookshelf, the rug, cluttered in the corners. In the sleeping nook, Grace found crinkled condom wrappers, and a Megadeth poster, and a stuffed animal bunny with a syringe up its ass.

Her deepest shock came when she reemerged in the main chamber and noticed what hung there. It was a piece of clothing nailed to the wall, an item that teenagers had spray-painted purple and black and green over the years. They'd written graffiti notes on it, too, many in red nail polish. One note said *Chris "Cannabis" Hackett* 95–99. Another said *Colonials Soccer*. Another said *No Iraq War,* and another said *Sara Aikenfield Goes Down*.

Grace petted the cloth memorial. It was her baptismal dress, she knew, but she preferred it this way, with fun and stupidity rubbed into it. She left it hanging, and decided to clean.

In the kitchen nook hung a garbage bag with Ho Ho wrappers in it. Grace moved through the rooms, filling the bag with the condom wrappers, the poster, the violated bunny, every last pipe and bong. In a corner, she found a tiny straw hand-broom and used it to clear the floors of dust and cigarette butts. She swept this detritus into the bag, tied the plastic sides together, dropped the bag off the porch. She watched the bundle crunch and careen off branches down to the ground.

Fetching the bearskin rug, she shook it over the porch edge, freed it of dust. After spreading it out again inside, she sat cross-legged on it, waiting. She spied something caught behind the bookshelf. Moving closer, she grabbed the trapped thing. It was Stewart's old crucifix.

Grace dusted it off, looked at the body on it. She set the crucifix on the bookshelf. Five minutes later, Stewart poked his head in the door.

"Grace! So it really is you."

"I guess you got my note."

"I thought that might be a joke from my crew. People said you skipped town."

Stewart stepped fully into the chamber. He wore a plain white T-shirt and jeans and a tool belt, his summer carpentry outfit. His left foot, as always, was shod in a green orthopedic boot. His other boot was a basic brown leather.

Grace stared, as she had each time she'd seen Stewart over the last twelve years, at his swollen biceps and forearms. They were still astonishing, thought Grace, but back in high school they'd seemed almost cartoonish. Now his limbs wore badges of labor. He had a scar above his right elbow, where a circular saw had bitten him. The sun had cooked and weathered his forearms, and hard gravel was trapped in the meat of one palm.

He works, thought Grace. *He works. He's a man.*

"I did skip town," she said. "But I'm back now. Will you sit with me a minute?"

Stewart looked at his watch. "I have to power-sand Pauper Jeckett's roof at eight o'clock."

"Just for a minute."

Stewart looked at her closely. Grace wore Timberlands and blue jeans and her Carlson's T-shirt, untucked. He thought her skin had seen some sun, but her hair was the same stammer-inducing torch.

"I haven't been up here in ages." He joined her on the rug. "Except for that graffiti-thingy, everything looks the same."

"I cleaned up a bit."

"Is that why there's a ripped-open bag of water bongs down in the Oval Office?"

"I guess so. Stewart?"

"Yes, Grace?"

It was a clear-sky Tuesday. Below Uncle Treemus, in the James Madison parking lot, buses were disgorging students who ached for summer.

"Stewart, why would your crewmen play a joke telling you to meet me? Why would they think signing *my* name would make you show?"

Stewart looked out the window. It was a window he'd fashioned, however crudely.

"Grace, if you left that note, why didn't you just wake me up? We could've talked at my house."

"I didn't want to startle you unnaturally from sleep."

Stewart adjusted his tool belt, moved a wrench that was gouging him. "But meeting in my old tree house, that's natural."

"Whatever it is, Stewart, here we are."

"Yeah."

She took his hand. Stewart was surprised, but didn't pull away.

"Stewart."

"Yes, Grace?"

"Let's tell the truth." She breathed in. The air tasted high, thin, slightly insubstantial. "On a morning like this, we should tell each other the truth."

"Okay. The truth is, I'm late for work."

Grace picked at the rug. She was frustrated, twenty-six, unsure. "I'm wondering if we should kiss."

"Yeah, right."

Grace kept holding his hand. She looked at him quietly. Stewart's face fell.

"You shouldn't tease a guy, Grace."

"I'm not teasing. I'm wondering."

Stewart waited for a punch line. When one didn't come, he tugged his hand from Grace's, set his jaw. He stared at his lap.

"Who do you think you are, Grace?"

Grace opened her mouth. "I—"

"I took you on dates these past few years, and you never even pecked my cheek. Now all of a sudden it's 'maybe we should kiss'? What the hell?"

"Not all of a sudden, Stewart. I've known you all my life. We've known each other."

Stewart glared at his addled foot. When he was angry, he did this, focused on his deformity, hating that his father had given it to him, hating the extra time and careful footing it demanded. Stewart knew what Janesvillers thought of him. They considered him one of God's fools, a cripple with a decent heart, a hard worker, a man who knew neither smut nor cynicism. He was the son of McFigg the butcher, the son who joined his father at mass each Sunday in St. Anselm's.

While some of these were facts—he was maimed, after all, and he did go to church—Stewart marveled at the community's blindness to his rougher edges, his failings. For years after high school, while Grace and so many others ebbed off to college, Stewart had stayed in Janesville, grappled with life. He'd taught himself carpentry and bought a house, but he'd also drunk himself to sleep countless nights, his heart suffocatingly lonely. He'd driven alone many weekends to Chicago, where he sat on bar stools, sulking down whiskey, waiting till some blowhard mocked his foot. He'd lured men into fights in this way, crumpled their ribs, earned fines and nights in jail, and all of it beyond the borders of home.

He'd had one-night stands, too, most of them during benders, often with women he'd found barely attractive. One summer night, in his early twenties, he'd left the Fracas Pub with none other than a bleary-eyed Periwinkle Danning. They'd driven to Lake Loomis in his truck and screwed in the truck bed, and afterward, Perry had begged him never to speak of it.

"It would ruin me," she'd sobbed, "if people knew I slept with a— It would ruin me."

Stewart carried these things in his heart. He carried his foot, his misdemeanors, his flimsy couplings with women. And because he, in spite of his efforts to the contrary, also carried goodness, he sometimes wept. He cried not like Perry had—cried not to public opinion—but to God and himself and, deep down, to Grace McGlone. Those were the persons from whom he wanted company and approval. So for Grace herself to call him out, to coax his care for her up out of its cave, was a lung-tightening fury of a thing.

"I'm not so sure you know me, Grace."

"Maybe not. But I might surprise you too. If you knew all that's happened to me, I bet—"

"Your little vanishing act?" Stewart snorted. "You leave town for a month, and you're a new person? What, you won the lottery?"

Grace looked at her baptismal gown, the mad colors on it.

"I married a man named Henry. I killed another man by shooting him in the head. Then I watched my husband die."

Stewart studied her. He read her eyes, weighed her words. He'd worked many years with hard-bitten men, and he knew the expression, the glance, the breath of a lie.

"Jesus," he whispered. "Jesus Christ, Grace."

"He might never have been in danger if he hadn't met me. I don't know. . . . I might've been what killed him."

"My God, Grace. God. I'm sorry."

"I'll tell you about it sometime. Not now." She tossed her head toward the corner. "Stewart. See that guy there? On the bookshelf?"

Stewart looked. "My old crucifix?"

Down at the high school, homeroom bells were ringing.

"I still believe in Him," said Grace, "but I don't want to talk about that now, either. I want to give you something."

She unlaced her boot. Her husband had died, but she was in the physical world, behaving physically. She peeled the boot off. The stone fell on the bearskin.

"It's a diamond," she said, pointing. "It's for you."

It was warm in the tree house, not hot.

"I just got back, and I haven't even seen my mother yet, and I have no idea what to do with my life. . . . But this is for you."

Stewart didn't look at the diamond. He saw only Grace's ankle, whose skin had become rough and resistant, like his hands. He brushed the gem aside, touched her heel. "You're hurt," he said.

"Just a little."

Stewart did something then he'd only done for doctors. His fingers shaking, he removed his left boot, showed Grace his atrophied foot.

Grace regarded it with alarm. Then her eyes softened. It was tiny and white but it could move, the ghost of something thought extinct.

"May I . . ."

Stewart looked away, his teeth set. He couldn't remember what he'd had for breakfast. He nodded, barely.

Grace touched the little foot. She held it in her palm. "It's fragile."

Stewart wouldn't look at her. Grace began stroking his foot as gently as she could. She didn't massage it, didn't kiss it, didn't move toward seduction. She simply stroked the man's foot, remembering its story, wondering.

Sun poured in the window. As Grace touched his foot, Stewart sighed. Then, involuntarily, he laughed. The laugh made him blush.

"It's all right," said Grace. "We're supposed to make noise."

"What the hell is this?" blurted a voice. "What in the freaking freak is this?"

Grace and Stewart turned their heads.

In the doorway were six shocked faces. They belonged to six seniors, six kids who'd cut first period to smoke dope in their lair at the top of the world. Two were girls, one black-haired and one blonde. In the fall, the black-haired girl would attend Emory, where she'd discover and admire Catherine the Great. The blonde would stay in Janesville to land the stoical, much older Jon Fracatto as a husband.

As for the boys, two were brothers who excelled at chess and loved Pink Floyd. The third boy was fearful of nuclear winter, and the fourth boy was Hanson Hackett, the broad-shouldered younger brother of Chris "Cannabis" Hackett, who'd ruled the Uncle Treemus reefer lovers of the previous decade. Hanson had long wheat-colored hair, and he would visit Laos in August with his parents and his stomach would tolerate the trip poorly.

For the moment, though, the young master Hackett was dating the future Mrs. Jon Fracatto, and he was standing in the doorway of what he considered his hideout.

Hanson stared at the man and woman on the bearskin. The woman was beautiful, the man enormous. They were dappled in sunlight, and one held the other's foot. Around them was a clean environment, except for the weird painted dress on the wall, the dress Hanson called the document dress, the dress he planned to sign next week, the morning after graduation, like his brother before him.

"Who are they?" whispered a girl.

Hanson held up his hand for silence. He was the leader, the one who'd first spoken upon seeing the transgressors. He felt it his place to address them.

But before the young man could form a complaint or a credo, the burning-haired woman hopped to her feet. She stood at her full height, and the teens stepped back, for in the woman's hand was a glittering stone, a ball of light catching sun from the window. She held the light up, held it out like a defense for the children to respect and remember, though she and the man would be keeping it.

"This place is ours," said Grace.

ACKNOWLEDGMENTS

With unending love for their unending support, I thank my wife, Martha Schickler, my parents, Jack and Peggy Schickler, and my three sisters, Anne Marie, Pamela, and Jeanne.

I take great joy in thanking for their encouragement the rest of my wide, wonderful family, especially the Schicklers, the Edds, the DeLaCroixs, the Moszaks, the Compisis, and the Ulrichs.

These people are my close friends and close readers, and God bless them for making me laugh: Chris Tengi, John Dolan, Ed Nawotka, Jennifer Danburg, Rebecca Donner, Erich Gleber, and Larry Mastrella. Chief of this clan is my best man, Cliff Green.

Thank you to these excellent colleagues: Bill Buford, Cressida Leyshon, Deborah Treisman, Michael Nozik, Margo Lipschultz, Barb Burg, and Theresa Zoro.

Thank you to all my readers and to those who attend my readings. I bow also to a certain terrifically named Manhattan social establishment.

I offer my final and strongest thanks to my three fairy godmothers:

Susan Kamil, my editor,

Shari Smiley, my film agent, and

Jennifer Carlson, my friend, literary agent, and daily paramedic of good sense.